S0-EKU-813

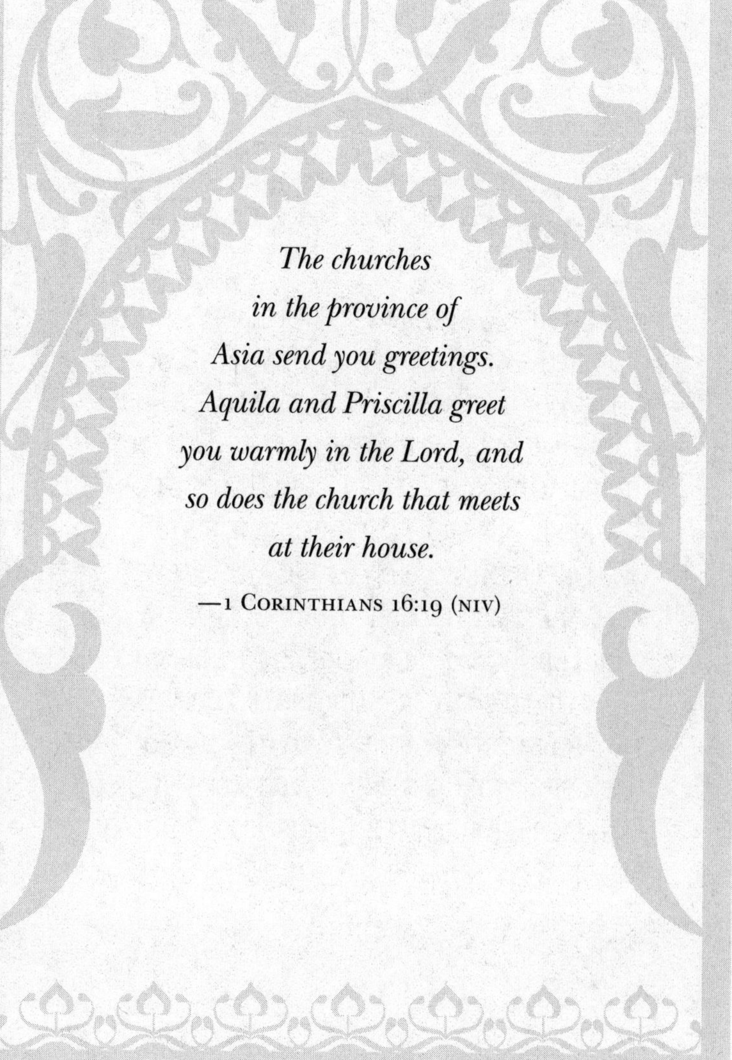

The churches
in the province of
Asia send you greetings.
Aquila and Priscilla greet
you warmly in the Lord, and
so does the church that meets
at their house.

—1 CORINTHIANS 16:19 (NIV)

Ordinary Women of the BIBLE

✦

A MOTHER'S SACRIFICE: JOCHEBED'S STORY
THE HEALER'S TOUCH: TIKVA'S STORY
THE ARK BUILDER'S WIFE: ZARAH'S STORY
AN UNLIKELY WITNESS: JOANNA'S STORY
THE LAST DROP OF OIL: ADALIAH'S STORY
A PERILOUS JOURNEY: PHOEBE'S STORY
PURSUED BY A KING: ABIGAIL'S STORY
AN ETERNAL LOVE: TABITHA'S STORY
RICH BEYOND MEASURE: ZLATA'S STORY
THE LIFE GIVER: SHIPHRAH'S STORY
NO STONE CAST: ELIYANAH'S STORY
HER SOURCE OF STRENGTH: RAYA'S STORY
MISSIONARY OF HOPE: PRISCILLA'S STORY

Ordinary Women of the BIBLE

MISSIONARY OF HOPE

PRISCILLA'S STORY

GINGER GARRETT

Guideposts
Danbury, Connecticut

Published by Guideposts Books & Inspirational Media
100 Reserve Road, Suite E200
Danbury, CT 06810
Guideposts.org

Cover and interior design by Müllerhaus

Cover illustration by Brian Call and nonfiction illustrations by Nathalie Beauvois, both represented by Deborah Wolfe, LTD.

Typeset by Aptara, Inc.

Printed and bound in the United States of America

10 9 8 7 6 5 4 3 2 1

Ordinary Women of the BIBLE

MISSIONARY OF HOPE

PRISCILLA'S STORY

ACKNOWLEDGMENTS

I would love to thank the entire Guideposts team for all the help they've given me in creating this book. I've read *Guideposts* magazine since I was a kid, so writing for the company as an adult is a thrill. My grandmother gave me my first subscription to the magazine. Although she's in heaven now, I like to think she's tickled pink to see me working with them. We're living in a world that needs every ounce of encouragement and hope, and the work that Guideposts is doing is more important than ever.

This book in particular was a big story to write, with a lot of moving pieces, so I appreciated all the helpful teammates and resources I had. I also found a lot of helpful information in N.T. Wright and Michael F. Bird's *The New Testament in Its World: An Introduction to the History, Literature, and Theology of the First Christians,* and Alberto Angela's *A Day in the Life of Ancient Rome.* Andy Stanley's *Irresistible: Reclaiming the New that Jesus Unleashed for the World* gave me lots of food for thought as I considered the transition from the Old Testament laws to the New Covenant of grace. Also, I'm thankful the internet allowed me to visit many historic sites, including virtual re-creations of cities and temples. Finally, the best part of writing biblical fiction is when a reader tells me, "I enjoyed your story, so I had to go find the woman you wrote about in scripture!" I hope this entire wonderful collection of books inspires you to do the same. —G. G.

PROLOGUE

66 CE, Rome

Mamertine Prison, the dungeon of Tullianum

Priscilla drifted between states of awareness. Sunlight did not exist here in the dungeon of Tullianum. The cold was a relentless adversary, never giving her a moment's peace. Every bone ached. Right now, her lower back ached as if someone pressed burning rods to it. The nerves that had gone numb in her legs had only made a cruel, temporary bargain. When she shifted position to relieve her back, they would reawaken in fire.

Was it a dream that she could still smell the sea air and still feel the waves that carried her so far from this city? She had landed in Corinth on a bright day with brisk winds coming in from the sea. She could taste the tang of brine that always hung in the air. Her hair had curled and frizzed the moment she stepped off the boat that day. She smiled at the memory, her dry lips cracking. That was the day she became a completely different woman, and she hadn't even known it.

And then Ephesus, oh Ephesus! She had imagined it to be a dark and terrible place, but the beauty of that city came back, even now. She closed her eyes, feeling the sunlight on her face. The beautiful mosaics, the limestone walls shimmering in the summer heat, and the breeze that passed through evergreen branches. Yes, evergreen was the fragrance of Ephesus.

Wiping a tear from her eye, she felt her sharp cheekbones under a thick layer of grit and dirt. How long had she been here? She did not know. A guard told her that Aquila had been here too but had already "met his fate." She had been too weak to disagree. Aquila had met his Lord, and that was an altogether different thing.

Tullianum was rumored among the guards to be the gateway to the underworld. Long ago, the guards whispered, unfortunate souls had been sacrificed in this spot during spring occult rituals. People always went to such desperate lengths to placate an invisible world. Why did they imagine the invisible world was an angry one? she wondered. If only she had the strength to tell them. Praise God so many letters had been written. The Word was in the world, and she had peace now as she left it.

Her mind turned to Aquila. Why could she not fully remember his fragrance? A tentmaker, he smelled of leather and sun and the rosemary sprigs he loved sprinkled over baked bread.

She closed her eyes and dreamt of him. He was the rarest of men. Fully aware of his strength and power and yet so willing to see her grow into her own. He had bought his freedom from serving her family as their slave only to spend his life granting her freedom that no woman dared dream of. All because this God-man they followed, Jesus, had given them all such radical new thoughts, a new vision for life, and a new covenant. But who among men had found the courage to act on Christ's words?

Aquila had. That was one reason why Priscilla had led a remarkable life. That was why, she knew, the tears fell as she dreamed. She was a woman who had been loved as no other woman had ever been loved before. Would there be others after her? she wondered. Would other women know such freedom? Would other women walk in both strength and love?

But one secret she must keep, she reminded herself. Even in sleep, she would not let herself dream of her son. She could never speak his name again, lest the guards pass this information on. No one was safe, no matter where they were. Even now, her son was on strange waters, his destination hidden from her.

She heard the guards whispering.

"Her hands move as she dreams!" a rough voice said.

"She is writing," another man answered. The two men laughed.

"Who are you writing, old woman?" the first voice asked. "No one is coming to save you."

Oh, but you are wrong. She smiled softly as she sank deeper into a feverish sleep.

CHAPTER ONE

Nineteen Years Earlier, Rome

The home smelled amazing. Priscilla peeked into the kitchen to watch the cooks at work. Thyme and rosemary had been chopped and prepared as a dry rub for the lamb to be roasted. Onions and peppers sat sliced and waiting in bowls. A cook set to work spicing the barley and lentil soup with dill, fennel, and thyme. First, she sautéed spices over the fire to release their oils, then added onion before putting it all in the soup pot. Another cook tucked rosemary into every pot for a burst of fragrance and then into the bouquets of flowers as well.

Bowls of celery seed and bundles of dill sat on the table, ready to be sprinkled over the flatbread. This was the bread used for sopping up the lamb's juices left in the bowl.

The meal will be wasted on me. I can't eat a thing.

The desserts looked lovely though with dates soaked in honey, plus raisins and pomegranates, alongside a platter of roasted chestnuts drizzled with honey. There were also tarts with honey. Three servants worked feverishly in the kitchen, elbow to elbow.

Maybe another bride would swoon with hunger. Were brides supposed to be hungry before their weddings? If only her mother were here to tell her what she should feel. Surely this cold dread settling in the pit of her stomach was not normal. Her mother would know how to chase it away.

She snuck back to her room and clutched her mother's wedding veil. The beaded linen had been recently bleached, but the family's crest embroidered in blue had lost none of its stark power against the white. Long ago, she had dreamed of the day she would wear this. She never imagined this day would come without her mother. What would Mother say about the man chosen as her husband?

"You did not come to the Trajan Forum yesterday."

"Father!" She jumped up. He stood at the door to her room.

He spoke in soft tones, all his strength lost since the death of her mother. He was a ghost of a man. Were the circles under his eyes darker? He so rarely slept. He cocked an eyebrow, waiting.

Priscilla exhaled, careful not to vent her frustration. "No, Father. I was hoping if you spent time alone with Marcellus, he would help you understand."

He cocked his head to one side, like a child. Her brother had obviously failed in the mission.

"There is still time to fix your mistake," she gently urged.

Stepping toward him, she reached out and rested one hand on his arm. He recoiled, then seemed confused. Father was not himself anymore. Was this still grief from losing Mother? But that was two years ago. Was this old age? She feared that a disease was at work, but Marcellus laughed at the suggestion. Just as he had laughed when she insisted Father would never allow her to marry a former household servant. Even if that man was Aquila.

Yesterday, Aquila had officially become a citizen of Rome. Two years ago, before she died, Priscilla's mother had granted Aquila a letter of freedom, his manumission. She had written the letter, and Father had signed it. Yesterday, appearing before the Trajan Forum, Aquila had been officially listed in the census among the citizens of Rome.

Tomorrow he would become her husband. It was unthinkable. She was destined to marry someone from the courts of the emperor, not a former slave. Someone educated, wealthy, and influential. Someone like her. In the meantime, she was going to serve in the courts as a historian. She had already arranged it with her tutor. Emperor Claudius adored history, and no one was a better scholar than she.

Her father did not move. His eyes stared into the distance, so she spoke kindly and gently.

"This marriage makes no sense," she said. "Reverse it. You are a wealthy man. You are Athos, supplier of exotics for the emperor's games. You are the man who dares to cage lions and bears. All the earth is afraid of you, Father. Giving your daughter to a tentmaker? A freedman?"

Her father's eyes cleared as he turned to her. "I did no such thing."

She moved in closer, her words rushing together. In her haste, her voice rose in volume. "But you did! You allowed it! Father, tell Marcellus to cancel the wedding. I have a chance to serve in the emperor's courts. I will work with Emperor

Claudius, writing the history of Rome. You know how he loves history. This is how I will serve our family and Rome. You've always wanted to leave a legacy to Rome! This is it, Father. This is how we'll do it. Now tell Marcellus—"

"Tell me what?"

Marcellus leaned against a pillar across from her room, his linen tunic freshly bleached and pristine. Whatever he had been doing today, it had not been work.

Athos looked between them both, his eyes glazing over again. Quickly, Marcellus closed the distance between them and took him by the arm.

"You've upset our father," Marcellus scolded her. "Are you really so selfish?" Turning to their father, he softened his countenance. "Come, Father, you need to lie down in your room." Lucian, the household steward, appeared and draped a shawl over her father's thin shoulders.

Marcellus and her father walked away, arm in arm, with Lucian following.

Her brother's words stung. She picked up the veil again and rubbed the soft material between her fingers like it had something more to offer, hidden beneath the beading and embroidery. Catching herself before she ruined it, she wondered why there was no escape from this misfortune. Her life had seemed so blessed just a few years earlier, her future secure.

Born and raised a Jew, she was one of God's chosen people. The religious festivals marked each season with gladness. In recent years, some in her synagogue had begun embracing a version of their faith that included a risen Messiah named

Jesus. They held that a second covenant was given through this man, a covenant of peace, and to live in this revelation of Judaism was called following The Way. Her mother had believed in this news, the Good Story, at once. Priscilla had followed. She loved the freedom the believers called "grace." She was free from sacrifices, from rituals, from hundreds and hundreds of rules, most of which she broke unintentionally and often before she even left the house in the morning.

But then the world unraveled at the edges. Marcellus, barely two years younger, came of age and joined her father in running the family business. That did not seem a reason for rejoicing, although she had never understood her misgivings. Her mother grew weak and slept in the afternoons. Tensions in the synagogue grew between Jews living under the New Covenant and the Jews who lived under the first. Slowly, every source of comfort and security was lost.

Her thoughts flitted to Aquila. *He follows The Way.* Her mother shared many conversations with Aquila about faith, especially as her strength waned. Roman law made certain that servants had no more rights than a chamber pot, yet at the end of Mother's life, she wanted Aquila and Priscilla both to pray for her. It was Aquila who was with her at the last moment, not Marcellus. Aquila and Priscilla together at the final, heart-wrenching hour.

That awful afternoon, when Marcellus discovered he had been excluded, he had slapped Aquila. When Marcellus swung his hand back to slap Priscilla next, Aquila grabbed his wrist. Their eyes locked but not a word was spoken. Marcellus's arm shook as Aquila remained steady. Service had made Aquila strong, stronger than Marcellus would ever be. Marcellus took a step back and Aquila released him. Marcellus left the room and did not return.

Priscilla was too grief stricken to remember anything else about that day.

Aquila was just a servant, after all, and not a man any woman would pay attention to.

If I had only known.

The servant's nimble fingers flew quickly through the intricate weave of the braid. Priscilla studied the reflection in her mirror.

"No." Priscilla shook her head. "Too severe. Heat the curling rod. We can try ringlets."

The servant, without expression or response, obeyed. Servants had no thoughts to express, not if they wanted to live safely in Rome. But followers of The Way had been agitating against this ages-old system. No one wanted their way of life destroyed, not even when they knew it was the right path to take, so no one liked the Followers disrupting the system.

Mother used to say, *"If you want to keep peace, never interfere with someone else's food or money."* Once she embraced the New Covenant of grace, she saw that the New Covenant interfered with absolutely everything. Jews were told it was acceptable to eat unclean foods. Gentiles were freely forgiven without paying the temple for sacrifices. It was no wonder that Jesus had said He stank of death to some but was the fragrance of life to others. And worse yet, servants and women were regarded as equals to men, regarded as fully human.

Not that she wanted to marry one.

Shame plucked at her heart. Or was it guilt that she didn't live out her beliefs? She didn't want to marry a former servant. Maybe it was pride. Aquila was several years older and not the most handsome man she knew. He had a brisk business in the center of town operating a cloth and tent shop. He serviced many clients in Rome, including wealthy patronesses seeking cloth sunshades for their gardens, which were in fashion. Now, all her friends would shop there and see she had become a shopkeeper's wife. After all her hard work with the tutors, all her plans to serve the emperor as a historian, and this would be her life?

"No!" Slapping her hand on her dressing table, she exhaled in frustration. She was a terrible Follower of Jesus. "I cannot help what I feel!"

"What do you feel?" Aquila was in the doorway.

Startled, she stood, knocking over a small jar on the table. She caught it, flustered at her clumsiness. He wore a toga over his tunic. She had never seen him in a toga before today. Servants did not often wear them. But then, he was no longer a servant.

"You shouldn't be here," she said. *And I need privacy*. Everyone was disrupting her as she prepared for the wedding.

"I came to see if you'd received the fruit I sent."

"No, but I am sure the kitchen servants have put it to use." Although guests had dropped off gifts—she'd seen them arriving all week—she'd not opened any of them. She didn't even know where they were. Marcellus had all of them.

He nodded, as if not surprised, and then held out a small basket. Lined in beautiful embroidered linen, fresh figs nestled inside, the morning dew still fresh on each one. Sighing, she accepted the basket and took one. She offered him one too, but he declined.

"I haven't eaten today," she confessed.

"I know," he said. "You're nervous."

She stood straighter. "I'm not. Why would you say that?"

"I was a servant in this house for more than ten years. I know you."

"You do not. You may know my routines and habits, but I am not those things."

"Your hair," he replied, a kind light in his eyes. "You always made the family late when you were nervous. You made the servants change your hairstyle over and over. Lucian complained endlessly about how you upended everyone's schedule when you were nervous about meeting someone. Or an event where people would stare at you."

Priscilla felt the heat creeping into her cheeks. "It's to be expected on my wedding day."

Aquila started to say something then seemed to catch himself. "It's not really your day, though, is it?"

"What?"

Her servant returned and was startled to see Aquila in the room.

"I will see you later today. Do your best to have a peaceful heart. Everything will be all right." He bowed slightly and departed.

The servant girl's eyes were wide, her curiosity plain.

"I have no idea what he meant," Priscilla said. "Now, let's try the curls."

Priscilla watched from the upstairs balcony as servants put fresh blossoms in the indoor fountain in the center of the foyer. Fresh bouquets graced the entrance and dining couches as well. The garden was in full bloom today, with sunshades stretched between trees to ensure reprieve from the sun for the guests. Ever since the emperor had used shades in his Circus, they had become a fixture of fashion for the wealthy. Aquila's shop made sunshades like these.

"Aquila makes a good living," Marcellus said. He had come to say his goodbyes a few minutes earlier. After the wedding she would leave the family home forever. Father was feeling unwell, he said, and would not attend the wedding. Priscilla wanted to question him, but something was different about Marcellus today. He carried himself differently. He did not walk, exactly...he strutted, as if he dared someone to challenge him. But why? For what?

Beneath them, a servant dropped one end of a couch as he carried it. Lucian screamed at the boy, and Priscilla flinched.

"Mother wouldn't want Lucian yelling at the servants like that," she said.

"Mother wouldn't have wanted a lot of things." Marcellus leaned against the wall, watching her, and crossed his arms. He had dressed in his finest red wool toga, with a gold clasp that sparkled in the light.

His eyes changed, darkened as if shadowed by a cloud.

"I've always been jealous of you," he confessed, looking away suddenly. "Mother talked of your beauty to anyone who would listen—and of your accomplishments and your brilliant mind. She knew you would make us famous. She knew the emperor would be a fool not to call you into his service."

Priscilla glanced behind her, checking to see if any servants were near. "She was proud of you too."

"No, she wasn't," Marcellus sneered. "She didn't understand me. I am a strategist. I have a plan. You are a dreamer, a girl with books and words. Everything would have been fine, but then Mother and Father converted to The Way, and you followed. The three of you spent so much time believing in the invisible that you never made any plans. Someone had to take over. Someone has to run this family."

Priscilla started to snap at him then remembered Aquila's words. She didn't need to be upset, not today. "You have done well, brother. The business is thriving. The family will be honored in Rome."

He stood to leave, then paused. Over his shoulder, he spoke quietly. "I arranged the match."

"You?" she gasped. "I thought it was Father. That he was not in his right mind. You married me off to a freedman who makes tents? You know it's beneath me. Beneath us. It's not even honorable."

"And Father is slowly forgetting you."

"This is revenge?" She hated how small her voice sounded, but she could not believe that her brother—or anyone—could be so coldhearted.

He shrugged. "I am not destined for greatness. I've always known that. When you speak, when you write and transcribe, you have greatness. You could do great things. But with this marriage, now I have taken that from you. If we are nothing else, now we are equals. You don't know what a comfort that is."

He walked to the doorway then turned back. "Oh! I almost forgot. My wedding gift to you." He dumped a bag on the floor. Out of the mouth spilled wilted, decayed flowers, brooches, small scrolls, and a ring.

"What are these?" She was afraid to move, afraid to touch the bag or inspect it. A deep and heavy dread gnawed at her as she stared at the contents.

"All the gifts and notes sent to our home by men who wanted to ask for you in marriage," Marcellus replied. "So many good, wealthy men. For over a year now, I've intercepted every message, every gift. So many lives you could have led, Priscilla. So many happy paths were open to you. Until one by one, I led you here." He smiled—but to himself and not for joy.

"Why are you doing this?" she asked hoarsely.

"Because I want you to know what it's like to live in the shadows." He looked at her, his eyes alive as she had never seen them before. Who was this man before her? What had happened to her baby brother? "I want you to live in the shadow of someone greater than yourself and know that if only God had been kinder, you could have been great too."

"I'm sorry," she finally managed so say. "I did not know you felt so ignored. I did not know any of this, Marcellus."

"When you leave today, you leave the family name too. From today, our family no longer has a daughter, and our family is no longer Jewish."

"You can't erase the past," she replied. "This is insanity, Marcellus. Jews outnumber any other group in Rome. Rome is Jewish, if you dare to look closely. The emperor knows it. He's never going to move against the Jews. If you want favor with Claudius, you do not have to get rid of me or deny our faith. You just have to be worthy of notice."

Her words hung in the air between them. A rueful smile played on his lips.

"That's always been the problem, hasn't it?" he asked.

CHAPTER TWO

Noise from the street caught her attention.

Embarrassed, Priscilla hid upstairs and watched as the litters arrived. Guests disembarked and entered the home. Murmurs of approval and comments about the flowers floated to her in her hidden perch. She strained to hear a note of disapproval or gossip about the match, but everyone seemed preoccupied with business. Peeking to see which of her friends had arrived, she was startled. No one had a familiar face. She recognized none of the guests, though she did recognize their striped togas, the bright colors, and jewelry. All were senators or wealthy men of influence.

"The wedding is a political event, for Marcellus to grow in influence," she murmured. Aquila's words came back to her. *"It's not really your day, though, is it?"* He had not been mocking her but trying to prepare her.

An hour later, Aquila's eyes betrayed no emotion as she descended the stairs, and her knees almost buckled with nerves. He nodded imperceptibly then, and she straightened her spine, lifted her chin, and proceeded down. He had tried to warn her. She could repay him by being dignified, at least.

She made her vows in front of Marcellus and his friends, paying them as little attention as they paid her. Instead, she focused only on Aquila and on his warm hands enveloping hers. His palms were calloused. She had never felt a palm that had callouses, and she decided she did not like them. His grip was strong, though, and steady. She was sure that if her knees gave way again, he'd be able to hold her up just by the strength flowing from his hands. His thumb ran back and forth over the ring she wore, her mother's signet ring, an olive leaf made of gold and set in the center with a wide emerald. He glanced at it only briefly, then his eyes returned to hers.

That surprised her too. She was becoming his wife and therefore, in Roman law, his property. This ring was worth a small fortune. He should have been delighted to see it on her finger, but he seemed not to care for it. He seemed only to care for her.

It was hard to remember that followers of The Way believed in marriage between equals, not in a marriage of man and his property. But any other man, surely, after being granted his freedom, would relish having property, and a wife to be his servant too? *Aquila is not like any other man,* the Spirit whispered to her heart.

That night, Marcellus seemed happier than he had ever been. Priscilla watched as he feasted and danced. When he had drunk so much he stumbled about, Aquila took her hand and led her to the door. A litter waited for one of the guests, but Aquila paid the driver, who agreed to take them to his tent-making shop in the *subura*, the center of Rome.

"I live above the shop," Aquila said, and color crept into his cheeks.

"*We* live above the shop," Priscilla replied, and without knowing why, without planning to, she slipped her hand into his.

"It's my wedding gift to you. I knew Marcellus stole the gifts from your admirers, so I waited to give it to you."

Priscilla looked at the engraved wooden box on the small bed. The torch on the wall in the shop below cast long shadows here in the loft. The smell of leather and oil, and fresh linen sheets on the bed made the loft seem unexpectedly inviting. She was surprised. There was hardly enough room to turn around, yet she liked the space very much. She stood at the edge of the bed, looking at the box, hesitant to open it.

Aquila was talking so much. He had rarely spoken when he was a servant in her home. "I did not want to buy this for you. I wanted something more traditional," he continued. "But a nagging voice inside said this was what would bring you joy. Since I became a follower of The Way, I seem to have a sense about things sometimes. But I am often wrong too. Still, I think…I hope…this is what you would need to see on your first night of freedom."

Is that how he views this marriage? Freedom? She flinched slightly and hoped it did not show on her face.

She opened the box and caught her breath in a sharp gasp. Inside sat a stylus and the largest piece of parchment she'd ever seen.

"You may be a tentmaker's wife," he said shyly, "but you will still use your gifts."

She looked away. "I cannot write a history of Rome, not now."

"I doubt you will use your gifts to serve the emperor. That is true. God may have other plans."

"Then why did I work so hard?" she suddenly asked, her voice rising. "If God knew this moment would come, why let me work so hard, so many late nights, so many early mornings, thinking I could serve Rome as no other woman has done? Why let me dream if the dream cannot be?"

"Because the dream kept you on the right path. Where that path leads is the Lord's business, not yours."

She brought her hand to her mouth and bit her thumbnail. Finally, she asked the question. "Are you on the right path, Aquila? Marrying me? Why did you do it?"

Maybe she wanted the truth or maybe she wanted to pick a fight. If he got mad enough, he would storm from the loft and sleep downstairs.

"That is a story for another night," he replied evenly.

"I don't understand how this happened!" she cried.

"What troubles you more, being married to me or the idea of being married to a former servant, a tentmaker?" he replied, clasping his hands together loosely.

The question stopped her from the anxiety rising in her mind. She had to think. And then, she had to see him, really see him for the first time. She looked at him steadily, considering his question.

"You are a good man," she said finally. "Noble and honest."

Aquila raised his eyebrows like a tutor hearing an answer that pleased him. "So it is only my occupations, both former and current, that offend you. Your pride opposes the match, not your heart."

He removed his outer cloak as he talked, and she realized he meant to undress.

Her swallow was audible in the tiny space.

The corners of his eyes crinkled with his grin. "Are you nervous?"

"Aren't you?" She sat on the bed, her legs too weak to hold her up any longer. What a day it had been. Her life turned inside out and sent packing. Now here with a former servant she had rarely spoken to. Married to him!

He sat next to her. "Of course." He kissed the top of her head.

She forgot how tall he was. He didn't really fit in this small space. Maybe he felt out of place in many ways too.

"Just answer one question," she asked abruptly. "Did you seek the marriage?"

"No."

He did not shy away from the truth. She appreciated that. He did not flatter. He really was a truthful man, she decided.

"But I always thought you were the most beautiful girl in all of Rome," he added.

"Oh!" she muttered. "And I had just decided that you were an honest man, one who knew better than to try flattery with a girl."

"I am an honest man and I'm not flattering you," he replied. "You were always too fond of your own opinions."

"But the whole time you served my family, you hardly said two words to me." She scooted back, determined to win the argument.

He leaned forward. "A smart man knows what he is good at."

"You were a servant. Surely you knew that was no chance we could ever be betrothed? My mother would have never allowed it. She was very protective of me."

Aquila took her hand in his. "You don't know everything about your mother. She trusted me. I knew she was ill long before any of you because she needed me to put her final wishes into place before she revealed her illness to your brother. She is the one who gave me the payment to buy my freedom. And she is the one who told Marcellus that a marriage to a recently freed servant like me would be absolutely unacceptable for you."

Her eyes widened as the realization became clear. Her mother had planted the idea in Marcellus's mind, knowing Marcellus would delight in betraying Priscilla. Which brought Priscilla to one other conclusion.

"My mother planned our marriage." Her voice was high, like a little girl's. "She intended me to marry you all along." With those words, a warm feeling rushed through her chest. Her mother had saved her from Marcellus, and Marcellus strutted and crowed, thinking it was his idea.

Without thought, she sat up and kissed Aquila, a fast, impulsive, joyous kiss.

It was not the last.

As the months went by, Priscilla settled into life as a tentmaker's wife. She learned to run the shop alongside Aquila. She even learned to prepare meals without the aid of servants or fire. In the poorer section of Rome, kitchen fires were too dangerous. Meals were mainly cheeses, figs, and bread bought on the street. Sometimes there was money for roasted meat, but usually she had to content herself with roasted chickpeas. Her wardrobe was a simple linen tunic, with a thin stola draped over it for modesty. Anything more and she'd never fit in with the other wives.

Aquila was still relatively new to tentmaking and learning from the guild. He was also learning the best practices of running a business. Overseeing the household of Priscilla's parents had given him wisdom and experience with bookkeeping, negotiating, and scheduling shipments, but owning his own shop was different. He had to get the sale, order the raw materials, transform them, sell the product, and work against deadlines.

He had come of age learning the rhythms of a household, but the world of business was different music altogether.

Priscilla understood. She had to learn the music as well. And if being a wife was a challenge, so was being a working wife. She was used to ringing bells for servants to attend her needs. What a new experience to wait on others! Customers expected her to fulfill their orders, give them discounts, and shorten delivery times. At night, she burned the oil lamps and learned to hold a needle and fasten leather into a tent. At first, none of her work was worth showing to a customer.

Aquila came home from synagogue only two or three times before he announced he did not want to return. The men in the synagogue, who still adhered to the Old Covenant, the Law of Moses, derided him for his lenient treatment of his wife. She could not cook, nor sew, and she had brought no dowry into the marriage except a signet ring that she would not allow Aquila to sell. That is how the men framed it. Write a letter of divorce and send her back to her brother, they urged him. She is of no use.

Priscilla knew this because the women at the public toilets gossiped. Public toilets were another daily embarrassment she had to adjust to, and the baths that were adjacent were little more than lukewarm dishwater. Still, this was how she met women who, like her, were shopkeepers' wives. Making friends was slow and awkward. Osira, the butcher's wife, was her first friend.

"Have you any thought of moving farther out?" Osira asked one morning, sitting next to her in the bath. Bored attendants sat on stone benches near the water, working for wages that would barely feed a child for the day. "No one likes leather workers in the center of the subura," Osira said. "If you move, I can send more business your way."

Priscilla's eyes widened. She got out of the bath, stung by her words and confused.

Later that night, Aquila explained. Leather tanning was a foul business. Scraping fresh hides to rid them of hair and flesh polluted the air and water near a shop. However, Aquila bought his leather already tanned. His shop was clean and bright, and he did a brisk business. Osira's husband, Cato the butcher, thought the location of the shop was blessed by the gods. He wanted it for himself.

"You should explain to her The Way," Aquila said.

"She pretended to be my friend!" she protested. Priscilla began bathing later in the day just to avoid her. She still hurt too much from Marcellus's betrayal to forgive anyone easily. In the heat of the afternoon, most of Rome took a nap. City streets quieted down. That was an ideal time to slip away.

Osira's suggestion that all leather shops stank was wrong. Aquila's shop smelled of warm leather and linen, of his beard oil made from evergreen trees, and Priscilla's bath oil made from aloe. Other shops, with huge families packed tight in the space, smelled of soil and sweat. Maybe someday, though, she'd have children too. Maybe then the cramped living conditions wouldn't bother her. She was determined to be brave, although she had not yet forgiven Osira and Cato.

What would Jesus have said about forgiveness? She had heard many different stories passed from the disciples who walked with Him. When she needed to know about one specific thing, like forgiveness, she had no way to know and no one to ask. The eyewitnesses—the disciples—traveled and told their stories, and other believers told the stories too. But unless a teacher was in their midst, or she had the story committed to memory, she had to just pray and allow God to reveal Himself.

Priscilla's hand cramped as she pushed the needle through the leather. She'd been working in the loft by the light of an oil lamp since the third watch of the night. Her leather goods had sold quite well recently. Aquila had been restless this night, though, unable to sleep. He claimed his heart seemed to be warning him, but he did not know what about. He left at dawn to go pray at the synagogue before the others arrived. She'd sharpened this needle to a knife's edge and set to work.

She did not like him going to there to pray. The men were divided in which covenant they followed, the old or the new. The advice they gave varied depending on their view of Jesus. Aquila was under grace, not law, and if anyone gave him advice that caused him to stumble back into works…

The needle sliced through the leather. Pulling from the underside, she stretched her thread out and placed the needle for the next stitch. The hair on the back of her neck stood up. Stopping, catching her breath, she listened to the night just beyond her door.

It is only the usual noise from the streets. Gangs of homeless youth calling to the prostitutes, the prostitutes calling to the men on their way home from the market or court, and women searching for drunk husbands. This was a side of her beloved city she'd never known until now.

My cooking upset Aquila's digestion tonight, that's all. If there is any foreboding, it came from his stomach. Besides, Aquila had followed The Way much longer than she had, and the New Covenant included the outrageous promise that the Spirit of God would live within each believer. Surely God would reveal His will.

A rush of footsteps past the shop door made her heart race. A woman's scream startled her, causing her to drop the needle. Scrambling to pick it up before it was lost in the dirt on the floor, sure to be stepped on, she was hidden behind a table when the shop door shattered. A trio of men stormed into the shop and the noise of the riot breaking out in the streets flooded in.

Priscilla scooted under the table, hiding herself completely, her hand sweeping frantically through the dirt to find the needle. The end pierced a finger, bringing blood, but she bit her lip and carefully wrapped her hand around the needle. Where was Aquila?

"Cato said to destroy it all," one of the men said.

"Just the merchandise and tools," another replied. "Leave the shop in good shape."

She only heard two voices, but she had seen three men enter.

Her hand flew to her mouth, but she did not reveal her position. *Cato sent men to destroy the shop?*

The riot outside continued. She could hear scuffling and fighting and men charging and cursing. She'd never heard such violence before. Her stomach knotted and clenched. Searing ice-cold pain coursed through her legs, making her want to run as fast as she could. She willed her body to stop its revolt, to remain perfectly still, to endure the terror without making a sound. But all the sounds were there, in her throat, threatening to explode in a scream.

"What do we have here?" a man sneered, standing over her. He had silently climbed the loft stairs and discovered her. He must be the third man she had heard.

She lunged out from beneath the table and jammed the needle into his cheek. He yelped, staggering back, clutching his face.

Aquila burst into the shop as the third man rushed toward the stairs, knocking over the oil lamp onto a stack of linen near Priscilla, and ran out the door. Aquila tackled one man, but the other ran rather than face him.

"Aquila!" Priscilla screamed to get his attention, her voice returning. Flames were already at the ceiling and moving to the stairs. She would be trapped in seconds. He let the man go and moved to the stairs.

"Come down, now!" he yelled.

"What do I save?" she called.

"There's no time! Run!" he screamed. The flames were at the wooden stairs, flicking up. She ran down, the edges of her thin tunic singed.

They ran out the door, only to watch as the fire spread to the shops nearby. Fire in the subura was a fearsome, merciless enemy, more ruthless than any emperor, hungrier than any beast in the Circus. In a matter of moments, it devoured the shops of many families. The fire brigade arrived, and Aquila assisted them, but it was too late for nineteen shops and residences. Those families lost everything.

Rumors and gossip made the next forty-eight hours unbearable. Violence in the city streets had been on the rise for years, but now people claimed the new sect of Jews who followed The Way were behind it. People demanded that Emperor Claudius punish those responsible. *Perhaps Cato and Osira started the rumors.*

A few friends stopped by the shop the first night to bring food and help salvage what remained. Priscilla marveled that one small household item could have ended so many lives, not just their livelihoods. And the men who came to loot the store had actually been bold enough to touch her! In her father's house that would be unthinkable. Any criminal would have known death would be swift for such a crime. But here, as a common wife, justice would be hard to come by. Since she had suffered no injury, there could be no arrest. But there had been a crime. And a crime unpunished was a crime in itself.

Isn't my God a God of law, of justice? Jesus upheld the laws. Where is God in this? Where is His vengeance?

"Do you have any salve?" Aquila interrupted her ruminations on the second night. "I burned my little finger and it gives me no peace."

"I do not. Where do I find it? Who sells it?" She had never bought medicine. It had always been sent to her home by the family physician.

Aquila popped his finger in his mouth and then blew on it, wincing from the pain. "I've had bigger injuries and ignored them. But this one little finger causes endless torment."

"Aquila! Where do I buy medicine?"

He smiled and grabbed a blanket left for them by a volunteer. After spreading it out on the floor of the shop, he lay down. "I'm exhausted. I'm going to sleep for a while." When he saw her expression, he sat back up. "It doesn't matter who sells medicine. No one will sell to us. Not until the truth comes out about who started the fire."

"But you're hurt," she replied.

"You know what the apostle Paul says," he murmured. "All things work together for good." He was asleep as soon as he closed his eyes.

Priscilla had never hated those words from Paul until now. Sitting in the rubble of her shop, with an injured husband she couldn't care for, those words were just salt in a wound. She never wanted to meet that man Paul. If his personal history wasn't terrible enough, his quotes were dreadful.

She sat on the floor next to Aquila, watching the door in case of intruders. The door did not fit in the doorway. It had been placed by volunteers from the synagogue, using a door from another shop that had closed last year. Noise and dust from the street flowed in. She wrapped a donated shawl around her shoulders. Her stomach was a pit of acid and her eyes were dry.

It would do no good to cry anyway. *What can I learn from this?*

In emergencies, she couldn't rely on other people to supply anything. She needed to stock supplies. Medicine, oil for the lamps, and a little food would be a good idea.

If trouble comes again, I will be ready.

CHAPTER THREE

The following month, as Priscilla was at market buying figs, steady vibrations in a one-two pattern shook the ground at her feet. The volume on the street grew in intensity and her ears seemed to stretch and open as if to take it all in. Everyone in the market stopped their haggling and calling, looking toward the sound of the distant thunder rumbling straight toward them.

The emperor's Praetorian Guard marched down the main street of Rome. Children ran alongside the soldiers. Young men cheered, and girls watched from behind their mothers. The Praetorian Guard was revered around the empire. Only the most elite soldiers could be considered for its service. She'd seen the Guard in the halls of the Senate and near the emperor many times. They were not only personal security for him and the politicians, they were elite fighting forces.

She marveled at the sight of their bloodred shawls, their bronze helmets, the shields with gold wings. Each man wore armor that covered his chest and shoulders so that he looked to be made more of metal than man. The noise they made as they marched in unison unnerved their subjects. She could feel every step in her belly.

She caught sight of one guard she had met at the office of the consul. His name was Marcus. Would he remember her? She stepped out to call his name, then remembered what she must look like now. She had no fine clothes, no pins in her hair. He was glorious, however, as he followed behind his leader, a man wearing a giant headdress made from a wolf's skull.

The crowd fell in behind the Praetorians, anxious to know why they marched. Priscilla counted two cohorts, at her best guess, about six hundred soldiers. Why would so many be dispatched to the center of Rome?

When the Guard reached the theater, one guard set a wooden box with stairs into place. The man wearing the wolf headdress climbed up to address the crowd, unrolling a scroll. As he read the edict from Emperor Claudius, Priscilla understood why the Guard had been sent to deliver the news.

Emperor Claudius had exiled all Jews. They must leave Rome at once.

The edict was met with a roar. Some were outraged while others rejoiced at their good fortune. The Jews would leave behind real estate, furniture, animals, their entire life's work and savings. Anyone who was not a Jew was about to become very rich—unless the emperor got his hands on the estates first.

The next morning, Priscilla still reeled from shock. Her hands felt heavy, as if the air had become thick and nothing she touched was real. Working with leather took more strength than her arms could give. Setting her work down on the workbench, she stood to stretch.

Aquila fetched water from the chipped crock at the back of the shop. "Here," he said, offering her the cup. Priscilla grimaced as she drank. The water tasted sour, which was probably why they had been able to afford it. *Maybe I should mix in a little wine next time. Oh, there is no next time. Not here.*

"This can't be happening. There are far too many Jews in Rome for Claudius to expel all of us," she said. She and Aquila barely had anything, and now they would lose even that.

"Quite a few of his advisors are Jewish," Aquila said. "Have faith. This will work out."

Her thoughts turned to her brother. "If Marcellus goes into exile, he won't survive," she said. "The crowds will kill him if they catch him leaving the city with his gold and his fine togas."

"And Marcellus would never go anywhere without being dressed in his finest toga," Aquila replied. "You're right to worry about him. The crowds will spot him at once."

Priscilla was thankful that Aquila knew her brother as only a servant could. Although Marcellus had betrayed her, she was happy. She wanted to tell him that. *Is that spite? Or the beginning of forgiveness? Maybe it is just the voice of Mother stuck in my head, urging me to try and reach him one last time.*

"If you want to go and speak with him, wait for me," Aquila said. "I have an important errand. When I return, if the streets are quiet, I will escort you to your family's estate."

The sun set across the soot-stained roofs of Rome, and Aquila had not returned.

Priscilla checked the oil for the lamp. It ran low. She had not thought to buy extra. She rationed her money so carefully, and with Aquila by her side she did not mind when the lamp burned out at night. Better not to have light than not to have food, she reasoned. But now he wasn't home and she was scared to lose the light.

A furious pounding on the shop door made her heart leap into her throat.

"Priscilla! Priscilla!" a woman's voice cried. "Let us in!" Priscilla went to the door and placed her hand on it. Did she know the voice? Was it a fellow believer? She had no other friends. If she was wrong, though…

The woman's scream pierced her deliberations. Priscilla swung the door wide and a woman from the Jewish community stumbled into the shop, clutching her young daughter. Slave traders, two of them, were at her heels. One grabbed the mother by her ankles. "We only want your child!" he screamed.

The other grabbed the daughter, prying her from her mother's arms. The girl bit the man, drawing blood, and he slapped her.

Priscilla, stunned by the violence, did not move. Forcing herself to breathe, she willed herself to grab a hammer from the workbench and swung it with all her might. The blow landed against the man's back but he only roared in pain. The blow did not stop him. Instead, he lifted mother and child and hoisted them to his shoulder.

"We'll take the both of you then," he spat. "Let the traders decide what to do with the woman."

And then they were gone.

Priscilla sank down onto the floor. Wind from the street swept into the shop from the open door. A woman was never safe in Rome, but now a woman was not safe in her own home, and a child unsafe in her mother's arms. What had Claudius done to her beloved city? What would become of the Jews?

And why was Aquila not back? If she wanted to warn her brother, she had to go now. She might lose her chance and he would be killed in the exile. He didn't know how violent their beloved city could be.

Draping the hood of a cloak low over her face, she prayed that the shadow cast over her features would give her some protection. She would be careful to keep her hands tucked into the folds of her cloak. A woman who worked with her hands was a woman who could go missing, and no one would care. The important women were kept protected behind walls and did no work.

Less than an hour later she approached the gates of her family's estate, as a litter passed by. Trying to stay in the shadows, she could not easily move from its path. The litter splashed mud and filth from the road on her cloak. The smell made her cover her mouth with one hand.

The litter stopped. Priscilla stopped, leaning further back into the night. A hand emerged from the shadows, holding a denarius that sparkled in the moonlight.

"My apologies for your tunic." It was Marcellus's voice.

Her heart pounded in her ears. He hadn't called her by name. Her cloak had been pulled low; he could not know her identity. He only knew his litter had splashed someone in the shadows, shivering and now coated in sewage, horse dung, and worse.

She edged forward. She needed the money. She could grab it and then present herself at the gates moments later. But no, he'd smell her cloak and put the pieces together. Still, a denarius! And just before she and Aquila fled the city with nothing.

He slowly withdrew the coin. "My arm grows tired. Do you accept my apology or not?"

Lunging forward, she reached to grab it, but his other hand shot out and took her by the wrist.

"I knew it was you!" he spat. "Huddling in the shadows like a rat! Why did you come back? To beg for money?" His eyes flitted to the ring on her hand. Releasing her wrist, he dropped the coin onto the street, where it sank into the mud and filth.

Tears stung her eyes. "I came to warn you."

He chuckled and sat back in the litter, so she could only see his profile.

"When are you leaving?" she asked.

"I'm not leaving."

"But the edict—"

"If I was a Jew, I'd leave. But I'm not. You could ask my father, but he does not remember anything these days." He wrinkled his nose. "You need to bathe. Let us finish our business. What did you want to warn me about?"

Her warning was pointless now. "If you're not leaving, what will you do?"

"Claudius loves bribes—everyone knows it. He and I have reached a comfortable arrangement." Marcellus shrugged then picked at a fingernail.

"You've always been clever." That was all she could think of to say. Maybe later there would be a hundred replies on her lips, but in this moment, the sadness and cruelty of her brother's nature had stopped her mouth.

"Why didn't you show your ring to anyone in the Senate?" he asked suddenly. "You would have gotten excellent treatment."

"Can I say goodbye to Father?"

"I can't believe I let you walk out the door with that," he muttered. He spoke quietly to his driver, and the litter passed through the gates into their family's estate. Only when she was certain he was gone did she bend down and search for the denarius. Shame inflamed her neck and cheeks as she sifted her fingers through the filth, but it was too much money to waste and the voyage ahead too uncertain.

She kept to the shadows as she went home. An old woman sat crouched against the Senate, shivering. Her eyes were milk white, her skin thin and wrinkled as wet parchment. As Priscilla passed, the woman held out a trembling hand. "Please, help me, for I am hungry and have no family."

Pausing, feeling the weight of the denarius in her hand, Priscilla's heart hurt. "I am here, mother," she whispered. It was only a term of respect, but as she spoke the words, she knew what to do. She pulled the signet ring from her finger and pressed it into the palm of the old woman. "Show this to the Consul in the morning. He knows this seal. It belonged to a woman he once knew. He will help you trade with it. Make sure you get lodging and food for a long time, for this ring is valuable. God be with you, mother."

"And with you."

As she approached the taverns, violence broke out, but she did not tremble in fear from it. Looters ransacked empty shops, as some Jews had already fled the city. She reached up and wiped the damp from her cheek.

She was crying, she realized. This was Rome, the greatest empire in the world, the model of justice for all nations…and now it had become a senseless, corrupt pit. And for what? What did Claudius hope to accomplish?

Aquila was less than pleased when Priscilla arrived home. He sat on a workbench, his face ashen with anger. She had risked her life in those streets. Again she felt the strange reversal of their relationship. She was answerable to her former servant. In Roman law, he could throw her in the street for disobedience and be done with her. Only in the eyes of Christ were they equals, and Christ had certainly not stopped the slave traders from taking that mother and child.

What changes the new believers could bring, what hope to women and children! But maybe that was the reason Claudius wanted them all gone? At the heart of fear was a fear of truth, and Christ was dismantling the old ways.

Clearing his throat, Aquila smoothed his tunic. "I have encouraging news." When he looked up, she could see his jaw muscles twitching. He was trying to control his anger. But to a Roman man, punishing a wife was a natural right.

Christ demanded so much more of men. For women coming to belief, they came to freedom. *It is easier for us. Freedom is instinctual. It feels right.* But for men, to walk away from a culture that defined masculinity as power, and power over a woman, that was a high price indeed. Aquila must have felt at times that he was less of a man. What faith it took for a man to fully embrace Christ's teachings.

"Priscilla?" he prompted.

"I'm sorry, husband." She smiled. "My mind wandered. What news?"

"Tonight, I met with the tentmaking guild to consult about where we should go. It's their recommendation that we go to Corinth. There is much work in that province. The Isthmian Games require many tents and leather goods."

"The games?" Priscilla replied. She'd never considered travel to Corinth, not even to see the games. They were much like the Greek Olympics, but Corinth had them every two years.

"Corinth is not a long trip by boat," Aquila continued, sounding excited. "The season is right for traveling by sea, and I was able to negotiate a private room on the next ship."

"We have no money," she said, then remembered the denarius. "Well, very little, anyway."

"But we do have something to trade. The captain won't have to pay taxes on something he can easily conceal at port. By wearing it as his own."

Priscilla shook her head. "I don't understand." And then she did. "I gave the ring to a woman who was destitute."

Color drained from his cheeks. If they did not have a private room, Priscilla knew, they'd travel with all the other refugees. They would suffer.

She ran her fingers through her hair. "I am so sorry. If I had known—"

"And if I had gone with you, it might not have turned out any differently."

After a long moment, he patted the bench next to him and she came and sat down, resting her head on his shoulder. "I probably would have given her the ring too. But at least then you could have blamed me instead of yourself."

She smiled at that. "I will not ignore your requests again," she promised. "It's always good to have someone to blame when things go wrong."

He laughed. Aquila was a very good man and an excellent husband.

CHAPTER FOUR

The Voyage East

Aquila had not secured better lodging, because on this boat there was none. They traveled to Corinth on a merchant ship, along with a handful of other refugees. Aquila had found a captain who needed work on his sails, and he and Priscilla were able to make repairs during the voyage. A bad storm from a previous trip had caused much damage, so there was plenty of work.

Priscilla sat above deck, needing the light to work and the fresh air to breathe. On the open water, sunrise was a glorious hymn of color, a praise that shifted and swirled as she watched. "I've never seen such color," she murmured. She had never realized how the buildings and grand architecture of Rome had blocked her view of the wider world.

The hold stank of sweat and old rotten grain. Above deck, the sun made the water sparkle and the wind cut across the ship, stirring her tunic and hair. Every hour or so, she set her work down and looked up. The horizon stretched endlessly in every direction.

Blackbirds flying low in formation raced past the stern.

"We'll be in Corinth by tomorrow," Aquila said, joining her on deck.

"I don't even know what that means," she said. "It's only a name to me. What will it be like? Will they hate us? Will we go hungry?"

He rested a hand on her shoulder. She reached up and placed her hand on his.

"Everything has worked out thus far," Aquila reminded her.

"But it's been painful," she replied.

"It has, especially for you. But consider the Christ whom you follow. He wasn't afraid of pain."

Priscilla removed her hand and stood up. "I know you're trying to encourage me, but you're only succeeding in making me irritable."

Aquila scratched his chin. "I'm trying to help. You seem unnerved at times. I know how much you've lost, how much change you've gone through—"

"No!" she replied. "You don't know. You never had a family, Aquila. You don't know what it's like to lose one." As soon as the words were out, she regretted them. Her stomach went sour. She had snapped several times on the journey and did not understand why.

He turned his back to her and walked to the ship's railing, dodging the men working to secure the rigging. She drew a deep breath before approaching him.

"I'm sorry," she said. "You did have a family, before ours, I mean. I never even asked you about them, did I?" Shame burned in her heart.

"I was brought to the slave market with my brother and sister when I was about four. They were older," he answered. His voice seemed small, and his eyes were locked on the horizon. "My father had gone into debt before he died. He could not face the debtor's prison, so he took his own life. My mother, of course, had no means to pay the debt, so the creditors took her children and sold us in the market in Rome. I had never seen a city before."

She hung her head. "What happened to your brother and sister? To your mother?"

"I do not know. I doubt they were as fortunate as I." He sighed. "The brothels, probably."

The next words would be bitter. "Was my father a kind master to you?"

He nodded. "He was. I was a fast learner, though. He did not need to whip me very often."

She blanched at the thought of a whipping and that he could be grateful it hadn't happened often. He should have been outraged it happened at all.

He reached for her hand and she quickly accepted.

"When the New Covenant was explained to me, when I came to understand what Jesus had done, do you see why I embraced it at once? When the message of Christ spreads, slavery will end. You cannot love as Jesus loved and crush the poor. Can you imagine what the world will be when His message takes root?"

"Perhaps someday your brother and sister will be free. Don't give up hope for them," Priscilla said softly.

"I looked for them, many times. What I cannot repair and I cannot understand, I choose to surrender." He kissed the top of her head. "That's how I live in peace."

I must control my temper. The voyage brought out an edge to her personality she had not known was there. *I am unused to the sea, that is all.*

The next morning, dolphins leaped in the water alongside the ship. A good sign, the captain commented as he passed by. He made morning rounds before dawn, checking the rigging and talking with crew members from the night watches. Priscilla had felt unwell and was above deck for fresh air. The hold's stench and heat, coupled with the rocking water, had made her violently ill more than once.

She leaned her head over the side, feeling she might be ill once more. In the distance the horizon had just turned pink. The sun would announce the arrival of the new day in shimmering rays of color. Catching her breath, she looked at the water below. A great eye rose from the depths, watching her.

Clutching her hand to her stomach, she gasped.

The captain sauntered over and peered at the water.

"Only a whale." He laughed and pointed farther out. "Look closely and you'll catch a glimpse of its family. They travel together." He lifted his finger toward the sky. "See those birds? They're albatrosses. My men believe them to be the spirits of dead sailors. We like seeing them guide our ship into harbor."

"What religion do you practice?" she asked him.

"I don't," he replied. "I don't mind a bit of superstition though."

"Have you heard of Jesus of Nazareth? Of His death at the hand of the Roman Empire and how He rose from the dead?"

The captain laughed again. "Now who is talking superstition?

Priscilla wanted to reply but was frustrated. Talking about Jesus and the Good Story was hard. It sounded outlandish. And this was a man who believed birds were dead sailors.

His face softened. "I didn't mean to insult you. Your husband has been very useful on this voyage, and your needlework has saved us a lot of money in repairs. But why would you follow a god who would force a pregnant woman out of her country and into a dangerous voyage?"

"I thought...I thought I was only seasick," she stammered.

"Before I took command of this vessel, I worked on a slave ship. You get an eye for those things. Sometimes a pregnant woman brings more money, and sometimes..." His glassy stare at the water sent a shiver down her spine.

He looked at her sternly. "Do not tell anyone on board. Sailors have superstitions about pregnant women on ships."

Aquila joined them, and the captain excused himself to finish the morning's work. Priscilla and Aquila watched dolphins leaping in the water alongside the boat. Priscilla did not speak a word of the captain's assessment. She wanted to find a woman, a midwife, who would confirm the news first.

I've never seen this color, not even in all the emperor's gems!

As Priscilla entered the port of Corinth, the first thing she noticed was the color of the water. It was dazzling, somewhere between emerald green and blue. She stayed at the edge of the boat, mesmerized by the water's brilliance. The land was dappled with cypress and palm trees, and the rocky cliffs had pale bands of yellow and white. The land itself was split in two, with the Corinthian Canal running in between the two land masses. The sight of activity on either side was like nothing she had ever witnessed.

Merchant ships were unloaded, then the cargo rolled on conveyers across the land. Then the ships themselves were brought onto land and rolled across.

The captain explained. "The canal is too shallow and narrow for most ships. But it connects the Ionian and Aegean Seas. This looks like a nightmare to manage for a captain and his crew but I assure you, they would rather do this than sail all the way around the coast. It's a much longer, very dangerous voyage. There are man-eating monsters in the water, teeth as big as your fist. They follow the ship day and night."

Priscilla's hand went instinctively to her stomach.

Aquila's eyes met hers and a light dawned in them.

The captain clapped Aquila on the back. "Welcome to Corinth. I hope she bears you a son."

Aquila took Priscilla in his arms and kissed her there, as the turquoise sea danced around them and the sun-washed city of Corinth rose before them.

Climbing up the stone steps into the city, Priscilla lifted her eyes, beholding a statue of the god Apollo. Nude except for a cascading bit of fabric, the statue spared no detail. Aquila nudged her along, and she laughed at his reddening cheeks.

He pointed to the mountain to their right. At the top was a temple with multiple columns on every side. Braziers with fire blazed on every corner, and pilgrims traversed up and down flights of steps up the mountain.

"Aphrodite's temple," Aquila said. "Goddess of love." His dismissive tone told her what he thought of that. "Hundreds of temple prostitutes are said to work there," he continued.

"Venus," she replied, more for herself than Aquila. Romans had different names for the Greek gods and goddesses, but at heart the pagan faiths were much the same. Both used young temple prostitutes, which believers of The Way had begun to protest against. Believers said it was wrong to use youths for this, and most of the temple prostitutes were really no more than children. Believers agitated against things that made no sense to their pagan counterparts.

As she climbed the stairs, she saw seashells littered on every step. She'd never seen one except in the shops back home. She stopped to pick one up.

"Look! Even the broken ones are beautiful," she said, holding it out to Aquila. The breaks afforded a look inside at the delicate work.

"And the air here is so different," she went on, but Aquila was already talking to a stranger. He'd picked up a few Greek words and was looking for directions to the tentmaking guild. The air was thick and salty but also clean. She had never realized how polluted Rome was until now, with its smoky air, human filth in the streets, and the people packed tightly together.

She quickly noticed here the men didn't wear long tunics but short chitons that stopped at the knee. The women still wore long tunics of linen, but they pinned another layer of material at their shoulders to cascade down the chest to the waist. The clothes looked cool and comfortable.

Lifting her eyes to the left, she saw the gently sloping hills as she felt the bracing wind sweeping in from the sea. This could be a good place to start over.

A man pushed his way through the throng of people at the port. "Aquila? Aquila of Rome?" he called.

Aquila lifted his hand. The man thrust out his hand and shook it, then pulled Aquila in for a loud, robust kiss on both cheeks. Priscilla bit her lip to keep from laughing at Aquila's wide-eyed reaction. He'd never been kissed in greeting. Romans didn't do that, at least not to freed slaves.

She took a deep breath of sea and sun. Aquila was not a freed slave, not here in Corinth.

Corinth really was a new beginning. They weren't running away from an emperor. God had brought them here. She could feel the difference in her spirit. A bird calling out overhead seemed to confirm it and she laughed at its timing.

"My name is Titus," the man said, then extended his hand to Priscilla. She took his hand and braced herself for a kiss, but he was gentle with her. A quick peck on each cheek and he continued. "I left Rome last year, after I sensed in the Spirit that I needed to minister to new believers here."

"Are there many of us?" Priscilla asked.

"Come and see!"

Within the hour, she and Aquila sat down to a meal at Titus's home. Stephanus, a synagogue leader, sat with them, plus a few families from the guild. Sitting on the floor around the table, she had trouble remembering all their names, and her eyelids grew heavy. But the food was a mercy that overwhelmed her. She was bone weary from the journey, frightened at starting a new life without friends or family or any of the comforts of home… and these strangers opened their home to her. They broke bread and set before her modest fare that tasted better than anything her father's wealth had ever bought. Fresh fish, hot bread, olives, figs drizzled with honey and spices. She sighed with contentment and silently praised God that she could keep it all down.

Titus's wife, Marianna, brought out clothes and sat them next to Priscilla. Priscilla looked up at her, not understanding. Marianna's expression was kind.

"You need a fresh chiton after a sea voyage. And a peplos to pin at your shoulders, like the women wear here. Plus"—she leaned in a bit closer—"you'll need a bigger chiton in a few months, yes?"

Priscilla's hand went to her stomach. *Why do I make that gesture without thinking?*

"How did you know?" she whispered.

"You wrinkled your nose at the olives. You remarked that the smell was too strong. But no one else can smell them at all." Marianna patted Priscilla's knee sweetly.

What does smell have to do with carrying a child? A sudden longing to talk to her mother swept over her so strongly she grasped the table for support. Tears must have fallen because she realized, to her horror, that the conversation had stopped. Everyone at the table stared at her.

Aquila was frozen, at a loss, it seemed, for why she was crying.

Marianna put her arm around Priscilla. "She is simply overtired from the long journey," she told the dinner guests. "I will lead her to the loft and let her rest there. Carry on."

Marianna did just that. She even stayed a few moments while Priscilla explained that her mother had passed nearly three years ago.

Marianna listened while she rummaged through her things and found a spare comb for Priscilla. "You will need it with the sea air here." Priscilla accepted the gift, the second gift Marianna had offered since Priscilla had arrived. Marianna and Titus were not wealthy people. But then, neither was she anymore.

"I cannot repay you," Priscilla whispered, too embarrassed to say it out loud.

"How long have you been a believer?" Marianna asked, sounding surprised.

Priscilla, her eyelids growing impossibly heavy once more, thought back. "About four years, I think."

Marianna tucked the linen coverlet around her shoulders. "You haven't understood everything yet, then. You don't repay me. You just go and do the same for someone else." Marianna took the oil lamp from the stand near the bed and padded down the stairs back to the dinner party.

Drifting into sleep, her belly full, her body so comfortable at last on a bed with clean linens, Priscilla could still feel the rocking of the ship and hear the cry of birds. *If this is how believers treat each other, why doesn't everyone want to follow The Way?*

Homesickness was a physical pain that lodged in her chest about two weeks later. Even her thick, frizzy hair struggled to adjust to Corinth. She longed for Rome, where she had hair oils and combs. On the streets here, every face looked so much alike. She had learned a few words of Greek, not the language of scholars but the words of the street, useful for bartering at the market. She went every morning before breakfast to the women's bath and met Marianna. After soaking and scraping the bath oil from their skin, they dressed for the day and compared thoughts. Marianna had been a follower of Christ for nearly a decade. She'd met the one they called Paul several times, plus Peter too.

"Paul murdered many of us, though," Priscilla said one morning as the steam rose from the baths. "How can you trust him?"

"I cannot explain that, any more than I can explain the ways of the Spirit," Marianna said, reaching for a towel as she exited the water. "We have the reports from the believers in other regions. He has done many miracles. People always remember that he was responsible for deaths, but do you know how many lives he saved? How many people he healed?"

After toweling off, Priscilla slipped a shawl over her chiton. Marianna handed her a brooch and Priscilla pinned the shawl into place. "I confess," Priscilla said slowly, considering it, "I never thought of Paul as a healer."

"And praise God that you have never needed one. He is most welcome in every town, except by the religious authorities. Paul is beloved among the poor. Children adore him too. Many signs and wonders accompany him wherever he goes. Goodness and love…"

"Will follow me all the days of my life," Priscilla said, finishing the psalm of King David.

Marianna nodded, pleased. "In a very real way, Paul is an example of that. Goodness and love follow him everywhere. It's a shame that people only know him by his past reputation. It grieves him endlessly."

Priscilla looked down and spied the pale space on her ring finger where her mother's signet ring once was. Like that pale skin, she felt exposed here in Corinth. Growing up, she had been prepared by tutors for life in the emperor's service. But no one had taught her how to start over. *The one skill I need more than any other is the only lesson I never learned in class.*

She caught Marianna watching her. Marianna reached over and covered her hand with her own. "You need sunshine and sea air to chase those cobwebs from your mind."

Together they climbed up the stone steps and into the morning.

CHAPTER FIVE

The following month, Priscilla joined Marianna as she went to market for the day's supplies. After this errand, she had to meet Aquila. He had found a space to rent and wanted Priscilla to look at it by first light. Even at this early hour, the streets were teeming with temple prostitutes, most of them very young girls.

"Well over a thousand of them," Marianna said, reading her thoughts. "These unfortunate girls work at the temple by night but come into the city during the day to supplement their income. They'll be returning before the markets open."

"Last night," Priscilla said, weaving her way around a vendor pulling his cart, "I went out to the edge of the city to breathe the night sea air and stood not far from such a girl. She could not have been more than fourteen or fifteen years old and stared at the horizon with tears in her eyes. I tried to share the Good Story with her, but she recoiled in horror and ran away from me. What did I do wrong?" Priscilla still had much to learn.

Marianna nodded knowingly, pausing as a group blocked their way. When the crowd parted, they continued.

"It's because she is Greek, I'm sure," Marianna said.

"Are they afraid of persecution?" Priscilla asked.

"No," Marianna replied. "They are terrified of resurrection. Some teachers of Greek philosophy—surely you remember this from your studies—teach that we are only material beings. To them, when we die, that is the end of fear, because that is the end of material existence." She paused and a radiance filled her eyes. "As followers of Christ, we don't just believe in the afterlife, like some religions do. We believe in redemption and resurrection. We believe in an altogether new life."

"The poor girls only want to escape their lives here," Priscilla murmured. "I'm not explaining why eternal life with Christ is desirable, am I?"

"Every culture has its own challenges," Marianna said. Stopping, she put her hand on Priscilla's arm. "Some here also believe that eternal life is only possible for those willing to die and be reborn three times. Their gods make eternal life a goal, not a gift."

Priscilla felt foolish. She had studied philosophy and religion. Jesus cut a wide path across all the teachings, and she forgot at times that His followers were on a brand-new road.

"Any advice for me, then?"

Marianna patted her arm. "Don't start your conversations with the hope of eternal life tomorrow. Start with who Jesus is and what He offers us today."

Suddenly Marianna dropped her hand. "I did not realize we were already so near. Keep your eyes down and stay close to me."

Priscilla looked around in alarm. Haggard men with narrowed eyes watched from every doorway.

"Slave traders," Marianna whispered. "Do not make eye contact. Walk briskly."

Priscilla glanced up only once, spying boys and girls on a raised auction block. Shuddering, she averted her eyes.

"It's my habit to come here. I'm sorry. I didn't think. I check every morning before the sales," Marianna explained. "We try to save who we can."

Corinth was a busy trade center. It was easy for people to disappear without a trace. In a few hours, a victim could be on either sea on their way to a port unknown. Ships and cargo made such fast passages across the canal, and so many day by day, that by the time a mother realized a child was missing, three or four ships might have already left the harbors on either side. Kidnappings were a regular occurrence, and she'd begun to feel sick whenever she'd heard tales of children disappearing from the street.

After another brisk walk, the pair arrived at the market. The shopping was quick, as neither had much money.

Marianna knew the way to the place where they'd planned to meet Aquila. Her face fell as she knocked on a door. "It's this one," she said.

Priscilla stepped back. This was not a shop but a hovel. Animals probably had lived in it at one point, though it was hardly fit for even them. Aquila emerged, his hands dirty, a leather apron tied around his waist.

"Welcome home," he said, his eyes watching Priscilla's for any hint of disdain.

Marianna's hand on her arm gave her courage.

Priscilla stepped carefully over the threshold and looked around. The entrance had not told the whole story. The interior was roomy, with a large downstairs work area. The loft upstairs was small, but their family had not grown yet, only her waistline. They would make room for the baby.

Dust covered everything, and old straw littered the floor.

"I'll get some women to come and help," Marianna said quietly.

Priscilla thanked her as she left.

"It's actually more than we can afford," Aquila said, "so we have to be careful with our money."

Priscilla's stomach turned sour as tears flooded her eyes. She'd never known the terror of being poor, but it was like a cloud that descended and swallowed her whole. "Then why did you rent it?"

"Titus told me that the believers have nowhere to meet," he said. He pulled a bench away from the wall and patted it, expecting her to sit. She watched the dust storm he had created and stayed where she was. He tried to swat the dust down, but that made it worse, and he disappeared in a murky haze, coughing.

She hung her head, laughing and crying at the same time. This place would not do.

"We need a place to meet," he said, the dust settling at last. She noticed the lines around his eyes. The long journey, the worry of her pregnancy, and providing for a family had all taken a toll on him. She sat on the bench and he joined her.

"The citizens here are not educated," he said. "They're athletes, tradesmen, seamen, and slave traders. No one ministers to them. We can have our tentmaking business during the day, and at night, host meetings. We will tell them the Good Story."

Slave traders? In her home? "No," she replied immediately. "Not in my home." Cringing, she realized she had just referred to this place as her home.

Aquila rested his arm around her shoulders. "I invited a slave trader to eat with us, and he turned me down. Do you know why?"

Priscilla glanced at him from the corner of her eyes.

"Because you and I are atheists," he continued.

She sat up, mortified. "What?"

"We don't believe in all the gods around us—Apollo, Aphrodite, and the rest. We only have one. We don't even make sacrifices to our god. We don't have an altar in our homes, we don't have sacred prostitutes, we don't have oracles or soothsayers. We just have tales."

"They are not tales," Priscilla said, her voice rising. "They are eyewitness accounts. Men aren't willing to suffer for stories they hear in the fish market. They're only willing to suffer for what they know is true."

"Did you see Christ crucified and resurrected?"

Priscilla glared at her husband then shook her head.

"Neither did I," he admitted. "But many have already memorized the eyewitness accounts. The stories are taught from memory."

"Many prophecies from Jewish scripture were fulfilled," Priscilla said. She sighed. "And we were taught to memorize God's laws, entire books at a time. But these new stories? Not everyone has heard them yet. Certainly few teachers have them memorized. And I suspect hardly anyone has written much down."

"You can understand, then, how we appear to outsiders," Aquila said. "They might fear we are adding on to God's laws, instead of resting in their fulfillment."

She searched his eyes. "Two things are needed, then. Those who can memorize must do so. We must also urge the eyewitnesses to write their accounts. If they have not begun already, we could help. Some of them were fishermen."

Many fishermen could not read or write. Priscilla and Aquila might have a role to play in encouraging the power of the written word, its usefulness, and its enduring benefits. And Priscilla knew many scribes; many had been her tutors. She could connect scribes and eyewitnesses wherever possible.

"I still don't want a slave trader in my home," she said suddenly, rubbing her stomach.

"I understand. But we need a base of operations." Aquila's tone was steady. "This is what the Spirit wants, Priscilla. Can't you feel that too?"

Priscilla looked up at him, incredulous. He was not budging from this horrid idea or this wretched place.

"I want a home, Aquila! Not a base of operations!"

"I don't know what to say," he replied. "When we left Rome, we didn't know what waited for us in Corinth. This is part of God's plan, I'm sure of it."

She stood, pointing to her stomach. "Aquila, we're going to have a child! I don't want slave traders or brothel owners in my home. I don't even want prostitutes in here. Everything is going to change when I have this baby!"

"Everything has already changed," he said. "We are only beginning to understand how much."

In the baths the next week, Priscilla sat in the warm water, her eyes swollen from crying all night. She missed sleeping on her stomach. She missed sleeping at all. She'd had nothing but dried beans for weeks, plus a little fish relish and rice when she could get it. Sometimes day-old bread. She thought that by saving her money, she and Aquila could afford a better shop with nice living quarters. Maybe one with a sea breeze.

"When are you going to see the Oracle?" A young girl eased herself into the water next to her, sighing from the warmth. The Oracle at Delphi was not far. The Greeks believed the temple at Delphi sat on top of the exact center of the physical and spiritual world. They believed it was a mystical place on top of a sacred spring, and that the priestess within, the Oracle, could answer any question…for a price.

"Oh, I don't know," Priscilla replied, looking away. What could she change the subject to? Glancing at the girl, she could not tell if she was a worker or a wife.

The girl's eyes grew wide. "You can't put it off any longer, surely. It's such a short voyage, anyway. Just across the channel. You need to know how to plan, don't you?"

Priscilla quickly smiled then cleared her throat. She didn't want to admit that she didn't believe in the Oracle. She felt so raw from so many changes all at once. She didn't want to be the odd girl out today. She didn't want to have this conversation at all. Being a believer sometimes seemed like being forced into one uncomfortable confrontation after another, and she was never sure how people would react.

"Is this your first, then?" the girl asked.

"Yes," Priscilla replied. The girl was not going to drop it. "What is the Oracle like?" she asked finally.

"Well, you stand in a very long line," the girl began, her face bright with eagerness to tell of what she knew, "and that gives you time to think of your question. You have to have a really good question."

"You only get one?" Priscilla asked. She didn't know the rules of approaching the Oracle.

"You pay for each question. The Oracle talks in general terms, and it takes a lot of money to get a specific answer. If you're smart, you craft a question that she has to answer specifically the first time."

"And women go when they're pregnant?" Priscilla asked. "Why is that?"

"Well, if it is a boy, they want to prepare for him. If it is a girl, they will tell their husbands and make plans to expose it. It's useful to know in advance. And you're how far now? Four, five months? Too late to do anything if it's a girl but you can be prepared."

"I think about that, yes," Priscilla said. Immediately Priscilla called for an attendant and stepped out of the water. The attendant wrapped her in a linen sheet and led her to a room to be oiled, scraped, and dressed. The girl frowned at her quick, silent exit, but Priscilla did not trust herself to make a reply.

If the child within her womb was a girl, she would keep it. The horror of that moment was not that people were still leaving infant girls to die by exposure, despite the believers beginning to challenge the morality of that, but that girls like this still spoke so casually of the practice. Priscilla had heard of believers in Rome getting involved in the fight against death-by-exposure for infant girls, but it had never been personal to her until now. How could anyone let an infant die for the crime of being a girl?

The casual, light way the girl spoke of death chilled her. Darkness was a commodity here. Slave trading, prostitution, idols that demanded money from the poor. People were traded in the darkness, sold in the streets, and shipped abroad.

"Forgive me, Lord," she whispered. "I thought I would be safe keeping people out of my home." She rested her hands on her belly, thinking of the child within. "We have important work to do."

As the next few months passed, Aquila gained a good reputation for his workmanship. The shop became a hub of activity during the day. Orders from the athletic games kept them busy making tents and sunshades to protect athletes and spectators. The ships always had need of repair work to their sails. Aquila and Priscilla worked from sunrise to sunset and hired an assistant, Niko.

Priscilla's abdomen grew wide and large. She met a midwife from the believers who estimated that she had perhaps six weeks or so left until she delivered. Priscilla was nervous about the birth and felt like she had nothing to hold on to. She wished for something to clutch; her life felt like it was floating.

Everything was out of her control. Childbirth was dangerous. She lived in a strange city, among people not her own, and would give birth among women she had not known for long. Maybe this was why so many Corinthian women clutched their household gods. Anything solid felt reassuring, even if it was a lie.

"How will we educate the child?" She sat up at night, unable to sleep, restless from the heaviness in her abdomen. "We do not have money for tutors. Does Corinth even have tutors?"

"When do you want to begin formal education?" Aquila sat up, rubbing sleep from his eyes. The chariot races that evening had been lively entertainment as the athletes practiced for the Isthmian Games. Aquila had worn himself out with cheering.

"When the child is six years old," she admitted. He did not reply.

"You think I am silly for worrying about that now," she said, trying to laugh. She settled back down next to him, adjusting her linens into a bundle to support her knees. "I cannot sleep. This city is too quiet at night."

"It's not a city at all," Aquila answered. The poor man sounded wide awake now. "The air is cleaner too. I think that will be good for the child. Less risk of fire. Maybe we will have a son, and he will compete in the games."

Priscilla tsked. "Not my son." The athletes who trained in Corinth wore hardly any clothes.

Aquila laughed. "Did you know what a runner told me tonight? He counted the temples in Corinth and lost count at twenty-five. It must be tiring work to appease all those gods."

"Plus the household gods and the deities on each ship," Priscilla murmured. "People are shocked when I explain that I believe in only one. Some feel sorry for me. Others are offended."

"Does it grieve you? Their reactions?"

She exhaled slowly, sleep beginning to descend upon her. "Yes. I wish they knew me."

Aquila rubbed her back. "Remember that tomorrow, will you?"

She did not have the strength to ask him what he meant. She was already drifting into blessed sleep.

CHAPTER SIX

Early the next morning, Niko arrived in the shop with warm bread from the market and a crock of broth.

"My mother sent this for you," he called to Priscilla as she carefully descended the stairs from the sleeping loft.

"You bought bread too," Aquila said, rising from the bench. Clapping Niko on the shoulders, he thanked him and took the food to the small table at the back of the shop. The little surface was the only one not covered with linen, leather, needles, and knives. The shop was flooded with orders this week. The port was busier than ever.

"We are expecting a large crowd at the meeting tonight," Niko said, glancing at Priscilla. "You need your strength."

Before Priscilla could ask what he meant, two men entered the shop. One was dressed in the Roman style, a tunic covered by a wide shawl. His clothes were torn and in need of washing and repair.

"We are looking for Aquila of Rome, and his wife, Priscilla," the first man said. "I am Silas."

The other had piercing sea-green eyes and brown hair. "It feels good to be in your shop at last! We've heard that you are building quite a church of believers here!" When he laughed, he had dimples that made her smile. He was young. "I'm Timothy," he said, noticing her gaze.

Not a Roman name, to be sure. He was dressed like a Greek in a short chiton, belted at the waist and stopping just at the knees. He had an additional layer draped over this, but like his companion's clothing, it was badly damaged. These men had seen hard travel. What did he mean "building a church"? Priscilla and Aquila let people gather here at night to hear about Jesus. This was not a synagogue nor a place of higher learning. This was just a home, and a poor one at that.

Aquila embraced Timothy at once. Silas stepped away from the attempt to embrace, and Aquila nodded politely. Why would Silas refuse the greeting?

"I heard from other believers that you had landed in Corinth yesterday," Aquila said, continuing as if nothing had happened. "I was anxious that you should find us. You are welcome here. The other believers will begin gathering tonight as the sun sets."

Niko busied himself pouring wine and breaking the bread. In Corinth, people drank diluted wine, not water. Priscilla caught herself staring at the strangers and moved to help Niko set the refreshment before them. The younger man, Timothy, came to her assistance quickly. Silas stayed where he was.

"Please, if I may?" Timothy asked kindly, taking the crock of wine from her. "You must be Priscilla. Allow me to serve you."

"But you are a guest in my home," she said.

He grinned, and those dimples charmed her utterly. She followed him to the main table, where Aquila was already clearing a spot for the men to eat. Timothy also set a plate for Silas and poured his older companion wine.

She looked at Silas, curious. "You are a Roman?" He looked like the men she had grown up with: black hair, strong features, a regal bearing. Romans held themselves with a certain stiffness in their spine, the pride of being a Roman woven inseparable from their very bodies.

He nodded. "I left before the edict." He studied her for a moment, then tenderness flashed in his eyes. She was confused. He had seemed so cold a moment before. "You and Aquila had no warning of what was to come. That must have been terrible. Everyone thought Claudius would be a reasonable emperor. A good one, even." He lifted a cup of wine, and Priscilla noted how he used both hands to grasp it. He raised it very slowly to his mouth.

"My life is here now." She shrugged. She reached for a piece of bread. Niko had done well to bring so much back from market. Silas was kinder now that he was sitting across from her. How strange.

"It is good for you to be settled," he said. A pinch in his words made her wonder if he had ever been settled.

"Tell us of Paul," Aquila urged the men.

Priscilla dropped the piece of bread she was holding. "Paul?" She looked from Timothy to Silas. "You know him? Many rumors circulate about that man."

Timothy laughed. "The rumors could not possibly do the man justice!"

Silas cut a sharp glance at the younger man. "What Timothy means is that life on the road with Paul defies all expectations."

"You'll see soon enough," Timothy said, lifting his cup for a drink. "He went in search of a physician. He is still recovering from being beaten with rods in Phillipi."

"Phillipi?" Priscilla scoffed. "That's impossible. Phillipi is a Roman colony. They cannot beat a Roman citizen with rods." Paul was well known to be a Roman citizen, which is why he once had been given such latitude in persecuting the believers.

Wordlessly, Silas stood. All at the table fell silent as he slowly maneuvered one shoulder out of his tunic, wincing as he lowered it. He turned, revealing his back.

Priscilla's mouth fell open. Silas's back was deepest red, with black and purple at the edges.

His face contorted with pain, Silas pulled his tunic back into place and slowly eased himself back down. "Paul got it so much worse," he said. "They beat his feet too. Broke the bones."

"Tell them the story, though, the good one," Timothy urged. He reached over and adjusted the tunic on Silas's shoulder where it had slipped. Priscilla smiled to herself, watching him, then caught Aquila's eye. He clearly felt the same way about Timothy. He was a kind soul.

Timothy's lightheartedness lifted the mood in the room.

"What story?" Niko asked, rising from the table for more bread. "How can there be a good story after that?"

"With Paul, there's always a good story," Silas said, a wry smile on his lips. "No matter how it starts."

"I'd love to hear it," Priscilla said, her voice softer now. "Niko," she said, lifting her head to address him, "would you bring the broth your mother sent? Silas might benefit from it as much as I."

Niko served the broth as Silas began a tale that was too outrageous to be believed. "In Philippi, a slave girl worked the market telling fortunes," he began. "She claimed to speak with the spirit of Python, which had intrigued many of the Greeks, of course."

Timothy interrupted. "Being a Greek, I can explain. Apollo, a god of the Greeks, defeated the mighty snake called Python at the site where the temple of the Oracle at Delphi now stands. But Python's mother is the earth goddess, Gaia, and capable of giving life. Some would argue that the spirit of Python endured. Perhaps an entity with that name speaks through the girl."

Silas cleared his throat.

"Sorry," Timothy said. "I thought that was important. Greeks have a lot of gods, you know."

Priscilla grinned at him. "Romans do too, you know."

Timothy returned her grin.

"The girl began to follow us," Silas continued. "She provoked Paul. She shouted everywhere we went, but it was always the truth." He lifted his eyebrows, as if trying to sort through the words as he spoke. "She didn't lie. It was the way she did it, though, that unnerved people and caused them to flee. She kept shouting, 'These men are servants of the Most High God, who are telling you the way to be saved.' No one would come near Paul to listen to him speak. We had to spend our time evading her, finding quiet spaces so we could teach."

"We tried talking to her masters," Timothy added, "but they said it was good for business if she drew a crowd. Didn't matter to them what she was shouting as long as people listened. Poor girl had that look in her eye." Timothy shuddered.

"What look?" Priscilla asked, leaning forward.

"The look of a girl who knows she is trapped and wants to die." Timothy's voice dropped and all were silent. "The message of Christ has to spread faster. Girls like her have no hope of freedom until everyone has heard of the New Covenant."

"Timothy is an idealist," Silas said, looking at the youth fondly. "Many have heard and don't want grace."

"What of the girl?" Aquila asked.

"One afternoon Paul became so annoyed he turned to her and said to the spirit, 'In the name of Jesus Christ I command you to come out of her!' The girl fell limp in the street. Her masters ran to her and lifted her by the arms. She looked right at Paul, and he nodded. It was as if the girl had asked him a question without words. But I think I know what the question was."

"*Who is this Jesus*?" Priscilla murmured. She'd heard the same question.

"But she didn't argue. She just took a deep, clean breath, her eyes never leaving Paul's face. You should have seen her eyes then." Timothy smiled. "She was free. Free in a way those men will never take from her."

"Of course," Silas said, "her masters were furious when they realized she had neither the ability nor will to speak for Python. They had the authorities arrest Paul and me. We were brought before the magistrates, but before we could be heard, the crowd waiting outside went wild with anger. The magistrates ordered us stripped and beaten with rods. After we were unable to stand, we were thrown in prison to wait for death or until we recovered enough to walk out. The guards didn't care which came first."

Silas lowered his voice. "We were in the innermost cell. Our feet were in the stocks. Neither of us was going anywhere. Paul's feet had swollen to twice their size and were turning purple. He was in such intense pain. He suggested we sing to keep our minds off our suffering, so we sang hymns. The other prisoners listened in. Some even asked us for prayer. Only Paul could turn a prison into a house of worship."

Aquila leaned back and wiped his mouth, finished with the meal. "That is a wonderful story."

"That's not the story!" Timothy said. "That's the setup!"

Silas rested his hand over Timothy's. "About midnight, Paul and I were still praying and singing hymns. We knew those prisoners faced death. No one was closer to hell than those men on that night. They knew they were going to die, and no one was coming to save them. But God sent us right into their midst. About midnight, the ground began to shake, and the walls trembled. Dust rained down on our heads. We feared for our lives. A violent earthquake rocked the prison. Suddenly all the chains collapsed to the floor and our feet were free. The doors swung open. Think of that—the foundations of the prison were shaken, but the doors still swung on their hinges. The jailer came running in and panicked. His life was forfeit if any one of the men escaped. He drew his sword, prepared to die. Paul shouted, 'Don't harm yourself! We are all here!'"

"Wait," Aquila said. "God sent an earthquake to free you. Wasn't it clear that God's plan was for you to escape?"

"I would have run the moment the chains fell away," Niko said, his eyes wide.

Timothy sipped his wine, eyeing them all with amusement in his eyes. "You don't know Paul."

"The jailer called for lights," Silas continued. "Men with torches came rushing in and the jailer fell down trembling, asking how to find God. Paul told him, 'Believe in the Lord Jesus, and you will be saved—you and your household.' God used the prison to save the prisoners and the earthquake to save the jailer." Silas shook his head in wonder.

"Then the jailer brought Paul and Silas to his house," Timothy said. "He fed them a huge meal and Paul baptized everyone in the family. I was still waiting with the believers at Lydia's house, hoping to hear a date for Paul's trial. Next thing I know, Paul and Silas show up, having converted everyone in the jail and the jailer too."

Everyone smiled at Timothy's easy good humor. But something did not settle well with Priscilla. Something gnawed at her later that evening as Aquila slept peacefully beside her.

In the silence and shadows, Priscilla questioned God. No miracles surrounded her life. No miracle saved her from fleeing Rome. *Does that mean God is not with me or Aquila?*

The believers often encouraged each other to think on things that were true. *What is true?* she asked herself. First, God hadn't changed. God never changed. *But is it possible that He works differently through each of us?* God hadn't done great miracles through her or Aquila. Maybe her path through life was a slow revealing, like a winding path through the trees that leads to a brilliant view. And others, like Paul, were shooting stars. Why could there not be different kinds of glory for God on the earth and among His children?

She thought of the blank parchment Aquila had given her. Sighing, she was surprised to feel a tear on her cheek. She had wanted to write great histories for the emperor, the words of Rome to be handed down for all generations.

How did I end up here, a noble daughter of Rome, lying on a stinking straw mattress in the dark of a tentmaker's shop? The burst of self-pity welled up unexpectedly.

This life was not anything she could have imagined. News of the exploits and miracles that these men did in the name of the Lord, she admitted, made her feel left out. What about the women like her, she wondered, who lived and prayed in the shadows, uncertain of God's plan for their lives…or uncertain that He even had one?

Wiping her tears away, she patted her belly. She was so emotional sometimes, especially at night. Why did the darkness tempt her to dwell on lies? She closed her eyes and willed herself to remember what was true. And what was true, right now, was that two new friends were snoring downstairs. Her beloved husband was beside her. Her child was due very, very soon. And tomorrow she would meet the apostle Paul. Whatever questions she still had in the morning light, she could ask him.

This was an unexpected life, to be sure, but it was still a good one.

CHAPTER SEVEN

The next morning, Priscilla went to the market to buy bread and fish relish. By now the shrine prostitutes would be making their way down to the shop, eager to see Priscilla and eat breakfast. Before Priscilla, they had pooled their money for food. Now Priscilla was able to help buy their breakfast, thanks to believers in other provinces sending collections. She felt uneasy becoming a mother figure to the girls only because she didn't know how to shepherd them well. She felt especially uneasy when conversation drifted to their clients. But serving bread kept her hands busy, and eating kept their mouths busy. She always had a few moments to steer the conversation in the right direction.

She approached the shop and saw familiar faces huddled together. Mist from the harbor hung in the streets. Distant cries of sea birds rang out.

Her heart clutched as one by one the girls smiled in greeting. They were so young. A disfigured man stood far off, under a torch. He did not approach, and the girls paid him no attention. Still, Priscilla did not like the looks of him.

"Come in," she offered as always. They held out their hands for the food but did not move to the door. Their masters would beat them if they spied them entering or leaving a home where "atheists" were known to gather.

"Last night I could not sleep," Priscilla said, handing out the breakfast, keeping an eye on the stranger. The girls ate quickly. "I thought of all the dreams I once had, that I know will never come true. I felt so sad, until I began to see how God is blessing me in unexpected ways." She hoped to learn more about the girls. "I woke up feeling renewed hope. Now, tell me of the dreams you once had for your lives."

The girls glanced at each other. No one spoke. Priscilla felt heat creeping into her cheeks. She had either offended them or embarrassed them.

"Did you have dreams for your future?" she asked, tentatively this time.

One girl stopped chewing and looked at the others before speaking. "Most of us were sold or donated at a very young age. We have no memories of life before the temple."

Horror must have shown on Priscilla's face, for another girl immediately spoke.

"You had hopes for yourself, Priscilla. Those must be lovely to look back on. I never understood why people grieved when dreams didn't come true. The real joy is that they had dreams at all."

"Of course, you're right," Priscilla said. She checked everyone's bread to see who needed more. The man had not moved any closer. She relaxed a little.

"You believed the world to be a good place, where good things happened," the girl continued. "Cherish that. We were born into this life, knowing we couldn't change the future. It makes no sense to me that you would grieve having a dream that didn't come true. That is like grieving that you were once a happy child. No. Be thankful for it."

Priscilla wanted to end this conversation. She didn't know how to steer it back to grace or anything else meaningful. These sweet girls had known so many hardships. No wonder they needed a mother. She prayed, quickly, silently, for a way to bring the conversation back to what would be helpful to them.

"The seashells on the water's edge are beautiful, are they not?" A deep voice startled them all. They turned in unison to see a man, his face gaunt and his cheeks covered in old scars. His dark brown eyes twinkled though, and were filled with youth and joy. No one moved. He reached for a piece of bread in Priscilla's hand and took a bite, leaving her speechless.

"Even the broken ones are beautiful," he added. "You see, I like to think the shells help us imagine that there is another world we cannot see, a world of mystery and breathtaking beauty...but a world we are not meant to live in. Not yet at least."

Did he overhear me when I first arrived in Corinth? Who is he?

He finished the bread. "Did I smell fish relish?"

Priscilla bit her lip, but she handed him the crock of relish and a ladle. He bent to smell it and his nose twitched. Several girls giggled. He looked up and winked.

Priscilla cleared her throat. "Are you the one they call Paul?"

Before he could react, the girls recoiled in terror. "We have heard of you! You murder people like Priscilla!" One girl put herself in between Priscilla and Paul.

Pain filled the man's eyes. "I did at one time." He held out his hands. "But see now? I have no weapons."

"Why are you here?" the girl covering Priscilla demanded.

"For you," Paul answered gently.

Her eyes grew wide.

"And you," Paul said, turning to another girl. Her mouth fell open. "Any of you who have whispered a prayer in the night. To know the truth. To be saved. To be loved. For they are all the same. His name is Jesus."

He craned his head to look at Priscilla. "Have you baptized any of these girls yet?"

"No," she replied hoarsely. What could she say? That she was still trying to earn their trust? That they already knew she was a believer in one God, and they weren't interested in anything but bread?

"When my friend here tells you of the Savior, listen to her. Don't be afraid to believe and be baptized," Paul said to the girls. They paid rapt attention. "Now, I think it's time I woke up Timothy. The boy will sleep until dinner if you let him." He smiled at everyone and hobbled to the shop door to knock.

Priscilla cleared her throat and started to laugh. Paul was unconventional. Intense. And entirely loveable. She had the sudden feeling she'd follow him to the ends of the earth, if for no other reason than to see what he'd do next.

At the edge of the horizon, the orange sun lit the sky with rays of gold. Dusk was a riot of color, and Priscilla savored the hushed calm that settled over the city. The moment in between labor's end and the beginning of night always worked its charms on the port. Sailors, merchants, and her customers in the shop paused in unison to look at the sky.

"This is my favorite time of day," she said to Paul, who worked beside her. He had settled in immediately, grateful for Aquila's offer of lodging and work. He was good with a needle and skilled at tent design. Paul had been their guest for two weeks now. He spoke kindly to the prostitutes who gathered for breakfast at the shop at dawn. He encouraged every customer who stopped by to visit him at the synagogue in the evenings. He taught about Jesus until almost midnight every night.

Business remained steady, despite their notorious lodger.

Paul looked up from his bench, squinting as the sunlight dwindled. His eyesight was terrible. "Why is that?"

The question puzzled her. Didn't everyone love dusk? "It's beautiful," she finally managed to reply.

He smiled, his hands nimble as they pushed the needle through the thin leather. "You see beauty everywhere, Priscilla."

She looked down at her work. Aquila glanced up from the bench he was at and nodded. "She had to, in order to marry me."

Priscilla threw a ball of string at him, which he easily batted away, laughing.

"You two are a good match," Paul said. "I marvel at God's ability to put couples together for ministry."

"It was not God," Priscilla said. "It was my brother. He thought the match would hurt me." She did not add that she did not consider herself in ministry.

Paul set his work down and looked at Priscilla. His gaze was riveting. Energy seemed to flow from him. "As our Lord said to Pilate, 'You have no power over me except that which is granted you.'"

She blinked, trying to understand his message.

He leaned toward her. "Your brother thought he was harming you, but God used your brother to accomplish a greater good. God works in all our circumstances. Consider this: if your brother had been an honorable man, what would you have lost?"

She was silent, flashes of memory playing out in her mind. If her brother had been honorable, if she had been cared for properly in those two years after her mother died, she would have missed living with Aquila the rest of her life.

"I would never want to relive some of those moments," she said. "But I would never trade my life today for better memories of the past."

"Because of Jesus, you don't have to trade," Paul said, returning to his work. "Jesus said He came to give life, abundant and overflowing. I have found that when I focus on Jesus, joy abounds until there is simply no room for bitter memories."

"I love to hear you speak of Jesus," Aquila said. "We have fragments of knowledge, you know. We hear from one teacher and pass that along. Then we hear something more and pass that along too. We long for a complete account of Jesus's life and ministry."

"Yes!" Paul said. "Many believers feel as you do. I was not an eyewitness of those events, of course. But the apostles who lived through them are beginning to work on their accounts. And that is why the Spirit has brought me here, no doubt. Very few believers can read or write. Very few understand right now how important that work is. Or will be. I feel strongly the need to write to the churches I have visited too, to share more of what I have been given."

Priscilla nodded as a little burst of joy bloomed in her heart. "I understand the written word. So does Aquila."

Paul stopped working, stunned. "You can assist me in writing a letter?

She nodded at once.

"My writing was never good," Paul confessed, "but after my hands were broken, it became even worse. My eyesight is not good either. I write with such large letters that I waste the scroll. Perhaps you can help? I must dictate a letter to the believers in Thessalonica. Timothy visited them recently but they need encouragement."

"Yes!" Priscilla exclaimed, then covered her mouth with one hand, embarrassed at her enthusiasm. "We all need encouragement. The written word would do that. If we had the word of the Messiah, of the eyewitnesses, and could read them to each other...that would help so much. Paul, that would change everything. The church could multiply and grow much faster."

"We will begin the letters to Thessalonica at once. The Lord has a plan for our time together," Paul said. "And a plan for you, Priscilla. And you, Aquila."

Her heart burned with joy. How had he known the words she needed to hear? She had been erased from her family but not forgotten by God.

"Now," Paul said, rubbing his eyes. "It will soon be time to teach. Tonight we are meeting at the water's edge."

"What? Why?" Aquila spoke before she could. How many people were coming to hear Paul? Had he already outgrown the synagogue?

Paul stood and slapped his hands together, as if eager to begin. "Tonight, I baptize a leader from the synagogue, Crispus. I hope to baptize his whole family too. I will preach to all those who come out to witness his public confession."

"But…it's only been…you just got here," Priscilla stammered.

"That's right," Paul said, then winked. "And I've only just begun."

A soft rain fell on the rooftop. Priscilla listened to it splattering in fat drops on the dry, dusty stones of the streets outside the shop. Wind swept straw along that came from ships' holds for animals and food storage. A dull cramp in her back had kept her awake for hours. The pain was not consistent, though, so she did not wake Aquila. Downstairs, Paul and his companions snored peacefully.

Only yesterday Paul had finished the letter to Thessalonica, with her writing the scroll as he dictated. Timothy and Silas often interrupted and offered their thoughts. She quickly learned to wait to write until Paul had listened to them, prayed through his own thoughts, then given her the final sentence. One short letter had been a surprisingly painstaking undertaking.

But now the time was hers.

She loved the quiet hours. She used the time to think. Daylight offered no chance for that. She never understood how busy the day could become without servants. She rushed before dawn to buy bread for the temple prostitutes. They were always waiting for her at the shop by the time she returned. She tried to buy poultices and medicines when she could, for they sometimes had bruises or cut lips. She never had enough money to sustain her household week to week, yet she never ran out either. After breakfast, she fed Aquila and whatever guests or workers lodged with them. The men stretched, yawned, and began their workday. Priscilla was well into her second hour of work by then. And the work never ceased throughout the day. She never complained, though, ever. She was certain that her brother would somehow sense that she was unhappy, and he would gloat.

She was determined to make this life work. Most days, it seemed, work was her life. But the evening hours, the dark and quiet hours, were all hers.

She shifted her body on the straw pallet, carefully, so Aquila would not be disturbed. The ache in her back intensified.

This cannot be labor. Women say the pains are sharp cramps in the abdomen.

The pain in her lower back intensified again. She groaned without meaning to. Sitting up, she tried to draw a deep breath. Her abdomen was so big, a deep breath felt impossible.

Downstairs, an oil lamp flared to life. One of the apostles was awake. She had probably awakened him making too much noise. She gritted her teeth, trying to be quiet. In the morning, she would find a midwife and ask if there was a remedy for this back pain.

The pain deepened. She shifted, trying to get a deep breath and relax her back, but Aquila sat up.

"Is everything all right?" he whispered, his face turned to notice the oil lamp, then turned to look at her.

"Fine, fine!" she whispered.

The door to the shop opened then closed. Priscilla caught sight of Paul quickly leaving. Where was he going at this hour?

The pain deepened again. She had not known that pain had so many levels. She hadn't known her body was capable of feeling this much pain.

Moments later, Paul returned with an elderly woman. Priscilla recognized her at once.

"You brought a midwife," she gasped as pain seared her back.

Aquila looked at her, his eyes wide in worry. "You did not tell me you were in labor!"

"I did not know!"

Paul helped the woman navigate the stairs, then motioned for Aquila to join the men below.

"Who should we wake?" she heard Paul ask Aquila. "Who is she friends with from the believers here?"

"Marianna and Vita," Aquila said at once. "Niko knows where Marianna lives, but Vita has not been here long. She is a wealthy widow who lives in Cenchreae, the village just outside the edges of the city. Priscilla met her last week, and they had so much in common. There was an instant bond."

Priscilla listened to the men below as the midwife slowly unpacked her supplies for the birth.

Paul woke Timothy. "Go find the woman called Vita and bring her. Tell her that Priscilla is in labor and needs a friend." Aquila woke Niko and sent him for Marianna.

Silas sat up, rubbing his eyes. "What can I do?"

"Go to the market, and as soon as they open, buy an extra quantity of myrrh." Paul reached into his coin sack and handed Silas two denarii with clipped edges. "She will need diluted wine too, so see what you can buy. And salt." One Roman denarii was worth slightly more than a Greek drachma; clipping the edges made trade easier in the provinces where the coins of the two peoples mingled.

Priscilla shook her head in amazement. The midwife pattered over to her side and began rubbing her back in firm, round circles.

"Paul is your friend?" the woman asked.

Priscilla nodded, unable to speak as the pain worsened.

"He has seen so much of life," the woman said. "He's a good man to have working for you."

"He doesn't work for me," Priscilla managed to say. "We all work for the same Master."

"Lucky master, then," the woman chirped. "Now, let's deliver a child, shall we?"

And so Priscilla gave birth to a son, born in Corinth with the scent of the sea and the distant calls of seagulls. She rubbed him with salt after his birth, then washed him with wine. He smelled of the vine and the sea, and she slept that first night with him nestled beneath her chin.

Priscilla watched as Aquila stumbled about in the shop for the first two days, dazed with joy. *He never expected to be a father.* Paul, Silas, and Timothy had been careful to bring the food from the market and care for the prostitutes while Priscilla rested.

Greek tradition demanded that she stay in bed for a full week with the newborn. Marianna had gone home after the birth to care for her own family. Her friend Vita stayed only for one more day after the delivery, eager to return to her work caring for the widows of her village.

"They have no one else to help them and nothing to live on," she said, as if apologizing.

Priscilla embraced her. "And I am so richly blessed, am I not?"

Vita kissed her on the cheek, then rested her palm against the cheek of the sleeping infant. "We both are, sister."

After she departed, Priscilla turned her attention to Aquila. He had risen early and was busy setting out the work for the day. The other men had gone to bring bread from the market.

So far, he had said nothing of the child's name. Perhaps he did not know what to say. Sometimes he felt his past like shackles on his feet, she knew.

"The naming ceremony is in seven days," Priscilla said.

Aquila nodded. He looked up at the loft where their son was asleep in Priscilla's arms. "The traditions here are much the same," he reminded her. In Rome, as well as Greece, no one named a child at birth, since many infants did not survive. In Rome, the ceremony was often on the ninth day. Here, the ceremony was on the tenth.

"Have you considered names?" he finally asked.

Priscilla pushed herself to sit up a bit without disturbing the infant. "Why would I?" The father had naming rights, and he selected a name from among his own family. Children, like wives, were the property of a man.

"We are doing a new thing by following Jesus," he said. "We do not observe the same traditions. After all, we do not hold to the Old Covenant." Aquila stared in the distance, then glanced up at her. "If you and I are coheirs of God's blessing, you should take part in naming him, Priscilla."

She blew a soft breath out from her lips. She'd never considered naming her own son. "How do we do that together? Do we still choose a name from your family?"

Aquila raised his palms as if to say he did not know. "We can choose a name that means something to us both, or a name that will mean something for our son."

"Manasseh?" Priscilla asked. "Joseph's son. The one who caused him to forget his suffering and his father's home."

"Or Ephraim," Aquila countered. "Joseph's other son. Named because God made Joseph fruitful despite his suffering."

Their eyes locked. These names were both good. But which one was best?

"Perhaps we will pray about it," Priscilla ventured. Aquila nodded.

The baby stirred, Paul returned with bread, and the day began.

CHAPTER EIGHT

The naming ceremony at dawn was attended by a handful of prostitutes, the local believers, and the three disciples from the shop. The prostitutes had pooled their money to buy a pigeon for the animal sacrifice.

Paul walked out to them, and Priscilla held her breath. Would he scold them for bringing pagan worship to her door? She cradled the baby in her arms, still marveling that Aquila had just revealed his choice for the name. His choice mirrored hers. *What a marvelous thing it is to pray over a matter instead of fight.*

The girl holding the pigeon between her hands stepped away from Paul nervously. He only smiled then gently wrapped his hands around hers.

"My sisters," he began, addressing the prostitutes, "and my friends, thank you for showing your love for Priscilla by offering a gift. God has shown His love toward you by offering a gift too. He offers you a new life, healing, and peace. Let us honor God's gift to Priscilla and Aquila. Let us honor God's gift of a new life to us by embracing the name of His Son, Jesus." With that, he opened his hands, and the girls followed.

The bird flew free. Everyone turned their face to the sky as dawn broke in pink and gold and the bird flew toward the east.

A holy quiet settled over the small crowd. "What will you name the child?" Paul asked Aquila.

Aquila rested one hand on Priscilla's shoulder. "Together we have chosen the name Ephraim for our son." Priscilla smiled.

With that, the crowd shared a breakfast of dates and fish then all dispersed back to work. Two of the girls stayed behind to talk to Paul. Priscilla knew he had led several to Christ already, but more and more people were coming to him in private seeking miraculous healings. He had great power to heal, but he preferred to spend his time in public teaching. Healings could be done anytime, without an audience.

Later that week, however, Paul surprised everyone. Priscilla was not there but only heard about it from Aquila as he prepared for bed. Paul had not come home that evening, nor had Silas and Timothy.

"They've gone to the house of the man called Justus," Aquila said. "From now on, Paul refuses to teach in the synagogue. He's grown tired of sharing the same message over and over and hearing nothing but arguments from the leaders."

"So he asked the Jews to meet at Justus's house instead?" Priscilla asked, confused. Ephraim was lying on his mat, wide eyes blinking in the lamplight.

"No, Justus is not a Jew. He's a Greek. Paul told the local synagogue that he would only preach to Gentiles from now on. Justus is a wealthy trader. He has a home with a garden as wide as the entire synagogue."

Priscilla's eyes widened too. Paul stoked a long-standing feud. Jesus was a Jew, and salvation was from the Jews, so salvation was for the Jews. Or so it had seemed. But Paul had pushed, over and over, for the Gentiles to be included. If he kept pushing, the argument would go over the edge and burst into war between the groups.

"For the first time since Paul arrived, I fear for him," Aquila said. "I fear he is making a mistake and provoking the Jewish leaders. We know that when there is unrest between religious groups, nothing good follows."

"My time of seclusion is almost up," Priscilla said. "Take me to Justus's house tomorrow. Let me hear this for myself."

Timothy barged into the shop the next afternoon. Paul and Silas had finished an order and were out delivering it. Aquila was at the bench working on a new shade for the games. Priscilla descended the stairs from the loft, Ephraim in her arms.

"Priscilla!" Timothy exclaimed. "I have news from Rome."

Aquila stood and motioned for Priscilla to sit. He brought her a cup of wine to drink, then sat beside her.

"What news, Timothy?" he asked.

"I stumbled across a drunk sailor in the marketplace. Truly, I stumbled across him. He was tasked with bringing letters from Rome to families in Corinth. But he's a drunk, and someone offered him a nice amount of money to read the letters, and now everyone knows what the letters said. Apparently, they were hoping for secret information about the emperor.

Claudius has made enemies among the ruling class. His nephew Nero is gaining power."

"Go on," Priscilla urged before taking a sip of her wine. It was safer than the water here but not far off from vinegar. It bothered her stomach at times to drink it, but the midwife said she had to drink plenty of fluids. Milk was too expensive and hard to come by.

"You have a brother named Marcellus?" Timothy asked.

Priscilla nodded, wary. She had not heard that name in so long. It roiled her stomach more than the cheap wine. Timothy's face softened.

"Your father has died," he said. "I am sorry to bring that news. Marcellus is constructing a family crypt outside the center of Rome. He has negotiated with Claudius for the land, but it is Marcellus and Nero who have become allies. If Nero comes to power, he said, Rome will be transformed. Building materials will be in high demand."

"Who was Marcellus writing to?" Aquila frowned.

"I did not find out." Timothy shook his head. "But it was a trader, that I know."

Priscilla absorbed the news in small waves. Her father had passed, but she had said goodbye to him two years ago. The loss did not feel like a sudden drop but more like a confirmation of a reality already accepted. Her heart felt only a dull ache at the memory of her father. The man, the real man he had been, had disappeared long ago.

Her brother building a family crypt, though, that news shook her. But why should it? She settled with the news for a moment to sort it out. The bitter truth unfolded slowly in her mind. Her brother built a family crypt...but her name would not be on it, would it? Even in death, her mother and father would remain separated from her.

Or so Marcellus thought. "Nothing separates us from the love of God," she murmured. Aquila and Timothy stopped talking and looked at her.

"What was that?" Aquila asked.

"Nothing separates us from the love of God. Paul teaches that," Priscilla said. "My mother and father knew Christ as their Savior. And so do I. Nothing could separate them from Him, and so nothing can separate us, not really. Only time. And time is not such a powerful enemy, is it?" She smiled. "For time itself is always passing away."

Later that evening at the home of Justus, before Paul taught, Priscilla watched in amazement as the crowd settled in. Jewish couples tried to distance themselves from the rough-looking sailors and notoriously crooked merchants. A few prostitutes crept in, trying to go unnoticed. None of these people had ever believed in the same god. Gathering together for religious instruction made them uncomfortable. The people who were most devout seemed to be the most uncomfortable, she noticed. Even if their religion embraced a dozen other gods or more, something about this one God made them nervous.

"Everyone wants to hear Paul," Aquila said. He stood at her side and offered to take Ephraim. Priscilla handed the sleeping infant to him.

"Paul has such intensity when he speaks," she quietly said. "But have you noticed? He's not polished. He does not charm the crowd or win them over with good humor. He never tries to impress them. He can be erratic too. His speeches wander from point to point."

"And yet the crowds come, in greater numbers every night," Aquila answered. "I'm glad your recovery is over so we can listen together."

"I am too," Priscilla said, leaning her head against his shoulder. "This day has brought hard news. I need this time spent listening to a teacher." More than once today she wished she had written down some of what Paul had already shared with her. *For dark moments, wouldn't it be nice to have a written record of Paul's teachings?* And when she taught the prostitutes or tried to answer their questions, it would be helpful to have written stories about Jesus. She always had trouble remembering what she'd been told from the eyewitnesses. There was just so, so much from His life. So many miracles. So many parables and stories. She didn't have the mind of Paul. He remembered anything and everything. Perhaps that is why his mind jumped from subject to subject so quickly when he taught.

Once more, she determined to urge Paul to write more. He needed to write everything down. All the eyewitnesses did too.

A great commotion outside alerted her that Paul had arrived. Women's voices, praising God in loud shouts, echoed through the room.

"I have no doubt Paul just healed someone," Aquila whispered with a wry grin.

"He likes to do that away from the crowds," Priscilla whispered back. "He does everything differently than what I had expected."

Paul entered the garden, moving carefully between people sitting in groups. Some reached up to steady him as he moved between them, and Priscilla wondered if they hoped for a secret healing too. The Spirit of God was rumored to rest so heavily on Paul that even the lightest touch could affect a miracle. She glanced at Ephraim, gratitude swelling in her heart. He was miracle enough for her tonight.

The sky above darkened, revealing the stars in brilliant depth and color. Making his way to the front of the garden, Paul then eased himself onto a bench that Justus had set out for him. Priscilla noted how Paul winced now when he sat. His wounds had healed, but arthritis was setting in. Too many bones had been broken and never properly set.

An expectant thrumming filled the air. Water from the fountain at the far edge of the garden splashed. Beyond the stacked stone walls, birds in the trees sang to the stars above. Justus's wife brought out platters of fresh cakes, still warm from the ovens, and servants passed them into the crowds. Priscilla's stomach rumbled as she reached for one.

"Justus and his wife are so gracious," Aquila said, taking a cake.

"They have the gift of hospitality," Priscilla agreed. But it bothered her a bit. She bought cheap bread for the women who gathered at her doorstep. It was the best she could afford. She didn't have a garden for Paul to teach in and she couldn't invite dozens and dozens of people to enjoy an evening under the stars.

Paul dispensed with greetings and began at once. His eyes filled with joy as he saw the mix of the humble poor and curious nobles all gathered to hear of the New Covenant. Sosthenes, the new synagogue leader, stood against the wall, arms folded but clearly interested. His hair was still quite dark and very curly. He had only a few lines across his forehead. *He must have spent most of his life indoors.* By now, Priscilla had learned to read faces, to know who labored under the sun and who reclined on couches.

Watching him, Priscilla felt she could read his thoughts. Crispus has been converted by Paul, so Sosthenes must have replaced him. None of the men at the synagogue wanted to listen to Paul anymore. Paul had left the synagogue just weeks ago in a fit of anger, determined to preach to anyone who would listen.

She felt caught between two worlds. Like the ships in the port, the believers were slowly moving between two bodies of water: the Old Covenant of works and law, and the New Covenant of grace and love.

She was a Jew but now she was something more, wasn't she?

"You are under no condemnation, not if you have accepted the Word of Christ," Paul began, his eyes alighting on the temple prostitutes attempting to hide in the shadows. "If Christ lives within you, no matter what happens to your body, your spirit remains alive because of His righteousness. Nothing that happens to you can take away what God has given you. Nothing will ever separate you from God's love."

Movement in the crowd signaled that people noticed whom he was addressing. Some men frowned in offense and turned their backs to avoid looking at the girls. Priscilla wondered if those same men had ever visited the pagan temple.

Paul held out a hand and waited. Silence fell over the crowd.

"Aquila, what's he doing?" Priscilla asked.

Aquila, being taller, had a better view. He smiled. "Watch."

She stood on her toes to catch a glance.

Paul summoned the girls and asked the patrons in front to make room. Paul gave the girls the best seats, directly at his feet.

"No more sitting in the shadows," he said. "No more hiding your faces. If you have accepted Christ, the old has gone. You have been washed clean. You are new creations. You are my sisters."

Sosthenes dropped his folded arms. Huffing in a rage, he left the garden, stepping over or on anyone who blocked his path. He was gone, refusing to hear any more.

Never, never had Priscilla heard a prostitute spoken to like this in public. Never had a man of learning and honor addressed a woman of the streets with such dignity. Watching the women, Priscilla saw them transformed before her eyes. Their faces radiated something she hadn't seen before. She had tended to their needs as a woman, as a fellow sister, but to have a man like Paul bestow honor and give them a place of honor in front of their peers?

"Their faces are radiant with love," Aquila said.

"He's made them whole," she whispered. Somehow, the kind, approving word of a man like Paul healed a wound they had carried that even Priscilla hadn't known about.

And at once, Priscilla saw the design of God at work. She had brought them and met many of their needs, and only when those needs had been met was Paul able to bestow grace to the broken places. She could not do her ministry without powerful men of grace. And men of grace would never reach the broken without women like her.

"Praise God," she whispered. "'God works all things together for good.'" Just as Paul had told her only this afternoon. *God doesn't just work things together for good, He works believers together for good. So many little miracles all around us.*

Paul continued, addressing the crowd now.

"Yes, although the body is dead because of sin, yet your spirit is alive forever. Why? Because Jesus's sacrifice has paid for your righteousness. Do you understand? This is the New Covenant offered to you. God offered the final sacrifice for forgiveness of sins. You are not responsible for keeping the old laws, not anymore. Believe in Jesus and love others. Everyone can partake of this covenant."

A few of the Jewish leaders glanced at each other. Priscilla caught their unhappy looks.

Paul's voice grew louder. "And there's more! In the Old Covenant, we did not speak of life after death. This is the Good

News of the New Covenant: the Spirit of Him who raised Jesus from the dead can also dwell in you. He does not live in a temple or tabernacle, not anymore! He can live in us! He who raised Christ Jesus from the dead will also give life to your mortal bodies through His Spirit who dwells in you. The New Covenant offers the forgiveness of sins, an intimacy with God that our ancestors never knew, and the promise of eternal life."

Goose bumps rose on Priscilla's arms.

Paul paused, making eye contact with a few people. Stepping carefully, he moved through the crowd, speaking as if to each person alone. "God wants to receive you as beloved sons and daughters." He reached out, resting his hands on people's shoulders and the crowns of their heads.

Tears flowed down cheeks. Sniffling and quietly audible sobs echoed through the garden. "You can cry out, 'Abba! Father!' God will listen to you as a loving father listens to His child."

Above them, a star shot across the sky, punctuating his words. Priscilla smiled. Only God could time the stars like that. Only God could time these people on this night to hear the words of Paul. And someday, she knew, people all over the world, across the generations, would hear these words too.

She was sure of that.

Paul limped back to the shop at the second watch of the night. Silas and Timothy helped carry him across the threshold.

Priscilla was waiting with warm bread, stewed beans, and wine. Paul's strength was nearly gone.

Timothy immediately filled a bowl with water and sat at Paul's feet. Working with delicate movements, he washed the broken feet of the man who had just preached for hours and healed many.

No one spoke. Paul's eyes were heavy with exhaustion. He did not move to take the bread set before him. Unsure if he would be offended, Priscilla sat at the bench next to him and tore the bread.

"You need to eat," she said softly. She lifted the bread to his mouth. He opened his eyes and accepted the bite. She fed him again, then offered a bit of the stew. After Timothy finished washing his feet, Silas helped lift Paul onto his sleeping mat then covered him with a cloak.

"Priscilla," Paul whispered before she backed away.

She lifted the oil lamp closer to see his face. "Yes, Paul?"

"When we entered the home of Justus, a shadow passed over your face. What troubled you?"

She hoped he couldn't see the embarrassed blush in her cheeks. "Nothing. Get some sleep."

"The Spirit prompted me to ask."

The Spirit? She frowned. Keeping the Old Covenant laws had been easier in so many ways! The law was only about judging actions. But the Holy Spirit knew her heart. And she had just lied to Paul.

"I was jealous," she confessed. "Justus and his wife have a huge home. They're wealthy. I don't show hospitality like they do. I can't." She sighed. "I felt embarrassed, maybe even ashamed. I should be able to do more."

He nodded, his eyes growing heavy again. "Someone has forgotten her long years of tutoring, using a wax tablet to study each word." Paul sighed. "Hospitality. What does it mean? What is the root?"

She smiled, understanding at once his point. "Good night, then, Paul." She hummed to herself as she climbed the stairs to the loft. Hospitality, translated, was "kindness to the outsider." Kindness was always within reach, no matter how poor she was or where she lived. She felt the jealousy fall away and contentment return.

Paul makes it so easy to forget the burdens of the Old Covenant and fly free into the new life of grace.

Moments later, she lay on her mat with Aquila on one side, Ephraim on the other. Downstairs, the disciples slept. Peace was palpable in the shop. It was a warm peace, nearly indescribable. Then she felt sadness enter, the sadness of losing her mother and then her father. She felt the grief so clearly she could almost trace the outline of the wound in her heart.

As the peace continued to flow, she felt the aching wound slowly fill.

Many people had been touched by Paul and healed of visible infirmities. But only God knew about the wound that ached in her heart, here in the dark hours of the night. God saw, and God healed, and what had she done to earn it? Nothing. She just received it, letting it wash over her, like a baby receives a blanket drawn up to its chin.

"Praise God," she whispered, and fell into contented sleep.

CHAPTER NINE

On a morning not two weeks later, Ephraim's cries startled her awake. Aquila leapt up from the bed and was halfway down the stairs before the disciples sat up. Outside, someone furiously pounded on the shop door. Priscilla stood and took Ephraim in her arms, rocking him side to side.

Aquila opened the door. Two men entered at once. Priscilla hadn't seen men like these in so long, but she knew the type at once. They each wore only a knee-length chiton, with embroidered scrolls at the edges and a wide belt fastened at the waist. A sprig of greenery was pinned to their shoulder and already at this early hour, their hair was oiled and styled into neat ringlets that fell to their shoulders.

These were men of wealth and influence.

"By order of the Proconsul, Gallio, Paul is charged with crimes against the Jewish law. We are here to arrest him."

Behind Aquila, the disciples had stood from their mats. Aquila held one hand up, signaling them to remain behind him.

Aquila held out his hand to the strangers. "I assume your charges are written and bear the seal of Gallio? May I see them, please?"

The men looked at each other, apparently at a loss. Finally, one spoke. "We did not bring the charges with a seal. Not many people can read."

His tone implied more. Priscilla knew he assumed that Aquila could not read or write because Aquila was only a tentmaker.

Never underestimate a man who works with his hands.

Aquila sighed then rubbed his brow. "My friends, Gallio is the ruler of this province and a man of great honor. He would want everything done properly. After all, he serves at the pleasure of the emperor. We must be very careful to do everything correctly."

The men looked at each other, as if uncertain whether to agree. The older of the men nodded in assent. "Honor is everything to Gallio."

Aquila clasped his hands together, as if delivering terrible news. "Gentlemen, you are surely aware of the kidnappings that occur so frequently here. The slave traders, the ship captains who need an extra man—well, anyone could claim to be Gallio and take a citizen off the streets. That would be a scandal that would undermine Gallio's authority. A scandal that would ruin his good name."

No one moved. "Your father is so wise," Priscilla whispered to Ephraim.

"Come back with a sealed warrant," Aquila said, moving the men toward the door. "If you are who you say you are, we will obey at once. We must all protect Gallio. These are such dangerous times."

When the men had left, Priscilla descended the stairs with Ephraim. She was tempted to laugh out loud, but Timothy and Silas were huddled over a bench, talking in low voices to Paul.

"You need to get out of Corinth!" Timothy said to Paul, tears in his eyes.

Silas nodded. "They're going to whip you. They always want to beat or whip you, Paul. You can't survive another one. Timothy is right. For the sake of the Gospel, get on a ship now."

Paul was having none of it. "Think! Gallio is appointed by Rome. A Roman proconsul. He would not care if I broke Jewish law. He has no jurisdiction. Who is trying to stop me, then? It is certainly not Gallio. I have nothing to fear from him."

"Sosthenes," Priscilla said. The men stopped talking and turned to look at her. "He left Justus's house in a rage. I think he is angry that Paul is inviting Gentiles into the faith. I understand his reasoning. If Gentiles join the faith, if we abandon the old laws, then we will no longer be Jews, will we? We're becoming something entirely new."

Paul nodded. "Just as I described. Entirely new creations. Every one of us."

"I understand more than anyone how hard it is to let go of who you once were," Priscilla said. "I wanted to hold on to my old identity, but it was taken from me. For some, to embrace this New Covenant must seem like a loss of their identity. It's not easy to change, even when the Good News is just that...entirely good."

The room grew quiet. Aquila nodded at her.

"The Gospel cannot wait for feelings to catch up to the Good News," Paul said, resting his hand over hers.

Timothy shook his head. "The Gospel has to wait until your body is stronger!"

"I'm nearly healed from my last beating," Paul said.

Silas rolled his eyes and looked around the room. "If you want to face Gallio, we will support you. But you might die here in Corinth. And we do not know your final wishes if that happens."

Paul motioned for them all to come closer. "Nothing will happen to me. I will not be beaten or whipped here in Corinth."

Timothy started to object, but Paul lifted one hand to silence him.

"I had a vision from the Lord," Paul said. "When I was praying, the Lord spoke to me. He said, 'Do not be afraid. Go on speaking, and do not be silent! For I am with you. No one will attack and harm you, for I have many people in the city.'"

"When did you have this vision?" Priscilla asked.

"Months ago, when I first made the local Jewish leaders angry," Paul said.

Silas threw his hands in the air. "And you're only now telling us?"

"Priscilla," Paul said, turning to her, "fetch your writing supplies, will you? I cannot teach in person, but I can still send letters."

Weeks later, a servant met them at the entrance to the council house, which the local Greeks called the bouleuterion, and escorted them to Gallio at once. Thankfully for Paul, the council house was in the same part of the city as the shop. Paul's feet couldn't have handled a long walk. His eyes were bleary from the letters he'd worked on while waiting. He'd made good use of the time he'd been in Corinth.

In the center of the small house, Gallio sat on a carved wooden seat, flanked by two officers of the court. He was dressed in finest Roman clothing, complete with a beautiful striped toga. The hard lines of his face told Priscilla he was unfamiliar with mercy.

Sosthenes was already there; scouts must have seen Paul leaving the shop and run ahead. Sosthenes stood, his hands clutched behind his back. He wore fine linen robes and an emerald pin at his shoulder to secure a fresh sprig of greenery.

Noises from the street outside worried Priscilla. Glancing at Aquila, she knew he shared her concern. A crowd gathered to hear what would be done to Paul. Crowds could never be trusted; she'd seen that in Rome.

Sosthenes wasted no time. "This man," he charged, pointing to Paul, "is persuading the people to worship God in ways contrary to the law. He claims Jesus was the Son of God, the Messiah, which is false. It has been proven false. He claims that anyone can be saved without following the law, which of course is against common sense. If he no longer wishes to be a Jew, he should denounce Judaism and the Jewish God. But he should not bring Gentiles into the faith and tell them to break every law."

"Which law are we speaking of, again?" Gallio asked, picking at his toga.

Sosthenes's cheeks turned red. "Jewish law, Gallio."

"I am a Roman," Gallio said. "I know only one law, and it applies equally to everyone. I know what that law requires of me today." Gallio motioned to a servant then whispered in his ear. The servant left and audibly called out for the next case to be heard.

Sosthenes stammered in protest, but Gallio cut him off. "If you were making a complaint about some misdemeanor or serious crime, it would be reasonable for me to listen to you. But since it involves questions about words and names and your own law—settle the matter yourselves. I will not be a judge of such things. Your charges against Paul are dismissed."

With that, the plaintiff and defendant of the next case came in. Sosthenes started to make a plea, but the servants grabbed him and dragged him outside the council house.

Many in the crowd were the very people Paul had healed and ministered to. Priscilla saw the glee in their faces at Sosthenes's humiliation. She gathered the hem of her robe and looked for a way through the crowd before the violence began.

The crowd turned on Sosthenes and began to beat him. She spied an opening in the crush of people and ran quickly for the shop. She heard Aquila and the other disciples behind her, not far back. She heard them struggling with something or someone but dared not stop or slow down to look. When she reached the shop, she closed the door, waiting for Aquila's voice before she opened it.

He arrived seconds later, blood streaming from a cut on his forehead. Silas, Paul, and Timothy were with him. Paul was untouched, as surely as the Lord had promised. But Silas and Timothy looked like they had been in a fight. Perhaps they had, for they helped Aquila drag Sosthenes's limp body into the shop.

Priscilla got them inside at once while the crowd shouted in the distance, calling Sosthenes's name, eager to finish the bloody business at hand.

Visitors streamed in and out of the shop all afternoon, eager to congratulate Paul on his victory over Sosthenes. No one knew how Sosthenes had escaped his beating. Most importantly, no one knew Sosthenes was upstairs in the loft, recovering from his injuries. As the guests moved in and out downstairs, Priscilla held a spoon of broth to Sosthenes's cut and bloodied lips. Wincing, he sipped. She checked the bandages at his ribs.

"You've bled through these again," she whispered. "I'll fetch new ones. Stay here and be quiet." She descended the stairs to the shouts of friends and fellow believers, and acquaintances from the harbor. It was a rowdy mix of people who loved excitement and those who were glad to see Paul acquitted.

Holding a finger to her lips, she silenced them. "Ephraim is sleeping!"

Aquila rested a hand on her shoulders. "My wife is right, friends. We should have quiet now so that Ephraim can sleep.

If Ephraim doesn't nap, we will all suffer, and no crowd will save us then," he said. Everyone laughed.

After the crowd of well-wishers dispersed, Paul spoke to Silas, Timothy, Aquila, and Priscilla.

"I'm leaving Corinth," Paul said.

Shock must have registered on her face because Paul reached for her hands. "I have a plan. You and Aquila are a part of it. There will be much to discuss tomorrow. But before I leave this city, there is one last man to convert."

With that, he ascended the stairs to speak with Sosthenes.

"Not Ephesus! Anyplace but Ephesus!" Priscilla said the next morning. "Paul, I have a child. I cannot take Ephraim to that cursed city!" She held Ephraim in her arms. The boy was content to look around the room as the morning light bounced off the tools laid across the work benches. He had slept wonderfully last night despite everyone else's unrest.

Even Aquila was speechless. Silas and Timothy sat at the table eating stewed figs for breakfast, not lifting their eyes above their plates. The tension between the men made Priscilla lose what little appetite she had left. Whatever she had heard about Ephesus, clearly it was worse than that.

Ephesus was the center of the empire for dark magic, superstition, witchcraft, and sorcery. Spell books were sold everywhere, sorcerers were as common as flies, demoniacs in chains were displayed in the streets as curiosities. One reason why was tied to the structure at the heart of the city—the temple of Artemis. The city was built to inspire awe for the goddess, which left no room in the heart for the true God.

The temple was twice the size of the Parthenon of Athens and considered one of the seven greatest wonders of the world. Pilgrims from all over the world traveled to worship Artemis, the goddess of the hunt. Romans called her Diana, but everyone knew she was nothing but cold hard coins for the merchants. Travelers bought silver statues of Artemis as souvenirs. They also bought spells written on scrolls, curses for their enemies, drafts, elixirs, and whatever was sold in the market. And in those markets, what was sold could not be spoken of without shame.

Ephesus had no shame, however. Second only to Rome as the largest city in the empire, she was incredibly wealthy. As a port city, she was the most important. As a trading center, she was the most profitable. If all roads led to Rome, all imaginations wandered to Ephesus.

Rome was meant to be the seat of government and the home of the emperor. Rome was pomp and grandeur. Ephesus was wild abandon plus money. Caravans crossed through Ephesus on the Royal Road, carrying goods from all corners of the empire. Whatever a man desired could be bought in the market, especially opium. People could easily choose whether they wished to forget their problems and slip into sleep…or just slip away into death. Either was possible and quite cheap thanks to the dealers.

Priscilla hated cheap deaths. She'd seen her mother fight valiantly to stay alive. Her mother had accomplished much good in those final weeks, despite the physical pain and suffering. The suffering had been so awful that it had been, in its own way, sacred. *What is beyond our understanding and ability to bear can be a sacred offering to God.*

"Will there be enough work for us in Ephesus?" Aquila asked, bringing Priscilla back to the moment. "How will I feed my family?"

Paul widened his eyes. "Enough work? What do you think your work is? You don't think you are only a tentmaker, do you?"

Aquila pressed his lips together in a thin, hard line, and Priscilla briefly feared for the apostle Paul. Aquila far outweighed him. Paul was a dear friend, but as a houseguest he brought court cases, mob violence, and the hiding of fugitives. *Most guests just bring a basket of figs.*

Silas cleared his throat. "Ephesus is a wild place, Paul," he said. "Here in Corinth, there is order. The proconsul is seen as an extension of the emperor, and his authority is respected. For that reason alone, your life was spared."

"For that reason alone," Paul replied. "And what of the Lord's will?"

Silas nodded quickly. "Yes, yes. Of course. My point is that Corinth is a town with a healthy respect for the Roman way of doing things. But Ephesus? Those people could tear you limb from limb in the streets before the authorities even knew you had arrived."

"The darkness of Ephesus scares me," Timothy said. Everyone turned to look at the young man. The plainness of his words seemed to reach Paul's heart. Paul studied him then sat at the table with them all. He filled a plate with dates and ate quietly, saying no more. As he ate, everyone breathed again, the idea of Ephesus slowly becoming real.

Paul finished then wiped his mouth. "Jesus said, 'It is not the healthy who need a physician, but the sick. I have not come to call the righteous, but the sinners to repentance.'"

"I have not heard that before," Priscilla murmured.

"Luke tells that story," Timothy said to her.

"Well, he has to write that down," Priscilla replied tersely. "I keep reminding everyone that these things must be written. All the eyewitness accounts must be written." She was upset with the suggestion of anyone going to Ephesus.

Paul folded his hands and continued. "Why do people go to Ephesus?"

"The temple of Artemis," Timothy replied quickly.

"Yes!" Paul exclaimed. "They long for wonder. People want to see a temple where a god lives. They want to worship. Do you understand?"

Naturally, Timothy spoke first. "No. Not at all."

Paul chuckled. "Ephesus has a terrible reputation for sorcery and witchcraft, that's true. With the temple of Artemis, many are reminded of Artemis's association with the goddess of witches, Hecate. But remember this: Ephesus is the one place where Gentiles from all over the world come to visit a temple and worship a god they do not know. Their hearts are more open than even they realize. And Artemis—what is she?" Paul blew out air, vibrating his lips.

Ephraim copied Paul, giggling.

Priscilla laughed, and Aquila's smile stretched ear to ear. Paul did it again, and Ephraim copied him again, making all the men laugh in return.

Paul completely stopped the discussion for several minutes to make silly faces at the baby. Ephraim giggled until he was red in the face and hiccupped. Paul wheezed and pressed a hand to his side but continued. Finally, Priscilla took Ephraim to the far side of the room and bounced him on her hip.

"He was having fun," she said, "but Paul, you were short of breath. I do not think your lungs are as strong as you would like. Didn't you say you had been shipwrecked? Did you almost drown, by any chance?" He had probably taken on more water than he knew. His lungs needed dry air, not another sea voyage.

Paul shrugged. "Shipwrecked twice so far. Everything is damaged. I do not worry too much about it, though. The Lord holds me together. Now, back to our discussion of Ephesus."

The mood immediately became more somber. Priscilla felt they were discussing a strategic military campaign more than a mission trip.

"We are not like everyone else, the people who can only see the darkness of Ephesus." Paul resumed his point. "We see with the eyes of the Spirit. And think of what we are bringing these hungry souls! They traveled to see a temple and a god who lived inside it? We will tell them of the God who doesn't even need a temple! But nonetheless, His glory filled the temple Solomon built. But not His image. No one saw an image of God. Not until they looked at His Son. And they have seen His face, walked with Him in our streets, watched Him die for our sins, witnessed Him resurrected in victory, and the most astonishing revelation?"

Priscilla couldn't help it. She had wandered back over to the table, and like the men, she leaned in toward Paul, spellbound, eager to hear the revelation. Ephraim reached his chubby arms out for Paul.

"Now, our very bodies are God's temples," Paul said, taking Ephraim in his arms and resting the baby on his lap. "His glory—the Holy Spirit—fills our bodies. Never again will they have to travel to visit a god. Their very bodies will be holy if God indwells them."

"I'll go," Timothy said.

Paul smiled. Everyone expected that, Priscilla thought. Whether Paul had adopted Timothy as a son, or Timothy had adopted Paul as a father, that was hard to tell. But the two were inseparable. Timothy needed Paul in many ways. Paul wanted Timothy to become everything he could not, for time was not on Paul's side. Even Priscilla could see that, no matter what events happened next, his body would not last much longer.

Silas reached for another serving of figs. "I hate the food on ships." So Silas was going.

"What is the distance?" Priscilla asked.

"Not as far as Rome to Corinth," Paul said gently. "We go across the Aegean Sea. I have made arrangements for us on a ship. We won't leave for a few weeks. Before we leave, I will first go to Cenchreae. I need to cut my hair." He had made arrangements for everything already, even a haircut to fulfill his vows and prepare for the trip.

"We made a home here, Paul," Aquila said. "This is where we planned to raise Ephraim. And I have clients and steady business. You're asking us to leave everything to follow you."

"I'm asking you to follow the Spirit," Paul said. He looked at each person in the room pointedly. "You're all going to leave everything you know to follow Jesus at some point in your life. It might be a small decision in a small circumstance. It might be a large one. But always, we will be asked to walk by faith, not sight. And that means to step into the unknown."

"It's hard," Priscilla said. Her eyes stung. She couldn't believe she was on the verge of tears, but she was. Suddenly she was sad with the thought of leaving this city.

"This is such good practice, my friend," Paul said. "Someday, far from now I pray, the time will come for you to join your Father in heaven. And do you want to be afraid, like a child at the water's edge who never learned to swim? No! You want to be like the child who is eager to dive headlong into the depths, because you spent your whole life leaping and jumping into your Father's arms." His voice grew very soft. By now, Ephraim had closed his eyes and was nodding off. "I feel sorry for the people who have never trusted Christ for even the smallest of journeys or the tiniest leaps. When the time comes for the greatest journey of all, they'll be so frightened they'll miss the wonder of it."

Aquila glanced at her and she knew their hearts agreed. They were going to Ephesus.

CHAPTER TEN

Nothing could have prepared Priscilla for the reality of Ephesus.

The ship arrived though the port gate on the eastern side of the city. In the harbor, their ship was surrounded by smaller boats, local fishermen pulling in their catches from the previous night.

Paul stood alongside her at the ship's edge. She pointed to a net filled with wide, silver fish. "What are those?"

"Sea bream," Paul replied. He'd traveled by sea enough to know many things now. "The best-tasting fish you'll ever have! We'll probably have some of those very fish roasted for breakfast in a few hours."

Onboard, the sailors around them rushed through their chores, darting back and forth on the deck. Priscilla was careful to stay out of the way. "Everyone is happy to arrive and anxious for a bath," Paul remarked. Hard work on a ship and a lack of fresh water had rendered the men unsuitable for society.

"Anxious to enter the city and see new faces," she answered. Aquila appeared from below deck with Ephraim, lifting one hand to wave. He carefully made his way over to them. The captain piloted the ship between vessels in the crowded harbor and prepared to dock.

Oil lamps dotted the harbor in the early morning darkness. Their flames flickered as a light drizzle of rain fell. Wrapping her arms around herself, she felt a slight chill in the air as mist rose from the water.

"Unusual to have rain here in Ephesus," the captain remarked as he walked past, supervising his men. "A good sign, though. Rain means rebirth."

Sailors and their superstitions! She said nothing, grateful they had not thrown her overboard. During storms, women were always the first passengers thrown overboard to appease the gods. Thankfully, even though they had only encountered mildly rough waters, Aquila made sure no one tried that.

The sailors worked for an hour to dock and secure the ship. The captain had to register the ship with the harbor master and pay a tax before anyone was allowed off. As the final arrangements were made, light rose over the city of Ephesus, burning off the mist. Ephraim was awake by then, babbling as Priscilla held him in her arms. He was eager to be set down on the ship, to crawl and investigate. Priscilla tried to distract him until they were off the ship. He fussed and whined and wrestled, eager to be free of her arms. Aquila reached for him and had no better luck. She took Ephraim from his arms and handed him to Paul. Ephraim immediately settled down, amusing himself with tugging on Paul's beard. Paul feigned great distress, which made Ephraim guffaw with laughter. The morning haze burned away as the crew made the final preparations to disembark.

At last, Priscilla could lift her eyes and look at the city in the morning light. Her breath caught in her chest. Aquila must have felt it too, for he rested a hand on her shoulder, then wrapped his arm around her and pulled her close.

Ephesus is exquisite.

White stone steps led up from the harbor into the city. From there, a wide, white stone street curved and ran as far as her eye could see through the city. Clouds parted and the sun burst through over a pair of stone elephants with intricate carvings on their foreheads. The elephants stood guard at the entrance of a building. Looking around, she saw statues like this everywhere.

Every building and every entrance was ornate and beautiful. Ephesus was a city built for the eyes.

As Priscilla looked up above the center of the city, she could see the outline of the temple of Artemis. Dozens of white stone columns, row upon row, outlined the massive temple. Hundreds of white steps led up to it, as if leading up to the heavens themselves. *Forgive me, Lord, but that temple is impressive.*

She bit her lip at the thought of trying to explain her unseen God to someone who had this temple to worship at. With so much grandeur and pomp, who would want to listen to what Jesus had to offer? "How will we reach them?"

"The Spirit will," Aquila answered.

She looked up, startled. "I didn't realize I said that out loud. I was overwhelmed seeing their temple, seeing their wealth. . . ." She looked down at her ragged clothes. "I'm not sure what we have to offer."

The captain returned, motioning for his passengers to disembark.

As Priscilla and her companions stepped off the boat, they were ambushed by children begging and selling necklaces of seashells, miniature statues of Artemis, and more. The noise and bustle overwhelmed her at once.

Ephesus was as busy as Rome, although the air was much cleaner. The breeze blew in from the Aegean Sea, passing through the cypress trees and over the low hills. An endless expanse of blue skies opened above them. The morning drizzle had stopped and the stones soaked up the rain. Birds darted in and out of the little puddles left behind. Cats perched on top of columns watched the people with lazy disinterest. Occasionally a cat would leap down to steal a fish dropped by a fisherman.

Priscilla did not want to acknowledge the thought, but she suspected she might even like it here. Since Ephesus was a Greek city, the people dressed in the same style as those in Corinth. She did not even need to buy new clothes. She just needed to wash and repair what she had.

Paul slipped a coin into her hands. Before she could ask what it was for, a young girl grabbed her by the hand, dragging her toward the center of the square, chattering in Greek. Priscilla was still not as fluent as she would have liked, but she did understand the words for *bath* and *law*. Glancing over her shoulder, Priscilla saw the men in her traveling party, including little Ephraim, being pulled in another direction. Paul was smiling, though, so everything must have been all right.

Within moments she understood. The law of Ephesus was that all visitors must immediately bathe. Public baths were located in the center of the market. The girl assisted her, and the coin Paul provided was for her payment.

A week in Ephesus had not changed her opinion for the worse. On her way to her daily bath, Priscilla marveled again at how fast the city had won her over.

The air blew in over the city clean and hot, carrying the scent of sea and evergreens. Above them were blue skies. In the distance were vivid green cypress trees stretching to the clouds. In some ways, the city was not so different from Corinth. Ephesus was a city by the sea too. However, ships came to Corinth only to pass through it, to reach the other side, while Ephesus was a destination. If someone came to Ephesus, whether as a trader or a tourist, they weren't eager to leave.

Ephesus was truly the most beautiful city she'd ever seen. Even walking in the mornings to the market was a luxury. The roads were works of careful craftsmanship. Each stone had been carefully cut and precisely laid. The streets were laid out in a careful grid, which made navigating the new city easy. Of course, the Ephesians had planned this, knowing a well-organized city is easier to defend. But now the threat of invasion was forgotten. The streets were lined with the peristyle homes of the wealthy and columned public buildings with ornate entrances.

And best of all, the Library of Celsus. Inside, scrolls and tablets—thousands of them—were available to anyone who could read. When Ephraim napped in the afternoon, Priscilla made her way to the library and gorged herself on words. Stories, treatises, philosophy...everything was there.

Someday, perhaps, the story of Christ would be there too. Words filled her soul in a way that nothing else did. Why shouldn't the most important words be written down like these others? *Wouldn't that be wonderful, if someone in a faraway land, in another age, could read His words?* Could she dare imagine how those words would fill the hungry souls of the world? But for now, she contented herself to feast on poetry and books of wisdom. And maybe the task of writing those words for God would fall to someone else. He hadn't revealed any plan to her.

She knew the darkness of the city was very real, and she knew there would be much work in the days ahead. But this was a city worth saving. She suspected that just as she fell in love with the city, she would fall in love with the people. Still, she felt guilty for loving Ephesus instead of hating it. Early in the morning, as she walked past the sorcerers and witches calling out in the market, she said a silent prayer for wisdom. *How to begin the work here?*

Paul had left already to continue his journey to Jerusalem. He'd stayed in Ephesus only long enough for a bath. His sudden departure had shocked her. Many things weighed on Paul's mind, but the believers had received news that Mary, the mother of Jesus, wanted to move to Ephesus to spend her last years. Paul was eager to verify the story, and if necessary, arrange it. She lived with John, one of the disciples, but as Mary aged, surely the clean sea air of Ephesus would be easier on her lungs than a crowded city like Jerusalem.

Paul had promised to return to Ephesus quickly, if the Spirit allowed. She wondered how he knew when the Spirit was speaking and how he heard such clear directives. She envied that. But perhaps it was consolation for the abuse his body endured.

At the bathhouse, she slipped the attendant a coin and entered. Thankfully the baths were not expensive. She undressed in one room and entered the steaming pools, only lightly filled at this early hour. Sinking into the hot, steaming water, she felt her muscles give way and relax. She took a few deep breaths and let her mind wander. This was the time she used for praise and devotion. With her body and mind awake but at rest, her spirit seemed to unfold, like a flower to the sun.

Ephesus is indeed a beautiful city, the Spirit seemed to say to her heart. A twinge of guilt shadowed her mind. She hadn't wanted to love this city. She had wanted to hate it. She hated the evil here but not the city itself.

I'm sorry, Lord, she whispered.

I know your heart, the Spirit nudged her. *I knew you would love this place. Now I will teach you to love these people.*

The muscles in her neck loosened. She hadn't even been aware of the tension she'd carried there, the stress of loving a city she assumed she was supposed to hate.

How do I do that, Lord?

Remember how I have loved you. My love for you is the beginning of your ministry. What a powerful witness a well-loved woman is.

And with that, a deep sense of calm overwhelmed her.

Coming out of the bath, she felt refreshed in her entire being in a way she hadn't felt for months. Women noticed the wide smile on her face. She stepped onto the gorgeous, ornately tiled mosaic floor of the bath and dried herself before walking back out into the open-air market.

Far to one side were the men's latrines and a brothel, but tourists had to look for them, and she certainly was not going to do that. She strolled instead toward the center of the market, with its large Roman water clock, knowing the hour for her own shop to open was almost here.

"I speak for the dead!" A girl extended her hands, beckoning Priscilla to enter a shop. "Come, sister! Speak to those you have lost!"

Priscilla shook her head and continued walking.

"Is your husband being unfaithful to you? Do you want to punish your rival?" an older woman called from a shop doorway. "Buy a curse scroll! Buy several scrolls for all his mistresses and I will give you a good price!"

"For all his mistresses? Can you imagine a man with that much time?" Priscilla smiled politely and walked on.

Eager for the day to begin, she bought breakfast and turned for home. Those who sold curse scrolls and other dark objects were not hard-hearted or cold. Their great sin was greed, and Priscilla knew that sin all too well after Marcellus's betrayal. She didn't see the point of meeting sin with anger. That was not how the Lord had met her sin. He had simply washed it away.

God's love for me is the beginning of my ministry. How He loves me is how I will love others.

Someday, she hoped, many of these same women would be believers. She would make it easy for them to turn to her to learn how. She would always be the easiest person to approach. That was her ministry, as best she could do it in this city, at this moment.

She paused for a moment to look up, watching as pilgrims began the hike to the temple of Artemis. *What do they pray for?* Artemis was the goddess of wild animals and the hunt. These people didn't look like hunters. Artemis was the goddess also of fertility, but surely not everyone here desired a child. So many people made the long climb up the white stairs every day. What was the allure?

Quickly, she ducked behind a curtain in a vendor's stall as her blood turned cold in her veins. Lucian, a steward from her old home—*from Marcellus's home*—wandered in the market. His long robe was clean at the hem so he hadn't been in the streets long. His chiton was tucked at the waist, and she spied a dagger. It was not an ornamental piece.

Why was Lucian here? What business could Marcellus possibly have in Ephesus?

The sun rose higher. Aquila and Ephraim would want breakfast. She glanced again at the market as Lucian ducked inside a silversmith's shop. Her heart pounded in her ears as she waited to see what he would do next. Was he looking for her? That didn't make any sense and it was a silly idea.

No, he wanted something here in Ephesus, probably the same thing all men wanted. When he exited she could see the linen satchel he now carried. He continued down the main street then turned toward the temple.

She dared to step out of her hiding spot and move closer to be sure. He walked toward the temple road, joining the other pilgrims making their way toward the long climb to see the wonder of the world and gaze upon the face of a goddess. Lucian was too old to hunt and he wasn't married, so he probably wasn't praying for a child. *What on earth would he be here praying for?*

Doubling back, she went to the shops. She had a sudden desire to do a little browsing—and make idle talk—with Demetrius the silversmith. Lucian may have said more than he intended, and restless shopkeepers always had a keen eye for intrigue.

CHAPTER ELEVEN

Ephraim was crying when she returned.

"He's hungry," Aquila said. "We all are." Several believers had joined them as hired hands. Aquila had a habit of hiring people and then discovering if they had any skills. Timothy rushed forward to help her with the food.

Priscilla thanked him then narrowed her eyes at her husband, who only winked. She shook her head, trying to suppress a smile. "My arms are only so big," she reminded him. "Any more workers and I'll need help bringing breakfast home every morning."

Timothy set breakfast on the table at the back of the shop as Priscilla took Ephraim from Aquila. Customers had already arrived. Sosthenes was busy taking their orders. Sosthenes had been a useful—if surprising—addition to their traveling party since Corinth. But after his synagogue members turned on him in anger and beat him, he lost all interest in being in their congregation. Joining The Way appealed more to him, especially since Jesus taught that enemies were to be loved, not beaten in the streets. He felt safer with the believers. Even if he didn't completely understand how to reconcile his Jewish faith with his faith in Christ, not yet anyway.

He busied himself writing their orders. Sosthenes was a scribe, like herself. Was it a Spirit-led coincidence that scribes seemed to be more common among the disciples suddenly? *Is the Lord planning something?*

Aquila stood at his bench, grabbing leather from one end of the table then dragging it across and pressing it flat. He was beginning a new pair of shoes. She could see the design on the leather.

"You're making shoes," she commented, shocked.

"Pilgrims wear out their shoes by the time they get here," he said. "No one can make the return trip home without coming to see us. The old shoemaker retired just last week. He was so grateful to rest his swollen knuckles at last."

"And they'll get more than a pair of shoes when they visit us," Sosthenes said.

She sat at the bench and put Ephraim on her lap. Tearing the morning's bread and roasted fish into small chunks, she set it before him. He grabbed at it impatiently, his chubby hands closing tightly around each bit. He insisted on feeding himself, and the cats outside the shop door meowed impatiently to be let in. They knew more would land on the floor than in his mouth.

"Wait your turn, you greedy beasts," Priscilla called to them, grinning. She'd been around so many Egyptians who still worshipped cats as gods. She'd seen the cat statues in the market. Those people needed to see how pitifully these cats behaved when they knew Ephraim was inside, spilling fish everywhere. Honestly, these cats would make a statue to Ephraim if they could, she laughed to herself.

Aquila glanced up. "We have more people who want to meet than we have room for."

"And there's no synagogue?" Priscilla hadn't been entirely sure until now. She was still exploring the city, and women weren't allowed to study or learn in synagogues. Her only refuge had been the library. Of course, she was one of the few women in Ephesus who could read, so that was an unhelpful distinction perhaps.

"No, thankfully," Sosthenes said.

Priscilla laughed without meaning to. "I'm sorry, Sosthenes. I know your feelings are still hurt."

"Feelings?" he exclaimed. "Priscilla, everything still hurts!" The curls around his ears bobbed as he spoke. Sosthenes was always intent on being heard. Even his hair cried out for attention. At least now he was their ally.

"As I said," Aquila continued, "we need a place to meet. Pilgrims here are curious, and since they are not at home or in their usual routines, they are willing to listen to what we might say. I found a hall in the oldest part of the city, on the far edges, about a mile beyond the amphitheater. We can have about two hundred gather at a time."

A sudden, frightful commotion outside made everyone freeze. The cats hissed and spat. Aquila put one finger to his mouth as he walked to the door then slowly cracked it open. He paused, then swung it wide.

At their threshold sat a hound. He looked like he weighed about forty pounds, with a scruffy brown coat, black muzzle and ears, and a wagging tail. His dark eyes were bright and merry.

The cats kept their distance, meowing angrily at being denied their fish. The dog waited, looking up at Aquila patiently.

Ephraim held out both arms, squealing. Priscilla hesitated. Roman households often had dogs as pets. Romans loved dogs and spent a great deal of time and money on them.

Priscilla and Aquila had neither at the moment.

But Ephraim's squeals become shouts of protest until Aquila took the boy in his arms and tentatively allowed Ephraim to touch the dog's head. The dog remained cheerful, its tail wagging, tongue out to one side, eyes dancing. It was as if the dog had been sent as a delivery. It clearly was here with friendly intentions.

"What should we call it?" Aquila asked.

"You're not serious?" Priscilla said. "We don't have—" But one look at Ephraim's face reminded her of what she did have—a child. And a child needed a companion, even if it was a dog. Maybe especially if it was a dog. Her thoughts went suddenly to Lucian roaming the streets.

"We'll let Ephraim decide," she said. Ephraim, still in Aquila's arms, burst into giggles as the dog licked his toes. "He is learning words."

Sosthenes picked up the fish scraps and went outside to feed the cats.

Later that night, after the workers had settled in on their mats in the shop below to sleep, Priscilla, Aquila, and Ephraim were lying on their mats in the loft. Skylos, the dog, slept at Ephraim's feet. Skylos was the Greek name for dog, and Ephraim had practiced repeating it all day. Both boy and dog had fallen into a deep slumber after a day of play and laughter. Ephraim was a toddler now. He'd be ready for lessons in another year or so in language, math, and history, as it was important to start young.

Priscilla watched them with surprised contentment. She had not known this gift was missing from her life and yet God sent the dog at just the right moment. She didn't know what to pray for tonight, but watching Ephraim and Skylos sleep, she didn't worry. God provided before she knew what to ask.

And now, Aquila was sufficiently sleepy and the streets were deserted at this late hour. She could begin the other necessary conversation without risking him lurching from the shop with a wild look in his eye.

"I saw a man in the market today," she began, keeping her voice soft and gentle, as if the conversation were routine.

Aquila murmured. "I saw him too."

"You did?" She could not contain her surprise. He sounded so calm.

"Yes. I want to invite him to our meeting hall."

"No, that is not a good idea. Did you see the knife tucked in his cloak? Why is he even here, Aquila?"

"After everything that's happened to Paul, who can blame him? Let's invite him to address everyone at the meeting hall. I heard him speak in the market square and was impressed. I'm anxious for Paul to return and meet him."

He was not talking about Lucian. That was clear. Who was he talking about? She couldn't ask, or she'd reveal what she knew about Lucian. Maybe she didn't have to, not yet. If Lucian was a pilgrim, he'd leave town in a day or two. There would be no need to mention it then.

She could hardly wait to hear this mystery speaker Aquila mentioned.

Ephesus had indeed proven to be an exciting city but for reasons that were entirely surprising.

The following week, Aquila led her and the disciples down toward the Lower Gate of the city. Aquila pulled a cart filled with leather shades and tools, though he did not explain why. Ephraim rode in the cart, dangling his legs off the side. Skylos ran alongside, barking for joy at the adventure.

The burning orange sun slowly lowered itself behind the dark green mountains, as the deep blue shadows lengthened and deepened in the valleys below. The afternoon's breeze had just taken on the soft cool edge of night. The whole world seemed tilted on the edge of a promise.

Something in Priscilla urged her to pause and commit this moment to memory. She looked at her husband and son, Skylos's unbounded joy, and slowed her pace, inhaling deeply. All of life was uncertain and unclear, but these tiny moments of light and grace burst through the darkness at such unexpected moments. God was in control. God was writing a good,

good story in her life and through her life. These were the moments that made her sure.

The walk continued for another twenty minutes with Aquila whistling as he walked. Priscilla was grateful that Aquila had secured a rental hall at the lower end of the city. Without stairs to climb, they could appeal to weary merchants and even the pilgrims who were sick of endless climbs.

"I expect a crowd," Aquila called behind him. "My friend cannot come to speak quite yet, but people will come nonetheless."

"Why?" Priscilla called back. She still didn't know who Aquila had met, and Paul had not returned from his journey to Jerusalem. She'd heard from believers who traveled through Ephesus that he had written a wonderful letter to the congregation in Galatia. She was so eager to see him and ask about the Spirit's prompting for what to say. But here and now, without Paul, why would a crowd gather in a rental hall?

"Quite a few are eager to see you," Aquila said.

Priscilla's step hesitated just a moment.

"People are curious about you," Aquila said, not breaking stride. "You are not a Vestal Virgin or an Oracle, yet you are a woman who speaks to God. And because many followers of The Way are known to have the ability to perform miracles, people wonder if you can do miracles too."

She exhaled forcefully. *Where to even start*? "God does miracles, not me. And I'm a woman, yes, but in Christ, all are equal. All are welcome. There is no special benefit to being either male or female. We are as He has made us, as a reflection for

His glory, not our own. I do not want anyone coming to see me. I can only point them to Christ."

Timothy behind her laughed. "And that's exactly why people will want to hear you."

She wanted to kick herself. Hadn't she just promised that when the Lord called her to do more, she would do more?

Aquila stopped and lifted his arm, waving it in presentation. "Here it is."

No one spoke. Priscilla hardly dared breathe, except to clear her throat. Before her stood three walls with falling stones. There was no roof. There was no place to sit. There was not even a front-facing wall with a door.

Her heart sank, though she tried to keep her face bright. This was nothing like the synagogue, with its stacked stones, beautiful arches, and inviting greenery. This was nothing like a temple, any temple, and certainly not like the temple built for God in Jerusalem. How had it come to this, that the mighty God was to be worshipped in a broken-down, disused place like this?

Aquila watched her. He nudged his toe against her sandal, chin lowered as he waited for her to say something. When she could only open and then close her mouth, he nodded.

"Do you know that I felt the same way?" he said. "When the Lord led me to this place, and I felt the Spirit urging me to rent this place, I resisted. I wanted a beautiful building. But what does that word mean, 'synagogue'?"

"To come together," she replied, fondly remembering a young Aquila eavesdropping on her tutoring sessions.

He grasped her hand. "We are the church now. Whenever we meet, that is our synagogue."

"The Spirit within us, Christ standing with us," she murmured, the full power of the new reality sinking in. She looked up, her courage restored. "Jesus promised that wherever two or more are gathered, He is in our midst."

"The weakness of this building is what makes it perfect, you know," Aquila said, pulling her to the edge of one crumbling stone wall.

"Do you remember how much we love a breeze at night?" he prompted her. "Don't you remember how hot the theaters got in Rome? No one wanted to rent this building but we can put shades across it, and the open design means people will have a cool breeze at night."

She stifled a smile at the word *design*. Aquila always saw things in a positive light.

"All those sunshades we've made recently?" Aquila asked. "Now you know why."

He walked the floor again, as if taking the building's measurement in his mind. "We can afford this place, Priscilla. I believe God will do great things here." He clapped his hands together. "Now, we have work to do."

The first few months, each of the disciples took turns teaching what they knew of Jesus's words and the teachings of Paul. Everyone had something valuable committed to memory.

Together, they offered the whole story as best they could. Occasionally, they had to double back and explain why things happened or the order of events, but with every meeting they were able to present the Good Story in a way that the people understood.

And week after week, the people returned. When Priscilla spoke, an uncomfortable ripple went through the crowd. She sensed it—all of the apostles did. No one had ever heard of a god who valued both men and women. Some gods here only spoke through women, some through men alone. But this God broke all barriers. Any person, any age, of any background or nationality was welcome.

There was no sacrifice to make—her God had made it for them.

There was no pledge of obedience—her God promised that He would supply both the desire and the ability to do what was right.

There was no war to fight in His name—her God promised that the Prince of Peace had conquered the enemy, once and for all.

After the first few meetings, Priscilla noticed a man in the crowd. She had not seen him in the marketplace before, and by now, she was well acquainted with most of the vendors. Even the sorcerers knew her name, and more than a few had been willing to come to the meetings. He had to be a visitor, she guessed.

He wore a smug, hard expression. With a square jaw and snow-white hair, his eyes watched her with a flinty glare as she told the story of the resurrection and the women at the tomb. Finally the man stood, interrupting her. "Men and women should not learn together. We should meet separately. Wives should be silent!"

Priscilla's heart dropped. She hadn't been verbally attacked in front of a crowd before and did not know what to do.

Aquila stepped forward. "We each have words we've committed to memory, the words and story of the Christ and teachings from Paul. We all need each other right now."

The man stood and left. The crowd looked down, or away, but not at her.

Aquila rested his arm around her shoulder as he addressed the crowd. "Remember what Christ said about causing offense. He is the true stumbling block. Not us. Sometimes, I think, we focus on each other, when what really makes us angry is Christ Himself and what He is doing."

Her very being had caused that man offense. She was a woman, though, and could not change that. She was called, and she could not change that either. She would not hide the light that had been lit within her heart. Not when the world was in darkness.

CHAPTER TWELVE

The next day she stopped again at the shop of Demetrius, bringing him a basket of figs.

"You return!" Demetrius exclaimed. He was a stocky man, with a white and black beard and darting brown eyes. His voice was commanding and deep, especially in the confines of his little shop. Everywhere stood tiny silver statues of the goddess Artemis. The body was a column of wild animals. It had dozens of breasts at odd angles. Wrapping around the top of its head was a replica of the Ephesian city walls. What exactly, Priscilla wondered, was worthy of worship in that image? It was as if the artist kept thinking of more things to throw in. And the only artists who backtracked over their work like that, cluttering the design until it was no longer recognizable, were artists who had no faith in the original plan.

Demetrius was a hardworking man who kept his family fed, plus many others at times too. He was the head of the silversmith's guild. He made the statues during the cool of the morning and ran the shop during the heat of the day. His hands had deep callouses and faded pink spots. He caught her looking at them. "From my days learning to work with melted silver. She is an unforgiving teacher."

He pulled out a stool for her and motioned for her to sit. He sat opposite. Taking the basket from her, he offered her a fig.

"What can I do for my lovely neighbor this morning?" he asked.

She sat and thanked him. "The man we chatted about last week…any news of him?"

Demetrius nodded, taking a bite of his fig. "Yes, but it cost me."

Priscilla reached for her coin purse tucked in her belt, but he waved her off. "No, put your money away. We will consider this a favor you owe me later."

Relieved, she settled back on the stool. She didn't have any extra money to spare. She hadn't even told Aquila yet that she had spotted Lucian. What was there to say?

"His innkeeper had the details," Demetrius said. "Apparently your friend Lucian is chatty once he's had too much wine."

"But Lucian doesn't drink." He only drank goat milk. He always said that wine affected him too strongly. "And he isn't my friend."

Demetrius shrugged, a mischievous grin on his face. "The innkeeper convinced him that Ephesian wine has absolutely no ill effects. And the more you drink, the better you feel." Demetrius laughed. "Which is true, in a way. Except that the next morning you feel like you're licking the floor of Hades with a boot on your head."

She chuckled. "What do you know?"

"You have a brother?"

"Marcellus," she replied.

"And your parents?"

"My mother died before I left Rome," she answered. "My father died sometime after I left. My brother remains in Rome, managing the family estate." She did not know how much to reveal.

"I was hoping the information was wrong." He shook his head. "It is the right family, then. I am sorry to say that Lucian was fired from your brother's service for being a thief."

"Oh," she replied, unsure what this news could mean.

"Servants can never be trusted." Demetrius scowled.

Priscilla forced a smile. "It sounds like you have had bad luck with your servants."

"Robbed blind more than once," he answered. "My parents were nearly put out on the street by a servant they trusted. I took over the family business after that. No one will ever threaten our livelihood again. Hear me on this—it is better to make an example out of your enemy than to forgive."

The darkness that glimmered in his eyes chilled her.

"Do you want me to deal with him?" Demetrius asked, lowering his voice. "Your brother would be pleased to hear that you avenged the family name."

"No, but thank you." She smoothed her robe and glanced at the door as a customer came in. "If he passes through again, let me know."

On the way back to the shop, she scanned the crowds, looking for Lucian. Her heart fluttered at the top of her rib cage as she pushed past people in the market. Lucian had never been a good man, but now he might be a desperate man. She did not want him to learn that she lived here.

Returning to the shop, she spied Ephraim sitting on the floor, playing with Skylos. She scooped up the little boy and held him tightly.

Aquila stopped his work, looking up from his bench. "What happened at the market?

"News from Rome," she sighed. "A pilgrim to the temple of Artemis is someone we know."

The following week while Aquila taught the Gospel message, Priscilla eagerly scanned the crowd for the man who had been so offended at her presence. He had not returned, but perhaps it was just as well.

Instead, another man caught her eye. Actually, he caught nearly every woman's eye. Priscilla was suddenly aware of his effect on the women in the room except for those too old and stricken by cataracts to see.

He won them over before he spoke a word. He had deep brown eyes and huge dimples. His smile conveyed a man genuinely delighted to be in the company of others, anyone and everyone. When Aquila paused, this man asked to share a word from the Lord. He had read a scroll, he said, containing the story of John, the cousin of Jesus, and wanted to share. Aquila hesitated but allowed him to address the crowd. Aquila knew enough of John's story to know if this stranger who called himself Apollos was a false teacher.

Apollos's rich, warm voice boomed through the open space for over an hour, every word like a carefully selected stone. Stone by stone he built a beautiful path leading to the undeniable conclusion that Jesus was the Messiah.

"For of the fullness of Christ we have all received, grace upon grace. The law was given through Moses, grace and truth were realized through Jesus Christ," he continued, as the hour grew late. "No man has seen God at any time; the only begotten God, who is in the bosom of the Father. Jesus has shown us the Father. This is my witness to you."

The crowd was mesmerized. Many professed faith in Christ. "If you repent of your sins, I will baptize you with water," Apollos said. "How good it is to repent."

Priscilla and Aquila looked at each other. Her heart stopped, then suddenly resumed.

"Apollos doesn't know," she whispered. "John was teaching them to repent of their sins but that was all. He did not tell them how to keep from sinning. He knew nothing of the indwelling Spirit that made all things possible. Oh my."

"It's like having a feast without wine or bread," Aquila replied.

"Or dessert." She smiled. "Yes, he is missing the best part."

"We have to help him," Aquila murmured.

Priscilla cut through the crowd, making her way to Apollos.

"Do you come to be baptized?" Apollos asked. His eyes had a slightly wary cast, the wrinkles at his brow deepening. He seemed hesitant to be approached by a woman but not offended. Priscilla liked that about him, though. He held a crowd's interest but didn't seek out feminine attention.

"I came to invite you to dinner with my husband," she said. Turning, she pointed to Aquila. "That's him. You can go with him now. I will finish the story and then meet you at the house."

Apollos's expression immediately brightened. "Finish? There is more?"

She smiled and nudged him toward Aquila. "Much more. We cannot wait to share it with you."

After the men had gone, she stood before the crowd. Some had wandered away, and she guessed they felt discouraged. Repenting of sins did that to a soul. That sort of repentance brought only momentary freedom, followed by heavy guilt and despair. Sin was unavoidable without the Spirit. Worse, sin was unforgiveable without Christ.

She gathered the ones who remained around her like a mother hen with her chicks. "Our dear friend Apollos has need of dinner and rest. I will finish the Good Story for him. And believe me, he has left me the best part to be told."

Back in their shop, the men gathered at the workbench that doubled as a table. Skylos wagged his tail furiously as his head rested in Apollos's lap. His charm even extended to animals.

Aquila maneuvered deftly in the cramped space to serve everyone. The men bumped elbows reaching for serving bowls and platters. Priscilla had long since stopped lamenting the lack of space or furniture. God was amazing in His provision. Workbenches made exceptional dining tables, long enough to seat eight to ten adults. And the benches? People usually sat on the floor to eat meals, but she discovered she truly enjoyed sitting on a bench. Plus, it made serving food so much easier. *Not so much bending down and lifting up.*

Aquila ladled stew into wooden bowls, and Timothy placed them before each guest. Priscilla was grateful she'd made a thick porridge of lentils before she'd left to hear Apollos teach. Stew and bread always seemed to stretch whenever she had guests.

Once every guest had a bowl, Aquila bowed his head.

Looking down, she noticed that Ephraim had clumsily carved a shaky line into the table. Aquila had mentioned finding Ephraim with a leatherworking tool from the shop. Catching Priscilla's eye, Ephraim ducked behind Aquila's robe, knowing he would be in trouble. She bowed her head, shaking it in aggravation.

"Our Father, thank You for this food. Bless it as it is broken," Aquila said. "May it serve us so that we can serve others. Amen."

She lifted her head again and looked at Ephraim. He peeked at her. She held a steady gaze at him. He tried his best smile. He looked so much like Aquila. A smile tugged at the corners of her mouth before she could stop it. He giggled, probably guessing that he would not be scolded in front of the guest, and dipped his bread into his bowl of stew.

Priscilla refocused on the men's conversation. Apollos did not seem uncomfortable having a woman sit with him at dinner. That piqued her interest even more.

"From Alexandria in Egypt," Apollos said to the men.

He must have been explaining his background.

"An Egyptian?" she asked. *That explains a lot.* Egyptian household customs were so different than Jewish customs. Egyptians did not strive to keep the sexes apart.

"Born and raised there," Apollos answered. "My mother is a Jew married to an Egyptian trader."

"So your mother taught you the scriptures?" Aquila asked.

Apollos blushed slightly. "No, but she urged me to learn. My mother does not read or write. I learned the books of Moses and later the prophets. In my teenage years, a scroll arrived in Alexandria containing the words of John from his teaching in Bethany. I committed those to memory."

She traced the outline of Ephraim's carving as Apollos spoke.

That makes sense. His words today sounded so familiar. Those were John's words at Bethany. She wished she could have read that scroll. She would like to revisit those words again, to take her time with them and savor them. That was impossible with recitals like Apollos's.

Apollos pushed his bowl away. "What happened today? What were those people waiting on?" He looked at Priscilla.

She nodded. "They wanted Jesus."

"But I told them of Jesus," Apollos sputtered.

"You told them of Jesus, yes," Aquila said kindly. "But they need to know Him."

Apollos blinked several times. "I am afraid I do not understand."

Priscilla held out her hand across the table. Apollos took it hesitantly. "But you will," she said. "And your life will never be the same."

With that, the friends set out to explain to Apollos the full revelation of Christ. Apollos understood well that Christ came as the Messiah and fulfilled the law. What Apollos did not understand was how the fulfillment of the Old Covenant meant that a New Covenant had come. The death and resurrection of Christ meant that Christ lived in each believer now.

His death and resurrection were a part of every believer's experience, by faith, and the indwelling Spirit of truth was now theirs as well. The old cycle of sin and repentance was abolished. Repentance was necessary, but walking in love was what mattered now. The New Covenant didn't focus on avoiding sin to please God—it focused on loving others and trusting God.

He was shocked. He stumbled over several points as he reasoned them out. The New Covenant was not based on what believers did but what Christ did. The new wine was poured into a new wineskin. Works couldn't bring anyone closer to God. Grace and truth reigned now. Faith and love expressed themselves best not in our acts for God but in believers' actions toward other people.

"Abram believed the Lord, and he credited it to him as righteousness," Apollos said, quoting from one of the writings of Moses. He sat back on the bench, a light dawning in his eyes. "Abraham believed. It was not about the law, not even for Abraham. God was hinting at this New Covenant all along!"

He stood, pacing. "I have felt this! But I had no words! Thank you!" He turned to Aquila and the others. "Thank you! Within me, my spirit burned at times when I taught, but I did not know why. Now I understand what I must teach."

"Oh my." Priscilla sat back, muttering, a smile playing on her lips.

Apollos pressed his lips closed, then held a hand over his mouth. "What is wrong? Do I have something caught in my teeth?"

"Your eyes dance now, my friend." She laughed. "When the Spirit lights the heart, a change comes over the face. I cannot explain it. No one can really, except that your very countenance is one of joy."

"That's a good thing, then," he replied, visibly relaxing.

Priscilla sighed. "I hope so. Apollos, did you notice that every woman there tonight was entranced with you? You must be careful never to encourage the girls that your attention is anything but pure."

His face turned brightest red. "I have no idea why anyone would think that!"

"Your hair, Apollos," Aquila said, wryly. "It's enough to make any woman stumble." With that, they all burst out laughing.

Aquila invited him to stay for the night and it was well he did, for they all stayed up late talking. Priscilla spoke long into the second watch about Christ, teaching Apollos on the New Covenant and Jesus's promises, but at last she had to sleep.

Early the next morning, Apollos was up and dressed for his day when she descended from the loft.

"Going back to teach? So early?" She kept her voice soft. Ephraim was still asleep upstairs.

He shook his head. "I'm off to Achaia tomorrow. I need to get my passage arranged today." Achaia wasn't just a city—it was the entire region of Greece.

Disappointment must have shown on her face for he quickly spoke.

"You and Aquila are capable of teaching here," he reassured her. "I am thankful for what you've taught me and anxious to share it elsewhere."

"But Paul will arrive soon from Jerusalem," she said. "You need to meet him. He is an apostle like none other. You and he will make a team that will hold every crowd spellbound."

"Who can explain the Spirit's commands?" he asked. He frowned, the sadness reflected in his eyes. "Meeting Paul is something I've dreamed of. I've prayed for it. But God is sending me on."

She twisted her lips, thinking. "Go make your arrangements then. Come back tonight for dinner, and I will have letters of introduction ready for you. You will travel through Corinth, and the letters will make it easier for you to find lodging and assistance to begin your ministry."

His face brightened. "Yes, thank you! I did not expect such a kindness."

"But I need the day to contact the disciples here to help me write them. Apollos, you are so gifted and well equipped for your ministry."

"But?" He cocked an eyebrow.

"Stay connected to the body of believers, especially other apostles. We desperately need each other. We are all members of the same body, and we cannot function without each other. Do you understand?"

He extended his hand and she accepted it, then he clasped his other hand around hers. "I do. I was teaching people to repent in Christ's name. You and Aquila taught me how to walk in Him. The power of the Spirit is good news, indeed. If I hadn't stopped in this city, if you hadn't taken pity on me..."

"There are no 'if's' in Christ," Priscilla said warmly. "There is only grace."

"Priscilla?" Apollos looked at his sandals, his mood suddenly somber.

She raised her eyebrows expectantly. At last he looked back up at her, but his eyes had a mischievous sparkle.

"Do you really think my hair is a stumbling block?"

She burst out laughing then covered her mouth with one hand to avoid waking Ephraim.

"Be back for dinner," she whispered. "And stay out of trouble until then."

As he left she thanked God for giving her so many brothers in Christ. Apollos was just one more, and she was so glad to know him.

Christ has given me an abundant life, indeed.

CHAPTER THIRTEEN

One by one that afternoon, Priscilla found the men she needed and helped them write short letters of introduction. The work was painstaking, and the ink took time to dry.

By four in the afternoon, she was hurrying home, tired and ready to begin dinner. Poor Ephraim was probably cranky and hungry. Aquila often forgot to stop Ephraim from playing with Skylos and to settle down for lunch and naps.

Demetrius saw her hurrying past his shop, and waved her in.

Gritting her teeth, she returned the wave. She did not have time for a friendly chat. A twinge of guilt hit her. Most of Jesus's ministry was about being interrupted. She could bear with just one interruption on this day.

"Hello, Demetrius," she said, entering his small shop. Walking toward the back, she was careful not to bump into the tables on either side lined with silver statues of Artemis. She hated them. They were grotesque, besides immoral.

"Your new friend? Apollos is his name?" Demetrius asked.

She stopped. "Yes?"

"The women in the marketplace? Their tongues are wagging about nothing else."

Poor Apollos. She'd never considered how his looks might distract people from his message. Besides, she wasn't sure why Demetrius would tell her this. "Apollos is a good-looking man, to be sure, but he is also well spoken. And you can tell everyone that he is moving on to another region."

Demetrius's face fell. "No! Tell him to come see me first. I want to hire him!"

"For what?" she asked.

"The festival of Thargelia approaches, of course." Demetrius smiled indulgently at her as if she were teasing him. "I need someone to stand in the market and call out to the crowd to buy my statues. I can pay more than other vendors. I can pay more than all the vendors combined."

She groaned inwardly. Thargelia was a festival of thankfulness and meant to be a blessing for agriculture. It honored Artemis and Apollo. However, it was also a miserable event in Athens that brought suffering and humiliation to the unlucky ones chosen as human sacrifices.

She had to tread carefully now though. Demetrius was the heart of gossip in this city. If she offended him, he would quickly have the city murmuring against her and the believers.

She swallowed, rubbing her lips together, preparing her words with caution. "His mind cannot be persuaded. I tried myself this morning. Plus, he comes from a wealthy family in Alexandria. I don't think any amount of money will interest him. And Demetrius?"

He motioned with his hand to move her reply along.

"Apollos is a believer, a follower of The Way," she said gently. "He would not want to sell these statues."

Demetrius recoiled. "Why not? Artemis is a goddess of fertility. Whatever your god is, I'm sure the two are quite different."

"Yes, they are. That is what I am trying to tell you. Would you be willing to come and listen and hear more about my God?"

Demetrius looked around the shop. Priscilla followed his eyes. All his money, all his time and effort were represented here. His life's work *and* worth were on display under this roof.

He took a noticeable step back, away from her. His face told her that his mind was settled. "If your god would get in the way of all this, then no. I don't want to hear about him."

"But my God has so much to offer you."

"Artemis has made me rich," Demetrius replied flatly, crossing his arms. A coldness came into his eyes, and he looked at her as if she were an unwelcome stranger.

Pain shot through her heart. Demetrius wasn't just ending their friendship. He was closing the door on a chance to enter a new life. He was backing away from grace. *For what? So that he won't have to admit he has misspent his years? That is what grace is for!*

Quietly, she thanked him for his offer and graciously made her exit. Her steps were not so quick for the rest of the day. Her heart was simply too heavy. Only later that night did she realize that without Demetrius, she would have no advance warning if Lucian was sighted again in the city.

In the dark hours of the following morning, Apollos was the first one awake. His ship would leave at first light. Priscilla rose to be sure he had breakfast packed.

"Tell Ephraim I said goodbye and to be a good boy," he whispered, then made his quiet exit. She watched him leave. Dawn broke over the street, illuminating the shadows as his soft footfalls echoed on the stones. Would she ever see him again? Achaia was a wide and wild region, and the emperor was not fond of believers.

"God be with you, friend," she whispered, unsure if it was a prayer or a promise.

The following months, Priscilla and Aquila went back to teaching on their own in the rented hall. Priscilla had the best mind among the disciples for memorization, honed by years of tutoring. She often recited Jesus's words from memory or the admonitions from Paul or accounts from the original disciples about healings and miracles.

But a darkness descended over the city. Or was that her imagination? She could not deny that she felt a steady sorrow after Apollos left. She did not miss him, exactly—she hardly knew him—but he reminded her of home, perhaps. He reminded her of the friendship she might have had with her own brother if he had come to faith instead of clinging to his money. Apollos was educated, funny, and witty. He had read all the same books she had read. He had received the same education. Had she secretly been holding on to hope that somehow, someday, she could return to Rome? Perhaps. The heart hid the truth, even from itself.

So she did what she could. She grieved the pain that pierced her heart and wept before God in her prayers. And she praised God for the blessings born of her sorrow. But somewhere in between the tears and the praise was a void that she didn't understand. She did the things she knew to do, but a heaviness remained—like clouds thick with rain and a sky turned the color of sea black. She waited for the storm to break or pass. Either would be a relief. But day after day, the heaviness remained in her heart.

"Are we making a difference?" she asked Aquila one evening. Walking home from the rental hall, Ephraim and Skylos were chasing each other back and forth across the street, investigating sleeping cats and causing minor mischief. Her son was no longer a baby, and somehow this made her sad too.

But with Ephraim chasing Skylos, Aquila and Priscilla had a rare moment to talk undisturbed.

"Are you focusing on numbers?" Aquila asked. "It's the scholar in you that does that."

"The number of people in this city who need to hear the message is a valid concern," she said in prickly defense.

He looped one arm around her waist as they walked. "You are right. As always. I meant only that harvesters and planters have different jobs."

"I don't understand," she replied. His arm felt reassuring, and her tone softened.

"We plant seeds. We do not make them grow. What good does it do to lose sleep over the seeds once they are planted? We would only lose strength. Do what you are called to do and leave the results to God. He knows who is in this city. He knows the need."

"Every day, I see an increase in witchcraft and sorcery," she said. "Just a few months ago, we were introducing a new message, and Apollos was here, and I thought the city was going to explode in excitement for the new Way. But instead, everyone quickly returned to the dark arts."

"Not everyone. We have many new believers. And those who fled back to the darkness might still change their minds. Not everyone is ready to accept the Word when it is planted. Didn't Jesus teach a parable about that?"

"Yes." She sighed. "But I didn't write it down when I heard it. Now I wish I had."

"Next time," he said, squeezing her closer. "Which reminds me, there is a story circulating in the market about Paul!" He laughed as he said it, so it must be good news.

The very name of her friend made her heart leap with joy.

"Paul? Why?"

"Just as there has been an increase in demonic possession, there has been an increase in exorcists trying to profit."

Priscilla had seen them. Exorcists charged a ridiculous fee to cast out evil spirits. They usually only resulted in relieving the family of their coins, not their problems. Especially when children suffered, families paid all they had for the hope of a cure.

"Tell me the story," she said, nudging him in the ribs.

"Sons of the chief priest were exorcising demons," Aquila said, "but using Paul's name to do it."

Priscilla's jaw dropped open in outrage. "After all the beatings and punishments they've inflicted upon Paul, they dare use his name? If they believe that he speaks for Jesus, then why—"

Aquila held a hand up. "Let me tell the story. The sons of the priest were exorcising spirits in the name of Paul and Jesus. It sounds unbelievable that they would do that, I know, after persecuting us. Anyway, they had a demoniac who was especially violent. Seven of these sons came against the demon using a prayer they heard that Paul used."

"Well, then it's just a meaningless formula they used, not a real prayer," Priscilla protested, "because those men do not believe in Jesus nor do they support Paul."

Aquila raised an eyebrow, and she pressed her lips together. He continued. "The demon spoke. It spoke! Witnesses in the room said the demoniac opened his mouth, and a foul wind swept the room. A voice like the sound of serpent scales rasping together shouted, 'Jesus I know, and Paul I know, but who are you?' Then the demoniac jumped up and attacked all seven sons. One man defeated seven! The sons fled from the house. Now everyone is talking of the incident, holding the name of Paul in great esteem."

Priscilla sighed. "That story is shocking but not surprising. Paul will be unhappy with the outcome. He does not want his name to be esteemed." She cocked her head. "Do you suppose that is one reason he is hesitant to write of his experiences? He did not want to be esteemed?"

"You are probably right. He has written to the believers in Thessalonica, and I know he is working on letters to other churches. The words do not come easily for him."

"I don't just mean letters to individual churches, about specific issues. He needs to record all that has happened to him on his journeys," Priscilla said. "And what about the apostles who traveled with him or at his direction?" She offered a silent prayer once more that God would provide. And somehow, hearing a story other than her own made her forget about the darkness troubling her heart. *Stories are medicine for the heart, even when we don't understand the malady or have a name for it.*

Three months passed without further news of Paul. A believer passing through Ephesus told Aquila that Mary, the mother of Jesus, had settled with John in the villages not far from here. Priscilla very much wanted to find out if that was true. Mary would be a wonderful woman to interview, to record her experiences for a scroll.

Thinking on these things, Priscilla greeted the sunrise as she strolled to the market, calculating how much to buy for the day. The workers Aquila hired often ate more than she anticipated.

Suddenly a boy she knew from Aquila's meetings came running full speed up the stone road, his chiton flapping at his knees. Pushing people aside, he cut in and out, racing toward her so quickly he bumped into her before he could stop himself. His eyes were aflame with excitement.

"What is it?" she asked, grabbing him by the shoulders to steady him. "Is everything all right?"

Clutching his side, trying to take a breath, he panted through his wide smile. "The harbor! You must come!" His cheeks were drained of color. Had the poor boy sprinted all the way from the harbor?

"The one you call Paul!" the boy said, grabbing her arm and tugging. "Paul has returned! That is all anyone is talking of!"

She nearly dropped her basket. Thinking quickly, she pressed a coin into his palm, urging him to run to the shop and rouse Aquila. Moving with a burst of energy, she bought bread and provisions for her workers, paying extra to have the goods delivered to the shop. Then, lightened of her chores, she hurried to the harbor. As she got closer, the tang of sea and salt reminded her of Corinth. She missed that city. She hadn't been back to the harbor here in Ephesus since her arrival here.

Peering down at the harbor, she scanned the crowds as they made their way up the great stone steps into the city. Each would have to go at once to the public baths, of course. She wouldn't have much opportunity to talk to Paul, but she was so eager to lay eyes on him. These last moments waiting to see him were agony. Being parted from a friend for so long had been bearable, but here on the steps, waiting to be reunited, she felt she could not wait another moment.

"Paul!" she shouted as soon as she recognized him. He was too far away to hear her voice over the crowd of merchants and sailors and city officials. He was assisted by another man as he walked. Priscilla's heart lurched, as every trip weakened Paul further. Still, she couldn't wait to kiss his cheeks and hear his voice. Her hands curled into balls and she shook them out, trying to dispel the tension.

"His hair is shorter," Aquila said.

She turned. Aquila had Ephraim on his shoulders. Skylos sat at Aquila's feet, tongue nearly dragging the ground as he panted.

"Did you race all the way here too?" she asked, delighted to be with her boys as Paul made his way up the steps. What a blessed reunion. Even the weather cooperated. The sun was bright and clear, the wind soft and cool. Ephesus almost always burned hot but not today.

Ephraim giggled. "Papa runs fast."

"I'm glad he did! We can all be together to greet our friend," she replied, grabbing Ephraim's big toe and squeezing it. She pointed to Paul. "Do you remember him?"

At that moment, as if he heard them, Paul lifted his face and waved. Ephraim waved back. Priscilla fought tears that stung her eyes. She'd said so many goodbyes she thought she was immune to tears. But she was wrong. Her tears had only been waiting for the reunion. She didn't mind. These were the best tears—the tears of a longing now fulfilled, a journey completed, and a promise kept.

The Spirit in her heart stirred. A wind blew from the harbor, and her mind stilled. She had a flutter in her heart that urged her to listen. Somehow, she understood that these same tears, the tears of seeing old and dear faces from a distance, and the contented relief of a promised reunion would be her final earthly reward. The warmth of the moment filled her with peace. The dark clouds in her heart scattered.

"He has to get a bath first," Aquila reminded Ephraim.

"Let's invite him to stay with us," Priscilla said, returning to the conversation.

"Looks like he is travelling with three other men," Aquila replied.

She scanned the crowd again. He was right. Paul walked with the assistance of one man, but two others followed close behind.

She would need to buy more food.

"You're staring," Paul said, chuckling as she served him at dinner.

"I'm sorry," Priscilla said, flustered. "It's so good to see you. I think I'm trying to memorize your face in case you go away again."

"Then I wish I had a nicer one," Paul replied.

Ephraim giggled. He sat next to Paul. It hadn't taken Paul long to reestablish the bond with Ephraim. Paul was impressed that Ephraim knew so many words now and could run.

Ephraim had spent half the afternoon showing Paul all he could do.

"But I am worried, Paul. You have new scars." She pointed to his arm. "Those look like tooth marks. Bites!"

He shrugged. "Wild animals. Here in Ephesus, in fact, but that is another story and not suitable this close to bedtime." He glanced down at Ephraim.

Aquila told Paul and his companions of Apollos and caught them up on the news of the city of Ephesus. Priscilla told them the story of the failed exorcism, and Paul laughed heartily. "I may need to ask forgiveness for laughing," he laughed, "but those same men gave me more than one of my scars."

After dinner, Priscilla helped the men settle into the downstairs workshop. Aquila pushed workbenches against the wall, while the men spread their cloaks on the ground for sleeping.

Priscilla watched as Paul's companion, the one called Luke, took special care making a bed for Paul. He unrolled a straw mat that he had brought and used his own cloak to make a pillow. Only after Luke had made a comfortable bed for Paul did he attempt to make one for himself.

She handed him a spare cloak. "You used your own for Paul's bed."

"He has aches. His joints hurt at night," he replied.

She nodded. "From his injuries," she said. "He is so young though, to suffer so much."

Luke nodded. "When injuries do not heal properly, arthritis sets in. I suspect the beatings and whippings he has endured play a part too. His body is always healing, but never healed.

He has an ailment, one that he never speaks of, that plagues him constantly."

She leaned against a workbench. "What else can I do? How can we make him comfortable?"

"I'd like to figure that out," Luke replied. He picked up a leather satchel he had carried in from the ship. He reached in and brought out small jars of ointments, a few scraps of parchment, and torn pieces of leather scrolls.

"There is a library here?" he asked.

She nodded. "An excellent one. You want to read the medical scrolls?"

His eyes lit with excitement. "Do they have very many?"

She held up a hand to slow his excitement. "Yes, but not many will be of use to you. Several are devoted to the study of the humors, and one or two more to medical philosophy. I have only found one, in fact, to be useful for everyday advice. But I do know there is one on surgery and another is a collection of midwife remedies."

"You can read?" Luke asked, his voice lilting in surprise. A pleased smile lit his face.

She liked him. That was the moment she decided. Some men recoiled, even if only slightly, when they learned that a woman could read.

"Born and educated in Rome," she replied. "Can you write also?"

He nodded.

"Good!" she exclaimed. She felt as if she had been given another brother. Grace upon grace, wasn't that the phrase Paul used? She took Luke by the arm and nudged him toward the door. The street outside was quiet. Overhead the sky was inky black. The stars had begun to shine, each piercing the darkness, dazzling in its place. Fireflies flitted around them.

"I'm concerned about Paul's condition," she said, grateful to speak freely. "My heart aches to see him so battered and weakened. And I feel like a wretch for pointing this out, but he is a treasure of words and wisdom that will be lost forever when he dies. Unless—"

Luke interrupted her, nodding kindly. "Unless someone were to undertake an account of his life. The acts and events of the life of the apostles."

"Yes!"

"But not just that, my sister. Believers need an account from the original disciples. Eyewitness accounts. The birth of Jesus is of particular importance."

"Why the birth?" she asked, startled.

Luke tapped a finger on his chin. "See? The story of the Messiah's crucifixion is told everywhere. Many people saw it, Romans and Jews, believers and Gentiles. Everyone is in agreement that it happened just as the story is told. The story of the resurrection is repeated everywhere too, because there are so many eyewitnesses who saw Him alive after His death. The eyewitnesses are from every community, not just those who profess to follow Him as Savior and Lord."

She clasped her hands behind her back. Perhaps it was an old habit from her years of standing before a tutor, but she had no answer or reply. She only listened, trying to follow his logic.

Luke paced, one arm supporting the other as he rubbed his chin thoughtfully. "The birth of Christ is a story not as often told. Why is that? Because it is a story with so few witnesses. A story of a family rejected by its community. The only eyewitnesses were angels and stable animals."

Her eyebrows must have lifted because he laughed.

"And documented by traveling sages," he added.

She placed her hand over her heart. "Tell me! I've never heard the details of His birth!"

Luke stopped pacing. "Tomorrow night, after I read over my work. I will even cook for us. And then we will all gather around and I will read to you from my scroll, for I have begun an account of the birth of Christ." He looked at her and a warmth passed between them, like siblings on a happy occasion.

"Priscilla, I am grateful to meet a kindred soul. Your encouragement means more to me than I can possibly explain. For months I have labored alone. I suspect there will be years of lonely work ahead too. Your enthusiasm for the idea of the written account is confirmation of what I have felt in my spirit all along."

She turned to go back inside but then paused, her hand on the door. "I once dreamed of writing for the emperor. All my energy was focused on serving him with excellence. And how I fretted that I would never be good enough! If I had only known who I would one day serve, I think I would have worked twice as hard and with ten times as much joy."

CHAPTER FOURTEEN

The next day was filled with such happy anticipation that Priscilla did not feel the usual exhaustion from walking miles for her errands or standing on her feet for hours as she worked. She could only think of hearing the story of how Jesus was born. What would it be, she wondered? His death had been so sad and tragic, a story that made her body ache to hear. The glorious news of the resurrection came at a cost, even now. She couldn't hear that story without suffering a mother's grief in her heart.

Again, she promised herself to find out if it was true that Mary, the mother of Jesus, had taken up residence outside of Ephesus. *What a wonder it would be to sit face-to-face with her.*

Luke prepared spiced stew that was truly exceptional. Of course, it would be though, as he was a careful man who paid attention to everything. He must have gotten this recipe from a cook on one of his trips. He had probably perfected it over time. Still, Priscilla found it hard to eat more than a few bites. She was so excited to learn how Jesus had been born, what signs and wonders had accompanied the King of the universe, the Son of God, as He entered the world of men.

As the shadows lengthened in the shop, a crowd began to gather. She had mentioned in the market that Luke would tell the story of Jesus's birth, but she had underestimated how many would be interested in hearing it. Paul lit the oil lamps and made a place for himself to sit next to Luke. He seemed to be enjoying watching his friend take the duties of teaching, Priscilla noted.

Guests packed the room and even the stairs leading to the loft. Aquila had made space for the workers to sit in the loft. More guests overflowed into the street.

Luke had more color in his cheeks than usual. Priscilla didn't know if the crowd made the room too warm or if he was unaccustomed to speaking before so many people. Opening the scroll, Luke cleared his throat. "This is only a rough draft of the account of the events in the life of Christ that I am undertaking." His eyes looked over the top of the scroll to the crowd. Catching his eye, Priscilla nodded eagerly, urging him to continue.

The crowd was hushed, focused on him.

"I started my account of the birth of Jesus with the birth of John," Luke said, "because that is where the story begins. John was Jesus's cousin, as you may know. And John will play an important role in Jesus's story." He glanced up again.

Priscilla pressed her lips together, willing him to find the confidence to read. She was so anxious to hear the birth story of Jesus.

Luke took a deep breath and began. "In the time of Herod, king of Judea, there was a priest named Zechariah...."

Over the next few weeks, Priscilla slowly absorbed the story, as a tree absorbs rainwater. Every nuance of the events had a word to speak to her, it seemed, and she pored over the story again and again with Luke.

She couldn't stop seeing the infant Christ, born in a stable, laid in a feeding trough, attended to by his mother and father. Only the animals and angels present. Why? Why did God not share His triumph with the world? People sleeping in the inn that night never even knew the miracle just outside their doors, in the darkness.

The kingdom of God seemed at times to be a kingdom of secrets. Secrets that she had to look for or she would miss the face of God too. In her prayers, she sought to know more of God and His ways. She prayed over her fears, especially Lucian. He had not been sighted again in the city. It was likely that he had only been a pilgrim like so many others.

Paul was gracious to her, never tiring of hearing Luke tell the story either, or of explaining the mystery of Christ to her. Like her, he enjoyed wandering through the city streets. Witchcraft and occult practices were everywhere, but this only opened the door wide for Paul to speak with boldness. People who dabbled in dark mysteries that they could not explain nor control were often open to hearing of another power far greater than the one they possessed. They never wanted to hear about sin or repentance, but curiosity nudged them back to the truth and back to hear Paul. His power to perform miracles and healings seemed to explode here, she realized, and it drew everyone's attention. Magicians who offered such miracles as making a feather dance were driven from the market in shame when Paul healed the lame and blind.

A few believers who had migrated here recognized and embraced Paul at once. They were eager to hear him teach. Like every Jew who had come to believe Jesus was the Messiah, they had spent hours going back over the books of Moses and the prophets, reading every story in a new light. Now every story was a foreshadowing and they listened carefully to find it. They loved to listen to Paul explain Christ as the fulfillment of these scriptures.

As Paul and Priscilla walked through the market, a young girl approached them. Their friend Gaius had come with them to help carry supplies back to the shop.

"My mother says you have the power to heal the sick," she said, handing Paul a handkerchief.

He knelt down to look her in the eye. "I do not, my daughter. Only your Father in heaven does. But if we ask Him together, He may heal your sister."

Her eyes popped wider open. "How did you know my sister was sick?"

He took her little hand in his and pressed it to the handkerchief. Holding his own hand over hers, he prayed. "Lord Jesus Christ, send healing to this household. Amen."

He released her hands, and she ran off with the handkerchief. Luke sighed. "That's been happening more and more, everywhere we go. People don't want to come and listen to him. They just want to be healed."

Priscilla's heart softened yet again toward her dear friend Paul. He hadn't sent that girl away, and apparently, he didn't refuse anyone who came to him in need. He just served them in Jesus's name. For a man with a fearsome reputation, he had the heart of a lamb.

Demetrius stepped out of his shop, curious. He caught Priscilla's eye. She smiled, hopeful Demetrius wanted to remain friends. Instead, Demetrius fastened his attention on Paul. People gathered around Paul, asking for healing. Asking about healing too, how it worked, and who it worked on. In a city of magic and witchcraft, they were accustomed to spells and formulas.

"It is a powerful name that I heal in, yes," Paul said, raising his voice to be heard. He remained good-natured though. The crowd was eager to learn more. "The name holds all power, but you cannot wield the name. Those who have tried have suffered greatly." Paul caught Priscilla's eye and she chuckled.

"Then who can wield the name?" a sorcerer asked. "What must we do?"

"Embrace Jesus as the Messiah," Paul said.

"But we are not Jews!" the crowd called.

Paul extended his arms. Somehow, Priscilla knew, he had the crowd where he wanted them.

"And yet you will receive the full inheritance promised to His chosen people!" Paul rested his hands on their shoulders, one after another. "You need not observe the laws or customs. You will receive grace upon grace, the forgiveness of sins, the hope of eternal life. An entirely new way of living awaits you. Come tonight, to the rented hall of Aquila the leatherworker, and I will explain how this abundance of life can be yours."

"How much money do we need to bring?" Demetrius called out. A few in the crowd snickered. They'd seen traveling sorcerers and salesmen who offered such miracles in exchange for vast sums.

"Nothing at all!" Paul replied. He stared at Demetrius, and a fire lit in his eyes that Priscilla had never seen. Here was the fierce and legendary Paul. "You sell idols to poor people who have no hope. Your money is filth to me."

Demetrius's face hardened. The two men locked eyes and Priscilla feared for Paul's life, until a mother took Paul's hand. She begged for Paul to heal her daughter. As the crowd closed in around Paul and his companions, she lost sight of him. Thankfully, so did Demetrius.

Weeks passed with peace. Believers became bold, speaking the name of Christ in the streets with joy, forgetting that many who listened hid anger in their hearts for Paul. The black arts of the city found it harder to draw a crowd, and without a crowd, there was no money. If a sorcerer attempted to conjure a demon, Paul walked past and cast it aside. If an occult healer attempted to cast a spell of healing, Paul simply said a prayer and the patient was restored.

Paul did not charge for his services either. His popularity grew immeasurably. From the believers, he did ask that they take up contributions for the church in Achaia. Apollos was hard at work there, and resources were limited. Many new converts were happy to supply for the work.

And the money that would have gone to Demetrius and his guild was being distributed to the poor, or worse to them—the poor overseas.

At night, Paul was exhausted, and his strength seemed to leave him entirely. Whatever the mystery ailment was, he kept it to himself. Luke attended him in privacy after buying poultices and plants in the market.

Priscilla readied the sleeping area upstairs one evening as Luke prepared a remedy at the workbench downstairs. Paul's feet had swollen and were giving him pain. Luke also prepared a second paste, but she did not know what it was for.

"Why does God not heal him?" Aquila whispered to her. Priscilla sighed quietly and shrugged hopelessly. The pair watched as Paul lowered one shoulder of his chiton and allowed Luke to apply a paste to an infected wound. Angry red lines shot from a pitted red slash, no doubt a wound made by a Roman whip.

"Some of the wounds from the forty lashes minus one have never healed," she murmured. "How many scars does he hide under that robe?"

Aquila clicked his tongue, and she knew by the sound that he was counting. "He's received that punishment three times, correct?" he asked. She nodded. "That's 117 scars across his back, just from that one punishment."

"And I've seen bite marks," she added. "He would only tell me it was wild animals. I think someone forced him to fight. And God did not shut the mouths of the lions for him."

Somber unease settled upon them as they watched Luke attend to him. A cold lump formed in her throat, and tears stung her eyes. "He's been shipwrecked and stoned. Beaten too. And Luke says there is another ailment, a painful one, that Paul will not speak of. Paul has pleaded with God to remove it but God will not. Paul tells me that God has said only that he must rely fully on God's all-sufficient grace."

"So must we all," Aquila said softly.

"The sorcerers in the marketplace who are jealous of Paul—" She sighed. "If they could see this, if they knew the price he paid... They want glory but would never pay the price."

"Isn't that why there is only one Christ?" Aquila rested his arm around her waist. "Who else would have dared to take the sin of humans into His soul and be nailed to His own creation to die?"

She leaned against her husband. "I hate that Paul's ministry comes at such a great cost."

"Paul knows he is not alone. He knows he is loved. That must give him great encouragement."

Luke finished attending to Paul then fetched his scrolls and a stylus to begin work. Priscilla watched as Paul took an interest in Luke's work. Her heart lightened. Paul had so much that needed to be recorded. Paul reached for a stylus but winced in pain and withdrew his hand. Reclining on his mat, he closed his eyes to rest.

Another night. He needs his rest. But one day, when he is not exhausted from preaching all day and performing signs and wonders, then he will write.

But with Paul, would there ever be a day he did not exhaust himself for the Gospel?

The following week, a messenger from the town clerk, Alexander, arrived at the shop. He was a young man with olive skin and brown eyes, typical of this town, eager to please and energetic.

Priscilla opened the shop door, inviting him in, but he declined.

"I bring word from Alexander concerning a guest in your home," he said, glancing at the ground. *He must feel some shame in the errand.*

"You mean Paul, I assume?" Aquila asked, leaving his work at the bench. Other workers stopped their tasks. Luke looked up from his scrolls with interest.

"Yes, the one called Paul," the boy said, grateful, it seemed, to address Aquila instead of Priscilla. She knew that some men preferred to speak only with other men, especially when dealing with official matters.

"Paul has been using the baths each day," the boy said.

Aquila nodded. "I believe every man in the city does. Am I correct?"

"Yes, of course!" The Ephesians were notoriously finicky about cleanliness.

Aquila crossed his arms. "Then what is the problem?"

"Alexander requests that Paul use the baths before dawn, before the baths open to the public. His appearance is troubling. Many find it distasteful."

Priscilla hung her head in her hands. Poor Paul. His body was covered in scars, and the other men found it repulsive. They'd probably never seen a man so sorely abused before and yet still alive.

"His body is his best witness!" She surprised herself by speaking out. "Don't you understand? How could a man who has suffered so much at the hands of others tell everyone that forgiveness is the gift of God if it wasn't true? His body bears witness that he is telling the truth. He forgives by the power of God." Suddenly she felt all the wind knocked out from her chest.

"They want to silence him," she said quietly, advancing toward the boy. "They want to cover the scars, hide the evidence of all he has suffered, thinking that his message won't have as much power now. But you underestimate our God. You will never silence Paul."

The messenger backed away, farther into the street, blood draining from his face. Clearly he had meant only to deliver an order, not start a fight.

Aquila leaned out the door, a wry grin on his face. "Tell Alexander that Paul will be happy to bathe at dawn, by the way."

The following week, Luke asked for everyone's attention at supper. "Paul has news."

Paul was pale, dark circles under his eyes. He desperately needed rest.

"I received a report today from a friend at the harbor—"

Gaius interrupted Paul. "Friend? Who?"

One of the workmen just laughed. "Paul has friends wherever he goes."

"Rome is not changing for the better. The city remains dangerous for believers," Paul said. "A woman named Flavia of very high status has been exiled. She was discovered to be a believer and professed the name of Christ when questioned."

Aquila took a plate of roasted fish and passed it to Luke. "We have no plans to return to Rome. Ephesus is a city with plenty of opportunities for work and ministry."

Paul nodded. "Yes, but the body of believers, the church, in Rome struggles. I want to help them. I also heard that in Corinth the church struggles under the leadership of Stephanus and Crispus. I want to write to them." His voice faltered and he paused to regain his breath.

Priscilla reached across the table, resting her hand on his. "We will. First, you must rest. Eat a good dinner and sleep. Sometimes, my friend, that is the best service to others that you can offer."

Paul shook his head, staring at his plate. *Elijah once faced total exhaustion too, didn't he? God fed him by the river with the help of the angels.* Of course, Paul wasn't running away from anything, not like Elijah, but the physical strength of any believer could run out. Good food and deep sleep restored the body and the soul.

She took the plate of fish and gave Paul a double serving, sacrificing what would have been her dinner. She didn't mind and no one noticed.

Sometimes the angels needn't bother showing up, she thought with a smile, *when believing women are already on the scene.*

At the market not a week later, Ephraim wanted a peacock's feather. Priscilla haggled good-naturedly with the street vendor.

"The feather is from the legendary phoenix!" the old man claimed, clutching the feather to his heart. "I cannot let it go for less than five denarii."

"A phoenix? Really?" She raised an eyebrow. "Before or after it burst into flames? I will give you half a copper coin and no more."

He shrugged, handing it to Ephraim, who waved it in the air like a sword. She paid the man, knowing he would have more treasures soon that Ephraim would beg for. She needed to explain to Ephraim that money was hard to come by, but it was hard to deny him little pleasures.

Skylos weaved in and out of their path as they walked, happy to be along for the outing. As she strolled behind

Ephraim, she spied a woman, her arms burdened with stained and worn scrolls, laboring through the center of the market. The woman had a fierce, determined look in her eye. Others fell into step behind her, men and woman alike. They all carried scrolls. Priscilla clutched Ephraim's hand, pulling him to her side, unsure of what she witnessed.

The crowd grew as they walked along. Making their way down the main road, they passed the turn to the left for the harbor. So they weren't taking these to a boat for shipping. They made a slight right, passing the library and then the office of the town clerk. Alexander came out to watch. By now, dozens were in the crowd. Each carried scrolls. Each wore an expression of grim defiance.

"Priscilla! There you are! What is going on?"

Priscilla turned to see Demetrius struggling to keep up. He had a knee that troubled him, so she offered him her arm to hold on to. He hesitated but accepted as they walked.

"I don't know, Demetrius. I've never seen anything like this. Where are they going?"

"Those are spell scrolls. I've sold a fair number of them," he said.

The crowd dispersed into a wide circle in front of the theater. One by one, they threw their scrolls into a pile. Shouting and cheering, they were eager to be rid of them. Priscilla wanted to clap but felt uneasy with Demetrius on her arm. The crowd was wasting years and years of wages too. How much money had they spent on these worthless pursuits? Her stomach turned as she looked at the vast pile of wasted resources.

Scrolls that could have been used for good works. Papyrus that could have carried words of hope or healing. Money that was spent on death instead of life.

"These are new believers in your god," Demetrius said, his voice tight. "This is Paul's idea."

Skylos barked as the crowd closed in around them, making it harder to move.

She watched the pile of works grow taller and wider. When a young man came forward with a burning torch, she could not deny that she wanted to be the one to tip it. He did it, though, and while the crowd cheered, she felt awash with conflicting emotion. She hated to see papyrus and leather burn. She loved the written word even if she hated what was written on it.

"Let's go." She tugged on Demetrius. His face was white with anger. It was not his products that were lost, she knew. He was witnessing the loss of business. These believers would never buy anything else from his shop.

He pushed her hand away. "Tell Paul he will regret this." Demetrius trained his searing eyes on her. "You will all regret this day."

Her mouth fell open as he limped away. She wrapped her arm tightly around Ephraim, keeping him close, grateful that Skylos would accompany them home.

Returning home from the market the following week, Ephraim ran ahead, chasing Skylos with his feather sword. Skylos paused every now and then for a play bow, allowing only enough time for Ephraim to get close. Priscilla thanked God yet again for the wonder of a dog. Ephraim had forgotten completely the adults who were angry at the burning of the scrolls.

As they approached their door, Skylos spotted a mouse and chased it into the shop.

"Wrong way, Skylos!" Priscilla yelled. She hated mice in the grain.

Mice in the working sections of cities were always a problem. Except growing up, she hadn't lived in the working section of the city. If she had, maybe she would have learned how to handle them. Now she had to battle mice and insects to keep the grain jars safe. As she walked toward the door, she mentally rehearsed a list of chores to do before dinner, including sweeping. That mouse would not find refuge in her house, even if it stepped forward and asked to be baptized!

Skylos charged back out of the house, barking angrily. Ephraim attempted to walk past him, but Skylos snapped at him.

"Skylos!" she gasped. Ephraim stood, frozen in place, his eyes wide. He pointed inside the shop, shaking his head. Skylos stood barring the doorway, his hackles raised.

"What is it?" she asked, picking up the edge of her tunic and running the last few paces. She looked into the shop and her hand flew to her mouth. She reached down to rest her hand on Skylos's head. "Shhh," she whispered. "It's all right." Skylos nudged his head under her palm, whining softly. She sagged against the doorway. Her heart ached at what she looked at.

"Ephraim, run and find your father. He should be returning from the tanner's shop by the far end of the harbor. Tell him we have been robbed."

Ephraim started to run, then stopped. Skylos was looking from Priscilla then back to Ephraim, his soft brown eyes in panic and confusion. Priscilla bent and gently took his face in her hands. "You go with Ephraim, Skylos. I will be all right." After kissing his snout, she whispered, "You are a true friend."

Ephraim ran, Skylos on his heels. She took a deep breath and released it. Ephraim would be safe.

She stepped into the shop, keeping her back against the wall. She had to, as the benches and tables were overthrown, supplies scattered across the floor. Crocks lay shattered, their contents spilled everywhere. No wonder the mice wanted in. The week's grain for the workers and family was ruined, spilled everywhere.

On numb and shaking legs, she pushed her way to the crock she kept hidden under the bowl of nails. It was gone. Searching the floor quickly, she spied it, crushed. Empty.

All their money, all their savings, gone. *Stolen. No food, no money.* Nothing to pay their workers with, nothing to feed their family with. The workbenches had been overturned—they had been strong men to do this, and more than just one.

She sank to the ground, unable to speak or cry. She waited for Aquila with dry eyes, her tongue sticking to the roof of her mouth.

She spied a scroll on the wall, one of Luke's personal accounts of Jesus's ministry. Someone had stabbed a dagger through it, nailing it to the wall.

CHAPTER FIFTEEN

No one claimed responsibility for vandalizing her shop, and Demetrius no longer greeted her in the marketplace in the mornings. Even if they had disagreed over her God, he had been cordial in the past. She refused the thought that he had done it, though. Instead, she blamed the growing unrest in Ephesus.

Egyptians had pushed the tourists to buy statues of the Egyptian sun god, and Demetrius had sent men into the market to steer tourists into his shop instead. Believers roamed the streets encouraging people to save their money and come to hear Paul and not waste time on either of the other gods.

A tense nervousness infected the streets. Priscilla could feel it clinging to everything like a thin film of oil on water.

Perhaps relief will come soon. Paul was not going to be in Ephesus much longer. He had decided to go on to Jerusalem as soon as he finished writing a letter to the believers in Corinth.

Priscilla watched the preparations for his journey with a heavy heart. Timothy would go on to Macedonia. Paul would go to Jerusalem and into other regions of Asia.

And did the Spirit expect her and Aquila to follow?

"I have prayed," she confessed to Aquila as she prepared dinner one evening. "But I have heard nothing. I do not know what the Spirit wants us to do. What do you think?"

"I have spent hours working side by side with Paul and Timothy. They talk a lot about God's grace and love," he replied.

She shook her head as she counted bowls and set them on the workbench. "What does that have to do with the decision to move? I know that God loves me, but I need to know what He wants me to do."

"Grace means this—if you are struggling with anxiety about hearing the Spirit, perhaps what you're really struggling with is anxiety over pleasing God," Aquila replied. "It's a subtle form of wanting to work to please God instead of trusting that God is already pleased."

"That's very true. Now, what does God want us to do?" She laughed.

Alexander announced a town meeting to be held in the theater. *Odd that it is not to be in a government building.* Walking from their home past the apartments and private houses of the wealthy, Priscilla saw the small altar to Artemis in the market loaded with offerings. The altar was used for those who would not make the greater pilgrimage to the temple for whatever reason.

As they approached the theater, noise from a crowd grew like a dull roar. Walking through the theater arches out into the bright light, Priscilla, Aquila, and the others looked up, trying to find an empty seat in the stadium. Paul was immediately seized by guards and escorted away. As Priscilla and the others called out and tried to help him, they were forced into seats in the shadows.

She spied Demetrius on stage with Alexander and government officials. Demetrius rose from his seat, lifting his arms in signal. He wore his money bag from the shop at his waist. *Smart. Probably worried his shop, too, could be robbed while he is here.*

"Great is Artemis of the Ephesians!" The crowd's chants were deafening. Alexander spoke but could not be heard.

"This is not a meeting. This is a public execution," Aquila said.

Luke cupped his hands around her ear. "I will get our things from your shop. You get Paul and get him to the harbor."

Luke must have seen this before. This was a trap. The crowd shouted endlessly, no matter what Alexander did. Even Paul was helpless to quiet them down. They grew louder. People bumped into her, shoved Ephraim. She was grateful they'd locked Skylos in the shop to keep him from following. The poor dog would have been trampled underfoot. Aquila stiff-armed men left and right, but they closed in just as fast.

Alexander still stood at the center of the stage, screaming for order. Suddenly the crowd overpowered the guards, rushing for Paul. A frenzy of violence and fear followed. She scooped up Ephraim and held him tightly. Aquila pushed through the crowd trying to get to Paul before the crowd tore him apart. She had never seen him driven to violence, and it turned her stomach as he forced men and women aside. Throwing Paul over his shoulder, he then rammed back through the crowd like an angry bull, running down the stairs and through the theater arches. Priscilla fled behind him, only putting Ephraim down when he had room to run.

As she set him down, he clung to her legs, crying. She bent to comfort him as she unpeeled his hands from behind her knees. "Run with me, okay? We will make it a game. How fast can we run if we hold hands?" She reached for his hand but their hold lasted only for a moment.

Lucian emerged from a shadowed doorway. She had forgotten about him, assuming he had left the city by now. He grabbed Ephraim and shoved Priscilla to the ground. She screamed for Aquila but he did not hear her. Ephraim kicked and screamed, terrified. She jumped to her feet and chased after Lucian, but he ducked into the men's gymnasium, a labyrinth of exercise rooms.

She did not even pause. Bursting through the doors, she heard the elderly men who had not attended the meeting gasp to see a woman in their midst. She followed their eyes. Unwittingly, they gave away Lucian's direction. Running hard, she took the next turn, plowing straight into Ephraim as he tore around the corner. He reared back to kick her.

She grabbed her son by the shoulders. "Stop! Ephraim! It's me!"

He blinked, then grabbed her hand and pulled her around to face the other direction and ran. "I kicked him!" he yelled. "Hard!" He nimbly navigated the corners and turns.

She forgot that he had been here with Aquila. Bless the Lord for that too.

A furious door guard held out his hands to catch her. "No woman is permitted—"

Priscilla punched him in the stomach, then pushed through the door. Aquila stood in the street, looking wildly side to side. Paul yelled her name. Aquila's eyes opened wide to see her emerge from the men's gymnasium. As she and Ephraim caught up to him and Paul, she wheezed, almost out of breath. "I'll explain later."

"Mama punched a man!" Ephraim yelled. Paul's eyes widened more as Aquila swept Ephraim up into his arms.

"We've got to find the ship called *Riverwind*," Aquila said. "Timothy bought a passage."

Racing down the harbor steps, she felt her legs burn as she tried to keep up with the men. "When?" she asked, a stitch in her side pinching off her breath.

"As soon as we arrived at the theater," Gaius said. "Your husband has a low opinion of crowds."

My husband is wise and experience has proved it so.

Paul used his hand to shield his eyes, searching the harbor. A bank of low gray clouds rolled in. This was not the season for travel. Worse yet, storms in the afternoon would make leaving the harbor safely more difficult. Paul had to be out of harm's way and quickly.

The men spotted the ship and moved to it, Priscilla following. The captain was waiting at the docks. Eyeing it, she guessed the ship to be a merchant ship, not built for passengers.

Paul and his companions would have another uncomfortable journey.

"Take good care of him," she said, grabbing Luke by the arm. He placed his hand over hers.

"I will. And you take good care of your household. You have one son, but you are a mother to many."

She held his gaze, wondering if she would ever see him again. There was no time for tears. Leaving him, she rushed to Paul as he approached the captain. Ephraim passed her in his panic. Both reached Paul at once, and both clung to him without words. Paul pulled back, out of their embrace, then kissed the top of Ephraim's head.

He leaned in to embrace Priscilla and whispered, "Did you really punch a man?"

Flustered, she scrambled for a reply. "Yes, but it is a long story."

The captain whistled for Paul.

Paul grinned. "Save it for me, will you? I look forward to hearing it!"

When Priscilla returned to the market a few days later, Demetrius stood at the opening of the street that led into the market stalls.

"I had nothing to do with it," he called to her.

She attempted to navigate around him, but he cut her off.

She planted her feet, squared her shoulders, and stared him down. "You nearly got my friend killed. My son was attacked too."

Demetrius folded his arms. "Nothing to do with me."

"And the coin bag at your waist?" She pointed to the purse on his waist. "I noticed you wearing it at the theater. Why would you bring money to a town meeting, Demetrius?"

He flexed his jaw. "I am afraid that someone might steal from me. I always keep this near."

"You paid people in the crowd to start that riot, didn't you? You wanted to get Paul killed."

"No harm came to him," Demetrius scoffed.

"How many people have you paid off in this city, Demetrius? You don't just make your money dealing in silver, do you? No, you deal in information. Men have come to my shop and vandalized it. Were they looking for Paul?" Her voice grew louder. "Lucian attacked Ephraim in the riot too. How did he know we would be there? Where do your loyalties lie, Demetrius?"

Demetrius looked at her coolly and patted the coin bag at his waist. That's where his loyalties were, he seemed to say. And betraying the believers was becoming good business.

In the fall of that year, Aquila ran out of money. It was as simple, and as heartbreaking, as that. He could no longer afford to rent the hall for the believers to meet. The believers collected offerings, but Aquila sent them on to other cities that had a greater population of poor and suffering. He prayed only for a place to meet.

With Priscilla acting as tutor, Ephraim's studies began. She loved their afternoons in the library, the dust motes swirling as the light shone through the open-air porticos. She loved the smell of leather, the rustle of papyrus, the soft footfall of scholars moving from one collection to another, the excited murmur of a new find. Most of all she loved seeing the library through Ephraim's eyes, a world of wonder and knowledge. Any scroll might open a new world, a new idea, a new challenge of mathematics or physics or language.

She loved to watch him read, his finger moving right to left across sacred texts. He read what he could of the books of Moses and thrilled to the stories. She learned them all again by heart too. His education was a rebirth for her, a reawakening of her first love, of words and stories and the sound of a voice reading in a quiet room. She praised God that in His mercy, He had not allowed her to miss this.

The air turned cooler as the breezes from the sea brought hints of the storms to come. Some merchants closed their booths and caught the final ships out of the harbor, to return in the spring. Voyages to homelands had to be undertaken now. In only a few more weeks, the sea would be treacherous.

As Ephraim studied a scroll, she walked from the table to the edge of the room, where the breeze from the portico was fresh. The tang of sea air blew past her, the chill raising bumps her arms. She pulled her shawl down from her shoulders, wrapping it around her arms and letting it hang loosely.

Paul. Where was he? Was he safe? She prayed he was not traveling by sea. This was the season of shipwrecks. He surely would not survive another one. She thought of Lucian too, and wondered where that rat had holed up for the coming winter.

The following week, Aquila led a group of believers through town, past the agora, theater, and government buildings. He led them up into the hills and finally into the caves. Questions bubbled among them as they walked then explored a dark cavern. Skylos ran into the darkness then circled back, barking. Priscilla grabbed Ephraim, pulling him to her side, and Ephraim held on to Skylos. Something hid in the darkness, something that Skylos did not like.

"What are we doing?" one believer asked.

Aquila opened his arms wide. "We are meeting. Here."

"In a cave?" Priscilla blurted. With a breath, she composed herself. "Why here?"

The group of believers formed a half circle around Aquila.

"Budget. We pay no one for this space," he began. "Security. We can see who approaches, and we know who attends. No one can eavesdrop and make a false report to Alexander. Finally, comfort. With winter coming, we will be shielded from the elements here."

She peered past him into the darkness. "What will you do about the uninvited guests?"

Aquila glanced over his shoulder. "Not much to worry about. There are cave spiders, lizards, bats.... I've seen a mountain lion, but they are usually shy around people. Unless there's a famine."

Priscilla clutched her tunic as several people in the group gasped. He waved his hands, trying to regain their attention.

"But no venomous snakes! That's the important thing!" he said. "And there's no famine here, so we don't need to worry about the mountain lion."

That was true. Living so close to the sea, with verdant green hills all around, both man and beast had plentiful food.

"There was a bear, though," he added, but softly, probably hoping no one would hear.

Skylos broke free from Ephraim's grasp. Running just to the edge of the darkness, he planted his feet and barked. A soft scurrying noise faded away. Skylos turned and plopped into a sitting position, tail wagging furiously, tongue hanging out one side of his mouth.

"Good dog!" Ephraim laughed. The believers laughed tentatively then with relief.

"God provides," Priscilla said loudly. Aquila met her eyes and mouthed the words *Thank you.*

"Let's have a meeting, shall we?" a believer said. He was the first to claim a spot in the dirt and sit. Others followed and soon Aquila alone was standing. While teaching might not be his natural gift, Priscilla knew these were not natural times. And the Holy Spirit was equipping all of them to do what they never dreamed possible. Even come together as a church with predators circling around in the darkness.

Suddenly she realized that the true predators weren't in the cave.

She hugged Ephraim close, ready to listen to Aquila share the Word.

Stirring a thick porridge for breakfast in the early hours on a late fall morning, Priscilla reflected on the changes in Ephesus. The cave proved to be an excellent choice for the meetings of the believers. Under gray skies, the believers trudged up the mountains and tucked themselves into warm groups while Aquila built a fire near the mouth of the cave. Ephraim often fell asleep in her lap, lulled by the sound of his father's voice and the heat of the fire on a chilly afternoon. Priscilla had enough room to pull the women aside for teaching especially for them. Since there was no rent to pay, she and Aquila had quickly rebuilt their savings, and she had been able to consider what other teachings she could offer the women. She wondered if their children would want to learn to read and write.

She hesitated to ask. Would the question only highlight the vast differences in class between them? Christ had abolished those differences, but the flesh did not forget so easily. She wanted to bless, not provoke. Sighing, she lifted the ladle from the pot and set it aside. She would pray about it. The children would need language skills. The future of the faith rested more and more with words.

And not just for histories that needed to be written. Everyday words were needed. Priscilla wished for a word like *synagogue,* for example. For those like her who followed The Way, what would be the word like *synagogue* that meant "coming together"? Some had taken to calling a group of believers the Body of Christ, and so a body of believers. The Greek believers referred to themselves as the *ekklesia,* or those called out of the others. But this did not describe a meeting of the ekklesia.

Here was the problem with this new faith, or the fulfillment of the old promises as it seemed—they needed a new vocabulary. They did not meet at the synagogue any longer, although they still came together. They were believers who no longer believed in the power of the Old Covenant law. They worshipped the God who dwelt in a temple that was their bodies, and when they came together in harmony, the larger body was made complete for His glory. They offered sacrifices daily, but sacrifices of praise, which were often so much harder than simply paying for a dove to be offered or incense to be burned.

And what would they be called? Christ followers? Followers of The Way? Disciples? Apostles? Believers in the Good Story? Apostles of the Good News? The language was becoming a barrier, she knew. She heard it every day in the market. It took too many words to explain who she followed and what she believed.

Perhaps the enemies of Christ in Antioch who called Paul and his disciples "Christ-ians" as an insult—perhaps they have done us a favor. Christ-ians was not hard to say or remember. She liked

His name on her lips. She liked the Name of God being her covering whenever she spoke of her faith.

With winter now at their doorstep, time was on her side. She would have three months to consider what new words would best fit the faith. Perhaps if Paul returned, she could talk to him in the spring. And she had one other painful consolation—Lucian was dead.

Demetrius would tell her nothing about it except that someone had paid to deal with that man. She knew it couldn't have been Aquila. She kept their money. She remembered thinking that whatever a man desired could be bought in Ephesus. She just never imagined that included murder.

Ephraim padded softly down the stairs, then made his way to her side. He hugged her briefly before taking Skylos outside. Wrinkling her nose, she called out softly behind him, "Make sure he doesn't roll in anything!" Skylos had recently discovered how much he enjoyed rolling in fish scales which were plentiful near the harbor.

Moments later, Ephraim returned, carrying a small piece of parchment. "This was delivered to us from a man from the harbor! I can read the letters!"

She would question him on the delivery later. He was thrilled to try reading with someone's words besides her own. Motioning him to the workbench, she sat and waited for him to sit across from her.

"'Greetings, Priscilla and Aquila...'"

Ephraim looked up, his face beaming. "That's you, Mama!"

She nodded, urging him to continue.

"'Herod Agrippa has...'"

She was a Roman citizen, and Herod Agrippa was king in Judea. Why would she receive news from his province?

"'The Apostle James has been mar...'" He frowned. "I do not know this word." He licked his lips and drew the parchment closer, studying it.

Lunging across the table, Priscilla snatched the parchment. "Thank you! Well done, Ephraim!" She tucked the parchment into her waistband, hoping he did not notice that her hand shook. She rose then took a bowl from a shelf and scooped a serving of porridge for him. Setting it before him, she tousled his hair. "Eat your breakfast then make sure you're ready to help Papa with his work."

"You don't want to practice more words today?" Ephraim asked, his shoulders sinking. He had read the parchment beautifully and he knew it. The only word he had stumbled over was the word *martyred*. He didn't know that word, thankfully.

Please, Lord, may that word disappear from our language and our lives.

When Ephraim went out to play moments later, she read the letter. James had been martyred by Herod Agrippa. James was one of the original disciples, and she hoped all his stories had been committed to memory. If memorized faithfully, the stories could be written one day too. The parchment gave few details of his death but warned the church in Ephesus that persecution of the followers of The Way was increasing. The letter was unsigned but gave details that Paul was currently in

Macedonia and had written again to the believers in Corinth for a third time. They destroyed his second letter because of its sharp rebuke. His recent visit to them had been painful for all, and he had shamed them for unspeakable practices.

What else did the Corinthians expect from Paul? Corinth was a city of sexual immorality just as Ephesus was a city of black magic. At least Ephesians could burn their magic spells and forget the words. Corinthians carried the memory of their sins within their bodies.

A shudder passed through her as her grip tightened around the parchment. If James could be martyred, she and Aquila were at risk too. Any church leader, anyone at all who spoke with boldness was at risk.

Of what? The Spirit spoke suddenly in her heart.

She had no answer. *Of losing this life?* Was that what she was afraid of? She closed her eyes, breathing deeply, feeling the morning sun begin to warm the room. Aquila stirred upstairs, and outside, noise from the street increased as women set about their errands. She opened her eyes and looked around the room. She could lose things, not people.

She would lose this home, these benches, these clothes. But not Ephraim, nor Aquila, nor Paul nor Timothy nor anyone in the faith. She couldn't even lose time, for God promised her eternal life, and whatever days she did not spend here would surely be fulfilled elsewhere, somehow. God was the God of the living, of eternity, the Alpha and Omega.

Her enemies could take material things but nothing else. Is that what those evil men devoted their life's energy to, depriving believers of chairs and sandals and common goods?

Priscilla sat, resting her head against the bench to pray. Moments ago, she had planned on spending a quiet winter here in Ephesus. What were other believers doing this winter? She lifted them to God in prayer one by one then rose to continue her day.

God could be trusted, and God was already at work.

CHAPTER SIXTEEN

Returning from the caves one evening as dusk set in, Aquila stopped in a tavern to make sure one of their workers would be at work in the morning. The man had been late frequently and hung over when he did show up. Priscilla waited outside with Ephraim in the gray chill. Aquila tarried longer than he promised to, and when he returned, his face was flushed.

"News?" she asked.

"Not about believers, but yes," he replied. Taking her arm, he nudged her back along the path toward their shop. She looked forward to the kitchen fire and the shelter of four walls to block the wind that blew in from the harbor. Kitchen fires were a luxury she would never again take for granted.

"Back in Rome, Emperor Claudius is dead, poisoned by his wife," Aquila said. "The tale is wretched."

"Which wife? I can't keep them all straight." Claudius had suffered two failed engagements and four disastrous marriages.

"Agrippina," Aquila replied. "That's his last wife, the one said to have poisoned him. She wanted her son to become the next emperor. But Nero, his great-nephew, is a much better statesman. He is a politician in every sense. How could Agrippina be so blind and foolish? Her son has no chance with Nero already in the wings."

"Will Nero be favorable to the Jews?"

"I do not know. Nero has already made his first proclamation as emperor. He proclaimed Claudius as a god. All in Rome must honor Claudius as such."

"To make Agrippina suffer for her foolishness?" Ephraim asked. Priscilla had forgotten how much he understood now. At five years old he was wise beyond his years.

"No, son," Aquila said. "Nero made Claudius a god in death so that, by extension, Nero as his successor is considered a god in life. Nero is his great-nephew, remember. Nero just proclaimed himself to be a god."

Priscilla sighed as she listened to Aquila recount the tale. Nothing about Rome had changed. Power was still preferred over decency.

Priscilla's thoughts turned to Marcellus. What role did he play in the new government? Did Nero still favor him? She wondered if he remained in the business of supplying wild animals for the emperor's entertainments.

Aquila spoke again and Priscilla shook her head, realizing she had not been paying attention.

"Will you think about it?" he asked. "We have the rest of the winter."

"To what?" She blinked.

"We can return to Rome," he prompted her. "Claudius is dead. His decrees are instantly repealed. Nero has not issued any decrees against the Jews. If you want to return home, to give Ephraim the formal education you want in the synagogue, to return to our shop there, we can."

She stopped walking. The very idea was a sharp slap across her cheek. *Rome betrayed us. As did Marcellus. Why would I ever return?*

Aquila stopped too and pulled her closer. "We will be safe there. Safer than we are here. We are Roman citizens. Think about what that means. The law gives us rights."

Without a reply, she looked at the tiny shop and saw the life they had built together here. They'd served so many believers and shared the life of Christ with many new faces. Tourists came to Ephesus to worship a Greek idol and left having encountered the living God of all creation. A city entirely given to sorcery and witchcraft had experienced the true Source of all life and light.

And Mary! She'd never made the time to visit her and record her stories. How she regretted that now. She didn't want to leave Ephesus, not yet.

Rome. The word sank like a rock in her stomach. The dirty, crowded streets, the smog from the fires. A city where nothing was sacred. There was only one god in Rome and that was the emperor. The worship of Jesus would not be viewed as religious faith.

Rome would see it as an act of treason. And yet, as they prayed about it, they sensed the Spirit telling them to go.

The day they left Ephesus, the sky was brilliant blue. Priscilla paused at top of the harbor steps and turned. Looking one last time at the city, she watched the morning sun dance upon the limestone and marble buildings, the ornate city stretching up into the deep green hills. Flowers along every path bloomed.

Aquila took her hand, and she knew it was time to leave. This was the city she had so feared, for all its darkness and sorcery, and yet this was the city that had held so many beautiful delights.

"Oh, Ephesus," she whispered. "You were once a city of darkness. But now, what an amazing harvest of hope you are producing!"

The fragrance of hyacinth drifted past her, the last memory she would have of this city.

Walking through the gates of Rome, she was overwhelmed by the stench and chaos of the crowds. Was this really the city she had once loved? There was no breeze, and the poor were crammed into apartments in wretched condition. Children without parents dashed through the streets begging. A few stole. The prostitutes here looked sick and thin. Their long tunics hung on their frail bodies.

Aquila's first stop was to exchange his Greek coins for Roman coins. In the capital city, bartering with Greek coins might prove more difficult. The brand-new Roman coins shocked him and he held one out to Priscilla.

"The image of Nero and his mother are on the same coin!" he remarked.

She inspected it closely. His mother was on the front. Nero was on the back. *A controlling mother doesn't bode well for his reign. Angry sons make terrible leaders.*

As they continued deeper into the city, she remembered the streets but not the faces. Aquila soon found their old shop, now occupied. She held one hand over her heart, looking at the tiny door on rusted hinges. What a small shop it had been, squeezed between two other shops here in the working-class district.

"We were happy, weren't we?" she asked Aquila. Ephraim and Skylos wandered nearby, exploring.

"We will be again," Aquila answered.

After two weeks, in their new home adjacent to their old shop, Priscilla stopped feeling the waves of the sea when she slept. After six more weeks, she recognized the room when she woke up and did not panic. But oddly, Rome did not feel like home, not anymore. She bought a secondhand stola to wear over her tunic and a long tunic for Aquila. It was hard to adjust to life here, and not just because here she drank water again instead of wine and ate cold food. No, the city itself was cold now.

Still, she was thankful that Aquila had secured this shop space. The renters who had their old shop were believers and so helpful as she got settled back into Roman life.

The shop owners brought them to the guild and to meet the believers gathering together in homes. Phoebe had arrived recently with a letter from Paul. To hear his name brightened everyone's spirits, but hers especially. Paul was alive and well. Meeting Phoebe was a delight she had not expected, and she cherished the visit.

The letter from Paul was helpful in explaining the faith to outsiders. Many Romans considered the believers, now commonly called Christians, to be philosophers. Christianity focused on following Jesus and how to treat one another and how to live, rather than formulas for worship and sacrifice. Romans didn't consider Christianity a religion.

One more thing here was unexpected—the new shop didn't have a door. It was part of a larger building, with one main entrance. The streets were so crowded that dirt and dust swirled into the building all day long. The shop was packed in between shops of leather goods, shoes, and clothing. One street over were the shops leading to the amphitheater, and those sold the gear for gladiators. A few sold wild animals, either for sport or pets. At night she could hear their growls and roars. It made sleep difficult.

All day long, children dashed between shops, hawking roasted chickpeas. Vendors with carts followed behind with roasted sausages and pastries.

The air inside the building was clotted with the stench of the city. Even at night when she retired to the loft to sleep, she could smell Rome on her clothes and in her hair. She longed for a cleansing sea breeze. The noise meant that quiet conversations had to wait for these night hours or else customers had to wade deep into the shop and speak loudly for Aquila's or Priscilla's attention.

That is why one morning she did not hear Marcellus enter the shop until she caught sight of him calling her. Her blood turned to ice in her veins as she saw her name on his lips. His eyes were a flat, dead brown with no sign of life within, certainly not the new life of Christ. He smiled, though, showing all his teeth, reminding her of a predator. He extended his arms and made his way across the shop, his gold rings glinting in the dappled light, the gold trim on his toga glowing as the dust floated in the air around him.

She took a step backward, bumping into a bench.

"Would you care for some drink?" Ephraim approached him, unaware of who the man was. Ephraim was a smart boy, though, and had immediately judged the stranger to be wealthy. *Ephraim will be a good merchant one day.*

Marcellus bent to look Ephraim in the eye. "A fine boy you are. What is your name?"

"Ephraim."

Marcellus straightened, cocking his head. "That's not a family name."

Ephraim frowned, then narrowed his eyes as he glared at the stranger. "It is now."

Priscilla stepped forward, taking Ephraim by the shoulder, suppressing a smile. "Go on and fetch your father. He is delivering an order to the Circus, but he will want to tend to this customer himself."

Ephraim scowled at the stranger and then left.

"I offended him." Marcellus chuckled. "I like his arrogance."

"It's not arrogance," she replied carefully, wanting to spit the words instead. "You questioned his place in this family."

Marcellus reached into his pocket, withdrawing a denarii, offering it to her. "Give him this for me. With my apologies. I was surprised by his name, that is all. I meant what I said. He is a fine-looking boy."

Priscilla did not move.

He set the coin on a bench next to him. "He may feel differently about my money."

"Did you know Lucian was in Ephesus?" she asked, studying his face. He had visibly aged. The lines around his eyes and mouth had deepened. The hair at his temples was gray. But he looked as strong as ever. His movements were quick and certain, and he did not look as if he had lost any muscle. He was an older enemy, who had lost none of his strength but had perhaps gained wisdom. If not wisdom, then at least experience. Though he looked weakened by age, he could be more dangerous than ever.

"I fired Lucian after you left," Marcellus said. "I caught him stealing. Why?"

I didn't leave. I was thrown out, twice. He had thrown her out, then Emperor Claudius had expelled her from Rome. Digging her fingernails into her palms, she said nothing, trying to keep her face blank. She couldn't give him any unnecessary information, not even what she was feeling.

"Lucian attacked Ephraim."

"Well, there are only two possible motives," Marcellus said. He had always been good at reading her thoughts. But she could not read his. Why did he not seem surprised at her news? "Revenge upon me, if he thought you and I were still close. Or he wanted his job back."

"Hurting Ephraim would please you?" she asked.

Marcellus gasped. "Never!" He cocked his head. "You don't know?"

She shrugged.

"I don't have a son. Ephraim will inherit my estate."

Her mouth fell open, then she turned away, clearing her throat. She had no idea he was childless. Without a son, he would lose control of the estate. Ephraim would get everything.

"He wanted to kill Ephraim to earn your favor?" she asked, keeping her tone even.

"Kill?" Marcellus burst out with a laugh. "No. You really don't see it, do you?" He sat on the edge of the bench. "If Ephraim inherits my estate, I would want the very best for him. The best books, the finest clothing, the most prestigious tutors. He would carry on the family name, you know."

"He has everything he needs." Her hands clenched to fists involuntarily.

Marcellus held up both hands. "Again, I am only speculating that was Lucian's motive. To get back in my favor." He stood and walked to the door. "I only came to say hello. I didn't mean to frighten you. Lucian is no threat to you now. You can rest in that."

"Do not come back here," she called.

He turned and looked at her. His face looked stricken. "It is well known you and Aquila are Christians. You preach forgiveness of enemies. Does that not include me, your own family?"

He caught her in a trap; she had no response. An oil lamp by the door caught his eye. He reached over and picked it up and moved it away from a stack of linens. "Be safe, sister. This is a dangerous city."

After he was gone, Priscilla replayed the conversation in her head a dozen times or more. When Aquila finally arrived, her thoughts and emotions were hopelessly tangled.

Marcellus knew much more than he was saying. Rome was a dangerous city, indeed.

The steaming bath water was murky green, heavy with minerals and fragrant salts. Priscilla stepped into the heated water, underneath the sign SALUS PER AQUAM, which meant "Health through Water." She soaked until her muscles felt weak and loose. Attendants with cool water and towels circulated as she chatted with the other women.

"Nero is performing at the theater tonight in the play," a woman said.

This was the daily reprieve from city life for Roman women. Without the sea, there was the bath. *The water always calls to us.*

Another woman scoffed. "He keeps raising taxes to pay for his projects, and all the while he expects us to come out every night to watch him perform? We are too tired from working all day to pay our tax bill!"

"He wants to build a new theater for chariot races. He wants to compete in those too."

A collective groan rose from the women.

"He's a poet as well and has commanded people to attend his poetry readings," Priscilla offered. *Is there anything more terrible than listening to bad poetry and trying to stay awake?* She kept that commentary to herself, although it was true.

Priscilla loved this one hour here in Rome. The believers often talked in groups. Here in the healing waters was a friendliness, a sharing of concerns, a cross-pollination of their lives. She told them of life in Corinth and Ephesus, of the gods and temples there, of meeting Paul and Apollos. She told them of traveling via ship, seeing dolphins and sea creatures.

And yet Priscilla heard other, darker rumors too. Nero was having a very public affair, angering his mother. His mother had then murdered two people in the government. Nero would not be content to amuse himself with chariot races and poetry readings for long. If his mother opposed him again there would be blood. But whose? That was the question that troubled Priscilla most.

Spring of 60 CE brought news of Paul's arrest. He arrived in Rome to stand trial, and Aquila quickly made arrangements for Paul to serve his time awaiting trial under house arrest with Priscilla and himself.

It was late in the morning when Priscilla heard the jeers and catcalls from the crowded street. She tucked up the edge of her tunic and ran with Ephraim to the threshold to see Paul, Luke, and several centurion guards making their way down the street to the shop. Her heart sank at the sight of her friends.

Paul was thinner, his beard longer and flecked with white. His arms had more scars too. She noted how his ribs rose and fell with each breath. His lungs worked for the air. When she embraced him, she felt like she was embracing a fragile bird, so thin and hollow did his frame seem. But the fire in his eyes blazed as it always had, and Luke was in good health.

A centurion was posted outside their shop. In his red short-sleeved tunic, his brown leather belt studded with gold clasps, and the heavy iron chest piece, he was a handsome sight. The girls in the street soon began walking back and forth in front of the shop just to look at him.

But he also had to wear an iron and bronze helmet and she felt sorry for the poor boy. His head was being boiled like a cabbage in that soup pot as he stood there in the full sun all day.

She brought him a drink every hour. At first he declined, but by late afternoon he relented. *These boys want to serve with honor, but there is no honor in dying of pride.*

That night at dinner, Paul began his stories. He had been shipwrecked yet again on the way to Rome for this trial. It had been his third shipwreck.

"What is it like to be shipwrecked?" Ephraim asked.

"First you are pitched about violently," Paul said then waited for a breath. He sat for a long moment, until he found his strength once more. "The sea becomes an angry monster, scooping you up in her hands, shaking you, dashing you to the ground then picking you back up, by the ankles this time, flinging you around her head." He coughed, then inhaled deeply and continued. "When the ship crashes and splits, the noise is like a great splitting of wood along with the screams of the crew. Crunching and splitting, then the sea sweeps the ship under and it disappears, as if it never was, and you can't believe what you saw."

Ephraim's mouth hung open, his hand with the spoon still hovering over his bowl. Priscilla suppressed a smile. Paul knew how to appeal to a boy's imagination.

"You are certain everything is a dream. And many survivors wish it were," Paul said, softly now. "Many cannot forget what they experienced. The power of the sea is not something that can be forgotten."

"But you weren't scared, were you, Paul?" Ephraim asked.

"No." Paul shook his head emphatically. "Shaken, yes, but not scared. Have you not heard the story of Jesus calming the storm?" Paul pointed to Luke. "Luke can tell you. I am tired, my son. I need to lie down tonight. But let me tell you this—the storms will come. Our ships, the things we count on, will break and disappear into the darkness. All we have is what we carry in here, in our spirit." Paul tapped on his chest. "And if that isn't enough for the courage to face death, it's not enough for the courage to live your life. Make sure you have the courage to live. That's what Christ is. If you choose to lay down your life daily, then facing death isn't the ultimate test for a child of God. No. It's life."

After Paul had gone to bed, Luke explained that Paul hoped to address Nero in person. He had been denied a trial before, and appealing to Nero should give him a chance to be heard.

"Nero is not a good emperor, nor a good man," Aquila said. "The city is on a knife's edge. Taxes are high, wages are falling, and Nero keeps gifting himself new buildings and projects. Nero is not a man who will listen to others, not even Paul."

"While we are waiting, then we will write, yes?" Luke asked, looking at Priscilla. "Paul needs to write to the believers in Philippi and Colossae. He also wants to write to the family of believers in Ephesus and to Philemon."

"That is a lot of writing to do," Priscilla commented. "He could not write one letter to be carried to all churches?"

Luke shook his head. "Philemon and the believers in Ephesus don't share the specific problems of the churches in Philippi, Colossae, or Corinth."

"Still, a circular letter would be useful," she replied. "A circular letter could be passed through all the churches. The specific challenges that Paul addresses in his other letters will be useful for future reference, always. But a circular letter, with general content, would be useful for everyone. He should consider this too."

"I agree. However, one challenge that we must contend with is creating unity. Believers aren't one ethnic group, not anymore. Each group has its own struggles. Some Greeks find our idea of eternal life detestable at first. The Pharisees hesitate to let go of the law. The women must take down their private altars to goddesses and begin to worship alongside men, knowing that the courts will support those same men stoning them for the least offense. How can a general letter of encouragement bring them all together?"

"It can't," Aquila said. Priscilla and Luke looked at him. Aquila smiled. "Only God does that. We are servants and stewards of His work and His word."

CHAPTER SEVENTEEN

A new youth appeared at dinner one night the following week, and the boy had a distinct appearance. The hair toward the front of his head was sparser and lighter in color. Priscilla guessed his head had been half-shaved, and his hair was now growing back, which meant he was a slave. Judging by the way he would not meet her eyes, Priscilla guessed he was a runaway. Paul introduced the young man as Onesimus.

Onesimus did not make conversation while at the table, except in quiet whispers to Paul. Priscilla and Aquila exchanged glances throughout the meal. It was obvious that Onesimus did not want to eat with them, and certainly not with Priscilla.

But then, slaves never ate with their masters. She excused herself as early as possible and retired upstairs until the meal was over. Late that night Aquila told her what he had learned about their new guest.

"A slave on the run," he said quietly. The men downstairs were arranging their pallets for bed.

"He wants Paul to intercede?" she asked. "What power does Paul have?"

"None. He has influence, though." Aquila stretched out, sighing with exhaustion from the day's work. "The boy better hope that his master listens to Paul."

Priscilla shuddered, thinking of what would happen to Onesimus if he was returned to the owner. He'd be branded, certainly. There were dozens of punishments for slaves who ran away. Even if Onesimus bought his freedom someday, he could never buy back his dignity. He would wear those scars for life. Shame would mark him for everyone to see.

She closed her eyes and said a prayer that Paul would persuade the owner to listen.

Day after day the centurion stood guard at the door. Paul did not escape. But neither did charges arrive from the leaders in Jerusalem, the men who had accused him of wrongdoing. The poor centurion kept a lonely vigil with no relief and no excitement.

Paul continued to teach as much as he could, only limited by the number of people who could fit in the shop. The vendors loved the arrangement. People bought food and drinks outside the shop as Paul was long-winded and the streets were dusty. People who came to hear Paul soon came here to buy their meals too.

Aquilla's tiny shop was overrun with guests during the daytime, and at night there was hardly enough room for everyone to stretch out and sleep. Privacy was a thing of the past. If she wanted to be alone with her thoughts, she had to go to the bath at a very early hour. Sometimes she soaked until her skin was as wrinkled as an old woman's, and she nearly fainted if she rose too quickly from the water. But still, it refreshed her just to get away. And she needed refreshment, for she was often worried about Nero's increasingly bizarre public behavior and Paul's declining health. Marcellus had sent a letter offering to pay for tutors if she was willing to let Ephraim live at the family estate. She had returned the letter to him with no reply.

She served dinner every night to whomever was at the table, as always, keeping her fears about the future to herself. Being constantly surrounded by so many hardworking men protected Ephraim in ways he did not know.

"Paul, can I ask you a question?" Ephraim suddenly asked one night at dinner.

Paul took a piece of bread, tore it, and handed the larger half to Ephraim. "Of course." Paul's arms were crisscrossed with scars. The teeth marks from the wild animals in Ephesus, the attack he would not speak of, had faded to dull red pits. If Paul would ever let her, she would look closely, only because she wanted to know the truth. She knew what a bite from a lion or bear looked like. Her family had traded in those animals for the emperor's entertainment for decades. If someone had forced Paul to fight a wild animal, that was a violation of Roman law, and she would make sure they were punished.

Paul had no interest in pursuing it or even confirming what had happened. He was a maddening friend.

"Paul," Ephraim continued, his brows drawing together, "if you can heal so many people, why can't you heal yourself?"

"Is this a matter of curiosity or faith?" Paul asked, setting his bread down then clasping his hands to rest his chin on.

"I don't know." Ephraim shook his head, and tears welled in his eyes. "It's just not fair," he muttered.

Paul's eyes sparkled. "You have a noble heart. You love justice and righteousness. But do not be so quick to hold God to human standards."

"But I am human. My understanding is limited, so why doesn't God make His purpose clearer?" Ephraim sat stiffly. "And I don't just love justice. I love you. It's not right to see you suffer like this, knowing you can pray over a stranger and heal them. A stranger who hasn't even done anything for God."

Paul continued to regard Ephraim thoughtfully as everyone at the table grew silent. "So, this is a matter of faith, then." Paul released his hands and pushed back from the table, his expression one of tenderness. "You can't understand God, but you are asked to trust Him. That is a lot to ask of a boy when he sees suffering."

Priscilla took a sip of her water then set down her cup. "That's a lot to ask of anyone."

Paul looked around at everyone sitting at the table. "If you haven't been disappointed and confused by God, you either just met Him or you are not true followers. Remember that the twelve disciples waited for Jesus to become a king and create a government in Israel. They had no idea what He was really doing and what He intended to give them. Are we any wiser than they? His story is still unfolding in each of us, my friends. All they wanted was a government." He sighed. "Think what they might have missed!" He paused then looked at everyone again, more urgently this time. "Whether or not we ever understand, always pray that His will be done. That is the only answer to prayer that we will never regret."

The table fell into silence. Without meaning to, Priscilla gazed at Paul's scarred arms again, her attention wandering to his hands too. Peering closer, she gasped.

"Are those puncture wounds?" she asked. Two small jagged edges, healed now but still an angry red, marked the top of his hand near the thumb. "Were you bitten by a snake?"

Ephraim's eyes popped open wide. "I want to see!"

Luke held out his hands as Paul tucked his hand into his cloak.

"That is a story for another time. Not a story for a boy who is close to bedtime," Luke said.

"Was it venomous?" Ephraim asked Paul, leaning across the table.

"Fangs as big as table knives," Paul whispered with a wink.

Priscilla clicked her tongue in exasperation. Suddenly she knew it would be hours before Ephraim would settle down for sleep.

The following week brought a visitor most welcome. Timothy arrived bearing news of the churches in Corinth and Ephesus.

Anxious to be reunited with Paul and the other believers, he was, Priscilla knew, also anxious to see the trial progress.

Her heart was full with these reunions. Strange, though, that being back in Rome was not what filled her heart. No, it was the people. She had once loved Rome more than life itself, or so she thought, but then her life had grown wider, deeper, and more meaningful than she could have dreamed of. She had trusted God with her disappointments, and He had expanded the size of her heart. He had given her the gift of love, of loving many friends and cherishing many moments. She thought Marcellus had doomed her to a small and insignificant life. But he had set her free, free from herself and her dreams, and when she let go of those, God caught her as she fell, lifting her to a new height.

Oh, the stories Paul and Luke shared at the dinner table. Ephraim laughed until he turned red and then grimaced when the story turned frightening. Paul had been shipwrecked again, bitten by a venomous serpent, and lived through much travel, more arrests, and a plot against his life with bandits lying in wait on the road. Paul told his stories well, mainly because he was fearless and thought nothing of it. God made him strong, he said.

Still, she cherished the quiet moments alone with her friend. Priscilla loved working in silence alongside Paul, watching him write or catching a quick nap between visitors.

Priscilla and Paul were in the shop together when the clerk from Nero's court arrived. Aquila and his men were buying a large quantity of supplies and were due back later in the afternoon. She had not anticipated that news of Paul's trial would arrive today. Something about legal proceedings seemed so formal that she assumed the weather had to be dreary to match. Today was a late summer day. The sun was bright and piercing, and though the streets outside were busy, everyone was anxious to conclude the day's business and retreat inside. No one could think in this heat, let alone hold court. The city was eerily silent.

When the clerk arrived with official papers, she invited him in, Paul at her side. The clerk declined. Instead, he handed a parchment to the centurion for inspection then spoke to Paul.

"You are released from house arrest. No witnesses have come forward to accuse you. You are free to go where you please, although the emperor would remind you that he does not tolerate challenges to his authority."

That was it. The centurion departed on the heels of the clerk. His job was done as well. Priscilla and Paul watched them depart and blend into the crowds in the street, gone forever. All the worry about Paul's trial and what he would say to Nero was for nothing. Paul was free.

"Some answers to prayer are more exciting than others," Paul said in a wry voice. Glancing at him, Priscilla chuckled.

"What happened?" she asked. She turned and went back to her work preparing food for dinner. Preparations for dinner were never ending. Paul, Timothy, Luke, Aquila, Ephraim, and whoever else joined them at the tables ate quantities of food that defied her imagination. She yearned for Jesus to come back and perform another loaves-and-fishes miracle, even if only to get out of cooking for just one night.

Paul followed and set to work helping her. In this heat, no one had arrived at the shop this afternoon for teaching or healings. Most would be taking a nap, preferring to venture out this evening. "For a Roman citizen, the law is clear. Without my accusers facing me in person, the trial cannot continue."

"I know that, but why did the Jewish leaders refuse to make the trip? They've wanted to end your ministry for years. This was their best chance, wasn't it?"

"I think the temple leaders are more afraid of Nero than me," Paul replied. "They may hear rumors from the senators that we do not. He has made decisions that seem unwise, at best."

"He is unpredictable. And he has a temper," she added. That was her answer. Nero was a dangerous man to appear before if he could not profit from the case. The Jews had only recently been allowed to return to Rome…why risk another expulsion?

Paul sighed, obviously disappointed. "I will not appear before Nero. What an opportunity has been lost."

"Your life has been spared," she said. "And we both know what you're going to do next."

Paul looked at her, one eyebrow cocked, then grinned.

Paul took the next available ship, hoping to arrive in Spain.

Ephraim didn't cry. He was closer to the age of manhood now, at least by the synagogue's standards, so he felt strongly that he had to resist tears. Priscilla cried enough for them both. Something about this departure felt different. Thankfully, Luke stayed behind, at Paul's insistence, to work on writing the acts of the apostles. She marveled how her faith had become a story about people, not a dry set of beliefs. Her heart seemed to expand in every season as she followed Christ.

Only later in the month when the legions of soldiers marched through the streets of Rome to remind the citizens of Nero's power, did she wonder if so much love might come at a price. Nero gained in power every season too. He did not act with his power, however. He paraded it. Strange that an emperor loved parades and peace. Peace usually came from conflict. Nero paraded in victory without the battle. *Strange emperor indeed.* And his was a strange peace in this city.

As fall arrived, Peter and Silas came to Rome and quickly found their way to Priscilla and Aquila's home. Priscilla extended her hand to welcome Peter into her home. As he grasped it, she noted the thick callouses on his palm.

"A fisherman's hands," he said, his expression serious. He seemed kind, though. "I still enjoy a day of fishing when the need arises."

"And does the need arise often?" she asked.

"More often than you'd know," he said with a barely a hint of a wry smile.

She welcomed him and Silas. The believers who gathered for dinner were overjoyed to receive them. By their conversation, Priscilla knew a few of them had met before. But to her, Peter was the first believer she'd met who'd actually walked with Jesus during His earthly ministry. She kept stealing glances at him. His face was weather-beaten like a man who had spent days in the sun. His arms were muscular too, which made her wonder how heavy those fishing nets were. Fish themselves were quite small, but maybe hundreds of them at a time weighed more than she imagined. She wondered, too, how a man who lived on the water for so long, away from the company of others, had adapted to life on land and a life among people.

The conversation hadn't taken long at all to turn to Paul. She chuckled and wished Paul were here. He had a way of dominating the room, even when absent.

"I never understood why Paul was called to the Gentiles and I was called to the Jews," Peter told the believers at the table. "After all, I was a fisherman. I spent my youth learning to catch fish. There is a moment when the water is calm, just before the sun rises and the mist hovers over the waters, you sense you are not alone. That was where I received my religious instruction. And that was all I knew of God before I met Jesus."

"Paul studied to be a rabbi, so it made more sense for him to go to the Jews," she spoke up. Peter glanced at her and nodded in agreement. She liked that—he did not recoil that a woman had joined in the conversation. He was a true follower of Jesus who treated women as colaborers.

"Ah yes. He did. He knew the law of the Old Covenant so well, every nuance, every twist and application. But back then, he did not know the Messiah behind the command. That's why you would think the logical idea would be to send Paul to the

Jews and me to the Gentiles. But God's ways are not our ways. I think I am unqualified for my role."

"When you are weak, then you are strong," she replied.

He looked up in surprise. "Yes, that is how I would explain it."

"That is how Paul explained it to me." She laughed. "I think we ought not look for roles where we can serve at our best or strongest. I think surrendering to God means we will be moved closer to weakness. It is an inside-out life, our weakness put on display becoming a display of God's power."

Peter raised his cup. "To weakness, then."

They all joined in the toast, and Aquila motioned for Priscilla to join them.

As the guests settled down to the meal, Silas leaned forward. "I have news of Paul."

Ephraim clapped his hands. "Tell us!"

Priscilla gently rested her hand on her son's shoulder. Ephraim assumed any news of Paul was news of an adventure. Priscilla knew the dangers Paul faced.

"Paul is in Spain," Silas said. "He arrived safely and without shipwreck this time."

"It's a wonder any captain will let Paul on his ship," Ephraim said.

Silas laughed. "You're right. When they take Paul on board, they don't know the trouble he might bring. But he is in Spain and writing a good bit. He has written letters to Timothy and Titus. And Mark, the disciple who walked with Jesus, is on his way here. He should be only a week behind me."

Priscilla inhaled sharply, and Aquila caught her eye. "Another disciple!" she whispered under her breath. She felt a bit light-headed. "Someone who actually walked with Christ!"

Peter raised his hand as if to stop her racing thoughts. "No, not one of the twelve. Mark is, however, my closest companion and did walk with Jesus. He began working as my translator, helping me in provinces where my language skills were poor. Later, he began prompting me to record more of my experiences with Jesus. He's been transcribing the stories ever since."

"A kindred spirit, then, to Priscilla," Aquila said.

"You can read and write?" Peter asked, his eyebrows raised.

"Yes." Priscilla blushed, which secretly annoyed her. She was blushing because she didn't want to embarrass Peter, not because she thought it was exceptional for a woman to read and write. The culture thought it was exceptional, and the culture was wrong. She was a Christ follower. She disagreed with the culture on nearly every point, after all.

She excused herself from dinner. She needed to plan. The supplies she needed were not sold in the market. She needed to go to a papyrus shop. The merchant there would have scrolls as well and stylus tools for writing, plus ink. She'd worry about the money later. This was an opportunity she could not waste.

Whether she wrote the words or Mark did, that was unimportant. Her passion was to ensure that every scrap of life was recorded. If Jesus performed a miracle of turning a small meal into a great feast for many, then imagine what He could do with a few written eyewitness accounts. Jesus could multiply their impact beyond anything they were able to imagine. She felt it in her spirit. And she knew it was the Spirit because she did not care who signed the letters and accounts. There was only one name that mattered now in the world. In this world of hostility and separation, only one name still had the power to heal.

Three weeks later, Mark sat on a workbench in the shop, reading a scroll in the morning light. Every so often, he'd rest his hands on his chest as if to pray, or tug at his beard, deep in thought. He was so different from Peter. How had the two men formed such a close friendship? His skin was entirely smooth and a perfectly rich nut brown. He'd never had pox or known hard labor in his youth. His beard was pitch black, shot through with gray, and his black curly hair trimmed close around his head. He blinked a good deal and laughed often. He was a man given fully to God.

Mark was hard at work on Peter's biographical material, the history of Christ. He frequently called upon Priscilla to proofread the account and point out what he needed to ask Peter about. As she tidied one evening, she noticed that her parchment, the wedding gift from Aquila, was missing from the wooden box.

"Do you know what happened to the parchment that was in here?" she asked, making sure to keep her tone light.

Mark, squinting, looked up from his work. "I used it this morning. Excellent quality. Here."

He handed her the parchment, still stiff from being kept in storage too long. She swallowed back tears of frustration. She really had meant every word of her pledge to the Lord that she would serve Him with words. She wanted to see His story written. But her wedding gift? Why did that have to be taken, and without her permission? That seemed cruel.

She sat next to Mark and began to read.

Mark looked up and leaned over. "It's the account of the... well, just read. You'll be the first."

And she read. After a few sentences, she stood and walked to the door, feeling the sunlight on her face. Her breath came too fast. She steadied herself and returned to the page.

"I only knew that He rose," she said softly, her eyes meeting Mark's. "I did not know what the women saw that morning."

Mark nodded, his face registering her astonishment. "The women are the first witnesses. Remarkable, isn't it? Women cannot testify in court. The law does not recognize their testimony as valid. Oh, what a new thing has sprung up, indeed."

"Who was the man wearing a white robe? Was he the one who rolled away the stone?" Priscilla stood and paced. "No, but that's impossible. The stone is too heavy for one man."

Mark crossed his arms and tugged at his beard. "I believe it was an angel."

Priscilla grabbed the parchment, clutching it to her chest. "Miracles." She lifted her eyes. "Thank you." In her heart she knew the Lord hadn't taken her wedding gift. He had given her one. One far beyond anything she could have hoped for.

She couldn't wait to share this with Aquila. If she had only known on that day so long ago.

Pausing, she remembered the girl she had been, dreaming of the words she would write on this scroll. Thank God she hadn't. Thank God she hadn't gotten what she wanted. And she thanked God for every broken dream that released untold blessings.

CHAPTER EIGHTEEN

Within weeks, her parchment was circulating among believers, sharing the Good Story. Peter's account of life as a disciple, written by the hand of Mark, had quite an impact on people. She wondered if Peter took more joy in it because it was his account of the events or because his spiritual son, Mark, had written the words. She suspected it had everything to do with Mark. The fisherman had mentored a brilliant young man. Mark's light burned brightly. *What an unexpected legacy for a fisherman.*

Peter and Mark, in the natural course of their lives, would never have met.

But the cross changed everything about a life, didn't it?

She enjoyed watching the men share dinner together at night. Worn from the day's labor, Peter would still have hours of teaching ahead. He would eat for strength. Mark would need to stretch, his back sore from bending over the table to write. His hands often cramped when he tried to tear the bread. Ephraim had taken to sitting next to him and tearing it for him. Ephraim, she noted, was growing quickly. Another year or two and the boy would be her height. In a few years after that, he might even be taller than Aquila.

Watching everyone bump elbows and jostle for room at the table, she wondered where she could have put another child. *Still, a daughter would have been lovely.*

But not here. Not in Rome. This was no longer a city for women. She took a nibble of roasted chickpeas and savored the cheerful flavor of rosemary. She loved the bracing flavor, although in Corinth and Ephesus it was adored more as a study aid. Students thought a fresh sprig would keep them awake and alert.

Do I need to stay alert? Her heart thrummed steadily on, but beneath the reassuring rhythm, she became aware of a tense and watchful soul.

Marcellus would turn thirty soon. *Is he the source of my unease?* He had not returned to bother her or visit Ephraim. He said Ephraim would carry on the family name. But if he wanted Ephraim to inherit his estate, why could he not send tutors here?

Or was her unease because of Nero? The emperor had proposed building a new palace, but the senators opposed him. Nero pushed new building projects every day. He taxed the wealthy in the provinces and kept prices low for the citizens of Rome. She did worry that he would forget that it was the wealthy who kept him in power, not the masses. But so far, although Nero loved entertaining the citizens and building the city, he did not love religious persecution. He had avoided making life unnecessarily difficult for Jews or Christians. He was eccentric, and he spent too much, but he was not a zealot.

Over and over, she turned each piece in her mind. Nothing was clearly, obviously wrong, so her unease made no sense.

And yet, every evening when the men finished the meal and at last the house grew dark and quiet, her heart grew restless. She knew then without a doubt that something was very wrong with this facade of peace that had descended in Rome. Something stirred in her spirit to warn her.

Something was coming. *But what, O Lord?*

64 CE, Rome

The sun rose, just as it had every morning of her life. But Rome, as she knew it, would not survive the day. Priscilla went about her morning errands and knew nothing of the unwinding clock, the last few minutes of life that passed and would never return.

The streets were crowded with shoppers and vendors. Ephraim was delivering an order with a few strong helpers while Aquila instructed workers on a new leatherworking technique. Priscilla watched Ephraim navigate through the crowded streets. Poor Skylos whined at her side, so she reached down to pet his graying head. He was too frail to keep up with Ephraim and not nimble enough to stay out from underfoot in these streets. Skylos returned to a mat Ephraim had placed in the corner, circled once, and slowly lowered himself for a nap. She could tell the poor dog's hips bothered him.

Priscilla set to work assembling the morning's supplies for Mark. After that, she would go to the baker for bread and then on to buy stewed figs.

Shouts came from the street, and Aquila looked up from his bench, his expression darkening. She followed him to the shop door, alarmed by the man shouting in the street. His words were that of a madman.

"The Circus burns!"

People whispered and hissed to one another, encircling him, demanding more information, until he broke free and ran. Aquila sent Priscilla back inside, but one of the workers volunteered to run to the Circus Maximus. Whatever Nero was doing, it was a grand spectacle to be sure. Perhaps they might all finish work early to go and watch, he suggested. Nero loved nothing more than costumes and pageants.

An acrid smell caught them all by surprise. Something did not seem right—this was fire, not a game or theater. Once more Aquila went into the street, where a crowd had swarmed, their faces turned toward the hills above. Just beyond the hills was the Circus. The sky was dark and it wasn't even noon.

"The Circus is on fire!" he called to Priscilla. She ran into the street, pushing through strangers to reach his side. Watching with a growing dread, she saw orange flames rise above the hills. And then, as if an enemy turning toward them in battle, the flames poured down the hill, heading for the valley. Heading for the people.

"Ephraim!" she cried. Aquila was already running through the crowd in the direction of the customer Ephraim had gone to see.

The flames ate their way through the trees with astonishing speed, methodically working their way toward the people below.

Those who could, ran. The very young and very old begged and cried out for help. And a few just stood and watched, unable to move even as death made its way toward them. Priscilla ran into the shop, working quickly. She got everyone out, telling them where to find catacombs on the outskirts of Rome. Those barren places of the dead might be safe, she reasoned. Nothing would burn there since they were just stone and dust.

She remembered the little fire she had faced years ago in the shop here in Rome, how Aquila's burn had caused such pain for days. She grabbed a satchel and stuffed it with coins, a jar of oil, herbs, her shawl, and shawl pin, anything she could quickly lay her hands on that might be useful for first aid or barter. In another satchel she stuffed bread and grain. Skylos whined, his tail limply wagging as he watched her.

"Oh, Skylos," she cried, and kneeled beside him. Resting one hand on his head, she gazed into his soft brown eyes. He was too heavy to carry. "I cannot leave you," she whispered, tears choking her as smoke slowly filled the shop. "God help me."

Peter appeared in the doorway.

"I told you to get the others to safety!" she gasped.

He didn't reply. His face was a grim mask, ash already collecting in his hair. He tore the hem off his tunic, soaked it in wine, and covered her face with it. He did the same for himself, then lifted Skylos into his arms.

He burst out the door, and she grabbed his tunic to keep from losing him in the crowd. Glowing red embers floated in the air. Landing on straw in the streets or on tunics or even in hair, they caused tiny fires to smolder and grow all around. Within moments her entire world was on fire. Smoke stung her eyes, blinding her.

Peter ran into walls and people, and she stumbled as she lurched against him. Frantically, blindly, they picked their way through the screaming people, making their way toward the catacombs. Everywhere she could dimly see figures shrouded by smoke and people aflame and panicking, beating the air. She heard children's cries in the darkness with no way to reach them. She felt they had been dropped into the depths of Hades.

With every step, she did not know if she was getting closer to finding Aquila and Ephraim or losing them forever in the flames. Her throat burned from the smoke, and she felt her airways closing off. If they had to run much farther, she did not think she would survive.

When they staggered into the catacombs, a handful of believers waited for her, speechless. Aquila and Ephraim were not among them. Peter gently set Skylos down at the edge of the group, but the poor dog's eyes did not open. And then Peter collapsed.

The fire burned for six days. Six days without night or day, sun or moon. Only the roar of flames and orange light, only gray smoke and scorched lungs. Priscilla tried to pray, but her tongue, dry and scratched, stuck to the roof of her mouth. Her body had not the means to pray and her spirit could find no words.

Aquila and Ephraim had not been found. She watched for them daily, waited for them to come staggering up the broken path to the catacombs, but they did not. Only dead shreds of the city blew past. Her skin held a layer of grit, and when she wrapped her arms around herself for comfort, her palms came away black with soot.

Embers floated from house to house below, continuing to set fires everywhere. No one, nowhere was safe. Of the fourteen districts of Rome, eleven were taken to the ground. If the fire had been a conquering army, there would have been a victory. But nothing was won. The fire only destroyed and ruined. And after the six days, when the fire at last died, the unthinkable happened. The unthinkable was allowed, or encouraged. Priscilla and the believers huddled in the catacombs did not know; they got such small snippets of information from the other survivors left in the city.

The fire reignited. Who did it, or what did it, was unknown. But the second fire burned for another three days. On the fourth day, a familiar figure picked his way up the path. The tears of disappointment and joy that mingled together on her cheeks were a strange brew to Priscilla as she called out his name.

"Luke!" She lifted one hand. "We are here!"

"Nero discovered the cause of the fire," Luke announced bitterly, working on organizing the supplies he had, adding them to the items Priscilla had carried out from the shop.

Priscilla watched the group as they waited patiently for him to explain. There were about seventy believers here. More were left in the city, hopefully hidden and huddled throughout. The believers here in the catacombs had been able to flee, and only a few were seriously wounded.

"Nero announced that the Christians are to blame," Luke continued. The shock seemed to freeze everyone.

"The Christians?" Priscilla echoed. "Why?"

Luke worked on tearing an old tunic in strips. "You fled the city quickly. You may not have seen, but some believers stopped Nero's firemen."

"I didn't see any firemen!" a believer spat.

"Firemen tried to slow the spread of the fire," Luke said. "I suspect they went to the wealthy neighborhoods first. But the winds carried the embers everywhere, so what did that matter? No one was safe because the fire came from the sky."

"But why does Nero blame the Christians?" Priscilla prompted him. "Because of a dispute with the firemen?"

Luke laid the strips out in rows, then worked rolling each strip up and setting it aside for use as a bandage. "No, not a dispute. The Christians, if they even were such, thought the end of the world had come. They welcomed the fire. They wanted to hasten the return of Christ."

Priscilla rested her face in her hands, momentarily forgetting that she would only leave soot marks on her cheeks. "We cannot hasten the kingdom of God by death and destruction."

"So many are suffering." Luke sighed. "I cannot stay long."

She nodded. "Of course. You are good to check on us. But we will manage. You are needed more in the city. Many people may have been trapped in their houses and shops. I fear what you will find there."

He looked at her, and his eyes were a depth of sorrow. "I do not fear it. I dread it."

She motioned for him to step outside for a moment.

"Any news of Aquila or Ephraim?" she asked, her stomach roiling with pain. If he said one word, just one confirmation of her worst nightmares, her heart would break right here. It was odd to beg for the answer that might destroy her, but she needed to know. She needed them.

Luke took both her hands in his. "No news. But that does not mean they are with the Lord."

She exhaled, and the ground under her feet wobbled. She closed her eyes to focus and try to stay strong. He hadn't used the word *dead*, but death was all around. Her faith seemed so impossible now, that her husband or son were alive even if their bodies were found in the rubble. She was terrified to know the truth of what happened to them in the fire…and she was terrified to know the truth of what happened to them with Jesus.

"The city smolders," she said, looking down the hill at the ruins. "Rome is gone."

Luke did not release her hands. Instead, his grip tightened. "God is our refuge and strength, a very present help in trouble.

Therefore we will not fear, though the earth give way, though the mountains should fall into the heart of the sea."

Luke's words and a deep breath restored her courage. "Yes," she said.

In the days that followed, new horrors unfolded daily. Each new flame ablaze in the city streets was not a torch but a Christian. Each game attended by the nobles had but one entertainment—Christians forced to fight wild animals. God did not close the mouths of the lions anymore, it seemed. Nor did He strike Nero with a wasting disease or send plagues and prophets to deliver His people.

Instead, His children suffered. Those with faith, prayed. Those with strength, cried out. But every day, more died. Every day as the centurions brought out the dead from the fire to be buried, the Christians added to their number. Only at night, if a cloud by chance rolled over the moon, did a believer dare stir in the city. Only in darkness did the children of light run for help. They needed medicine for their burns, which inflicted such pain as they'd never known and then grew infected. Their children needed bread and milk.

Still, no mercies or miracles from God seemed to ease the nightmare. Priscilla crept to the edge of the catacombs at night, shepherding believers into safety when she could. She traded information when she had it. No one had word of Aquila or Ephraim. The city had thousands dead. Most were still inside smoldering buildings or underneath rubble that could not be moved for weeks. She had to live with not knowing.

Strange to walk in darkness. The grit of the burned city lodged in her mouth, and smoke stung her eyes. Had Lot's wife felt like this in that last final instant?

The hardest part, to her, was that God knew where her husband and son were. God knew and said nothing. She remembered the story of Jesus standing at the tomb of Lazarus, weeping. Jesus wept and then performed the miracle.

Had Jesus's back been turned to the sisters? Did they think He was silent as the tears flowed? *Maybe, maybe I cannot see His face right now. Maybe it is streaked with tears. But even so, can I believe in miracles?*

She did not know. She only knew Ephraim and Aquila were out there, in the city. Whether they were alive or dead, she needed the truth. If she couldn't have a miracle, she needed at least to know. She knew what she would do the next evening.

She would go to Marcellus.

Moving in blackest night, her arms and face covered in soot, Priscilla escaped detection. She was dehydrated and weak by the time she reached her old family home. She had seen enough terror in the street to sear her eyes open. She would never sleep peacefully again. She rested only once, when from a distance she spied the gates to the family estate still standing. Marcellus and the estate were fine. He had escaped with his wealth. Nero had probably had something to do with that. Somehow the richest houses seemed to have fared well, but maybe she had only noted houses with pools and fountains in the gardens.

Approaching the gates, she paused one last time to reconsider her idea. If she asked for Marcellus to help find Aquila and Ephraim, he would demand a price. The price, of course, would be Ephraim. Marcellus would want to raise him and educate him as his own. She would trade Ephraim for his life. Marcellus could keep him safe and well cared for now, while she could not. Marcellus was in favor with Nero. Christians were hunted.

But the unknown risk was this—if Marcellus no longer wanted a son, he could turn her in to Nero. Marcellus made his money supplying beasts to the Circus. He'd make a nice bonus supplying beasts plus a Christian. She'd probably give away the location of the other believers if she was tortured.

A centurion walked out of Marcellus's house. She ducked behind a scorched evergreen as his familiar voice carried in the night.

"I don't care," Marcellus said. "Nero has coated his palace in gold and mother-of-pearl! He has to pay his debts! And I have to pay my suppliers, or it is I they'll feed to the lions next."

"Why sell animals then? Can't we sell more Christians?" the man asked.

"I know where they're hiding," Marcellus replied, his voice a low growl. "I could always cut you out of the deal."

"I'll bring you more animals," the guard said.

"Find the boy called Ephraim, and I'll double your pay."

Her heart sank. Marcellus didn't know where Ephraim was. The guard left the estate, his face a mask of fury, passing in front of Priscilla as she hid. She knew him. He had a wife among the believers hiding in the catacombs. He was trading in lives too. She was too broken in spirit to be angry at him.

When she no longer heard her pulse thundering in her ears, she fled back to the catacombs.

CHAPTER NINETEEN

Ephraim was not found, not by Marcellus, nor by Priscilla. In the time that followed, many of the believers did not survive their injuries from the fire. Priscilla did all she could to help ease their suffering. So did Luke. But it was Peter, that roughened man of the water, who brought them all the most comfort. Peter wrote for them a beautiful letter about suffering. After he finished, Priscilla gathered the believers still hiding in the catacombs. Mark read aloud to the frightened, hurting survivors.

"'You are protected by the power of God through faith for a salvation ready to be revealed in the last time,'" his deep voice read, echoing in the darkness as many gathered around. "'In this you greatly rejoice, even though now for a little while, you have been distressed by various trials, that the proof of your faith, being more precious than gold which is perishable, even though tested by fire, may be found to result in praise and glory and honor at the revelation of Jesus Christ.'"

Mark's calm, rich voice soothed her as her eyelids fluttered closed. Shaking herself back awake, determined to listen, she sat up straight. Peter had been hard at work on this letter for days now. The believers gathered around Mark, with Peter near as well, soaking in every word.

The letter, which would go to believers throughout the world, would comfort them in any trial. She wondered how many would face such a tragic loss of life, and how many would face such evil persecution. She sent prayers along with each word. When believers heard or read these words, would they sense the community this letter was born from? Would those believers know they were not alone and that so many others had gone before them in prayer?

"'Casting all your anxiety on Him, because He cares for you,'" Mark continued.

Priscilla's eyes were heavy again. She would sleep tonight. For the first time since being separated from Aquila and Ephraim, she would truly rest. The comfort of God had touched her spirit and brought the healing she had not known how to pray for. She smiled as she drifted off later that night, her head on her arms. The healing she had needed was simply called sleep.

Tomorrow she would know what to do next. *Somehow, I will know.*

The next morning, Priscilla prepared breakfast. She made a small fire at the far edges of the catacombs. Smoke at this distance would not be noticed in the city, not when a cloud of smoke still hovered over the ruins. Still, it was best to do the cooking as far from the catacombs as possible, to avoid giving the location away.

A man approached the camp with food. Priscilla greeted him with a nod, then recognized him as he passed. He was the centurion guard. His wife was hidden here with the believers.

When he left, she made sure he saw her face. If she ever needed a friend among Nero's guards, now she had one. She knew where his wife was hidden.

That same week, the catacombs were raided. Peter was arrested along with many others. Priscilla escaped with a handful of the women. She now had less than a dozen believers with her and still no sign of Aquila or Ephraim. Her heart constricted further every day with fresh panic.

The world had changed before her eyes, and she knew it would never be the same. The streets were gone. Buildings and blocks incinerated. Friends whose beloved faces she would see no more in this life all swept away.

In that moment she was profoundly grateful she had never achieved any measure of success in the emperor's courts. For if she had known success, she would have had wealth too, and wealth had a strange way of narrowing the circle of true friends. Marcellus was alone now in his sprawling estate. If his wife had ever loved him, then she was the only one who might still.

But the hardships Priscilla had faced had cast a wide net in her life, bringing back friends from far places. The common people who labored with her had opened their homes, and where the home was open, so was the heart. Had she known that when she crossed those thresholds, or when they had crossed hers? God had denied the prayer that she might serve in the courts so that she might serve in the shadows…and how rich she had become.

She prayed for her friends now, the ones who remained and the ones who faced death as they waited in prisons.

Word came the following day that Peter had been crucified. She nodded mutely, receiving the news. Rome was gone, and slowly, her family of believers was being picked apart, one by one. She'd spent a lifetime building these foundations, and Nero razed them in days. Tears seemed never ending. Apollos sent word through a messenger that he was at work on a letter to stir faith. She sent word back, with directions for him to find her if he wanted assistance.

When the messenger returned the next day, Priscilla thought it was news from Apollos. But it was not.

Ephraim had been found alive. He was in prison, sentenced to die.

Priscilla arrived at the prison called Mamertine in the second watch of the night. She judged that the first watch guards would have fallen asleep by then, grateful to be done with their duty, but the third watch guards would still be asleep, desperate for every last hour.

The second watch was a lonely vigil and she well understood it. Any mother did.

Watching the two guards posted at the dark entrance, she could hear the screams and cries of the men imprisoned within. Many still suffered burns from the fire, she knew. And Nero favored tortures that made her heart fail within her to even consider. But she had to find out if Ephraim was here. If not at Mamertine, then he was well out of Rome and out of reach. She could do nothing to save him if he was not here.

Nero liked to put political prisoners here, though. So if Ephraim was inside, then his fate was sealed. He would die for being an enemy of the Roman Empire. No matter what he had done to cause arrest—if he had done anything at all—he had no way out now. No way except her.

The stupidity of what she was about to do stunned her. If Aquila was here…her eyes clouded with tears and she hung her head. Where was he? What would he want her to do? *God, save us,* she pleaded.

Wiping her eyes with the backs of her hands, she breathed quietly through her open mouth, careful to make no noise. As her vision cleared, her mouth still hung open. She was too shocked to close it.

The guard who secretly visited the believers hiding in the catacombs was on duty at the entrance, just as she had arranged. Quickly, she squatted, her hands running across the surface of the soil. She picked up a wide rock, pulled back, and launched it as far as she could throw it.

It scattered across the stones in the opposite distance, immediately catching the attention of the guards. Breathing another silent prayer, for everything depended on the choice made next, she watched eagerly.

The guard she did not know walked away to investigate. Stepping quickly out from her hiding place, she motioned for the guard she knew to approach her. He hesitated. She stepped farther into the torchlight, an assurance that she was alone.

"I am going to have a look around over here," he called to his coworker, advancing toward her.

"Did you verify it?" she whispered.

The guard glanced over his shoulder, then nodded. "Yes, Ephraim is here. I thought you would want to rescue Paul first, though."

"Paul is here too?" Her heart felt the news like a dagger had plunged through her.

"I can't get them both out," the guard whispered. "I can get someone in, though."

"Not yet," she whispered, thinking quickly. "I will contact you with the arrangements. Meanwhile, do as I asked. Change the boy's name on all prison records."

"What should I call him?"

"Manasseh," she whispered. *If Aquila were here, he would smile at that.*

She sank back into the darkness. She had an impossible task to accomplish and no money. But the Lord had provided in the past, and He would provide again.

That was her only hope. *The future is unknowable, but God is not.*

Arranging the transport took days, days Priscilla feared that Paul and Ephraim did not have. She managed to get word to Luke that Paul was in Mamertine. Paul had managed to get a letter out of the prison to Timothy, so someone in authority there was sympathetic to the believers.

She could not reveal the identity of the guard she knew, not even in a letter to Luke. Nero's spies were everywhere. God knew how to get Luke in to Mamertine if that was His will. The guard knew enough about Luke to be on alert, and that was all she could do.

Meanwhile, she had to find passage to Asia. Convinced that only in the Asian churches would her son and the believers be safe from Rome's persecution, she sent messages to her old friends in the ports, looking for a ship that might carry him and the others away without question. *Without question and without much money.*

One captain sent a message back that shocked her. It shouldn't have. Nero set the fire himself. After building a palace so grand that it dwarfed every other building in the city, Nero had decided to destroy the city and rebuild a new palace. The new palace would be the size of Rome. The entire city would become a palace for one man.

Apollos sent word and a manuscript he was working on. He was recording a list of the mighty faithful in the scriptures. While she added her thoughts, she did not want to add her name to it. Too many people were suffering for the name of Christ, and she could not distract anyone from the hope of salvation, even for a moment. And still, even in the ruins of an empire, a woman's name was a distraction.

She worked long hours on the letter, holding the stylus until her hands cramped, adding suggestions and memories, corresponding with Apollos about what believers most needed to remember about true faith. The work steeled her for the days ahead.

She had one consolation—her son would be safe from Marcellus.

When the guards broke down the door to the cellar Priscilla was hiding in, she set down her stylus and stood. Her only regret was that they had taken so long to find her. Were her directions not clear enough, she wondered?

Arriving at Mamertine an hour later, she was forced to stand outside the gates while the warden attended to an execution in the courtyard. Lifting her eyes to the sun, she squinted at the bright clear light. A cool breeze swept past, and she realized it was the first pure wind to blow through this city in weeks.

"Ephraim," she whispered, as a bird cried out overhead. She closed her eyes and stood silent.

And then the rush of the world's noise returned, and she was dragged by her arms into the prison.

As she was pulled deeper into the pit that was Mamertine, she caught sight of a familiar head of hair, a familiar frame, a man she would always remember as a boy.

True to the captain's word, she had been allowed to catch sight of her son as he was led out of the prison. Ephraim had not seen her being led into the pit.

Priscilla stirred. How long had she awaited this day? *Too long.*

The guards jostled her roughly as they walked her to the execution block in the open courtyard. Paul had died here. She had heard the rumors of Aquila's death here.

The sky was a clear blue as a bird called out, flying overhead.

"Place your head on the block and keep your eyes down," the executioner said. The captain stood next to the executioner, as a witness. He nodded, only once, to acknowledge her. In the blinding sunlight, she recognized his face. *I hope his wife is safe.*

"I am a follower of Jesus," Priscilla said, her voice hoarse. "I keep my eyes up."

"And this is why the emperor is killing your people," the guard said, kicking her in the back of the knees. She fell at the foot of the wooden block.

"Just tell me, what happened to my Aquila?"

"Who?"

"Her husband," the captain said to the guards, sounding bored with the prolonged ordeal. He grabbed her by the elbows. He whispered in her ear, "Ephraim made it safely onto the ship. But Aquila…" He cleared his throat, trying to finish the sentence. Instead, he stepped back.

"I will see him soon, then, won't I?" she murmured.

She heard the executioner slap on his leather apron. Another guard took her by the neck to force her head onto the block. She struggled to keep her face toward the heavens. But suddenly a great and blinding light overwhelmed her, and only from a distance was she aware of the guards still preparing for her death. A quiet peace filled her as she let the guard move her body where he wanted it, for she was no longer there.

She stood at the edge of a garden, where all things were in bloom. In the distance, a huge stone had been rolled away from some forgotten place and rested just off the path. Children sat upon it, singing. Her mind was slow as she took another step on the path. *Where am I?*

The light in the garden was so bright. She shielded her eyes as she heard his voice. The voice of Aquila, and he was looking at her, his arms extended. Restored, he smiled as he waited for her on the far side of the garden's path. Behind him…could it be? Was that really Paul? Restored too? His body whole, unbroken, the marks of cruel men gone. Paul waited for her too. And behind them...

Oh, standing just behind them, the Glory of all Glories. Jesus.

And she felt the tears running down her face, the joy of seeing old and dear friends from a distance, and the blessed promise of reunion. And this, the realization she had but to take a few more steps and she could touch the face of Christ.

Paul had been right. Nothing could separate her from Jesus, not even death, for Jesus was nearer now, in this moment, than He had ever seemed.

When the blade fell it was too late to hurt her, for the heavenly joy coursing through her body made earthly pain impossible to feel.

And so Priscilla stepped into the garden,

where the stone is forever rolled away,

where Jesus is King,

where beloved family and friends wait,

where she waits even now to welcome her sisters and brothers into the kingdom.

EPILOGUE

In the coming months, Jerusalem would fall. Emperor Titus would lead the Roman army to destroy the temple. The Old Covenant would no longer hold, as there was no temple at which to offer sacrifices. The temple, that center of Jewish life, was gone forever.

Even as the Roman army marched down the streets, the ground trembled under their feet. If they did not notice, it was because men do not always know when the earth is changing. Mighty Vesuvius in Pompeii was preparing for her entrance on history's stage.

Beneath their feet, Vesuvius dreamed, and it was a fitful sleep.

AUTHOR'S NOTE

The Roman world was a world of gods and emperors. Everywhere you went in the empire, the streets were lined with monuments and altars. To an ordinary soul, it must have seemed that the world was filled with men who achieved great deeds, and deities whose demands would survive the ages.

Yet to the Roman mind, Christianity was a strange sect, destined only to be quickly crushed and forgotten. But today if you walk the streets of Rome, you won't find a busy altar to those ancient gods. The Vestal Virgins aren't in business, and not far away, the Oracle at Delphi has long since shuttered up shop too.

We remember very few of the emperors. And no one worships the pantheon of Greek and Roman gods. (Well, some probably do, but there are always some who dig up what history has thrown out.)

When I walk the streets that once fell under the shadow of the emperors, I am aware of two things especially: the souvenir shops feature crosses and images of the crucifixion, and tourists flock to visit the sites with any connection to the apostles.

Rome belongs to Christ now, and it always will. The whole earth does.

I remember visiting the jail where Paul was held prisoner—Mamertine. Mamertine is open for tourists, and many will pay for the privilege of standing in an empty stone-floor room, where Paul might have slept. We long for a closer connection to the people and events of the New Testament.

Priscilla would have understood. She was an eyewitness to everything—the growing church, the mesmerizing people, and the historical events. What most intrigues me about her story, however, is a puzzle that has never been solved.

Did Priscilla author—or coauthor—the book of Hebrews? Scholars have included her and Apollos at the top of the list of possible of authors for years. Many reasons would have prevented a woman from claiming ownership of the letter. And Apollos was so gifted in speech that he could have easily dictated the letter, with Priscilla writing.

What a beautiful mystery to ponder. Someone among the ancient believers created this letter for us and left out their name.

And the grace flows. Their work endures. Whatever their name was, it is not lost to God.

In our world obsessed with fame and followers, we can remember that God has our names written on the palm of His hands (Isaiah 49:16). Whether anyone ever knows our name, let's pray that grace flows from our life's labors. Let's pray that the work we do in love endures, even into the ages to come.

Your sister in Christ,
Ginger Garrett

FACTS BEHIND *the Fiction*

TROUBLE IN ROME BRINGS FRIENDS TOGETHER

Priscilla and Aquila might never have met Paul had it not been for Emperor Claudius expelling Jews from Rome. Luke, author of Acts, a history of the early church, reported the expulsion: "Claudius Caesar deported all Jews from Rome" (Acts 18:2 NLT).

Luke stopped short of explaining why the emperor did that. Three Roman history writers of the first century confirm that Claudius expelled the Jews: Suetonius, Pliny the Younger, and Tacitus. One of them explained why: "Jews were constantly causing disturbances, instigated by Chrestus. So, he [Emperor Claudius] expelled them from Rome" (Suetonius, writing in *Divus Claudius* 25). "Chrestus" is an alternate spelling of the Latin word for Christ, *Christus*. Suetonius sometimes used "e" instead of the "i" when writing about Christ or Christians.

Paul's letters along with Luke's stories in Acts report the kind of disturbances Suetonius probably meant. Tradition-minded Jews abhorred hearing fellow Jews like Paul teach that God had a Son and that Jesus was His name. Jews saw that as undermining one of their most basic teachings: there is only one God. "The LORD is our God, the Lord alone" (Deuteronomy 6:4 NLT). Most Jews at the time considered the growing Christian movement blasphemous and thoroughly disrespectful of God.

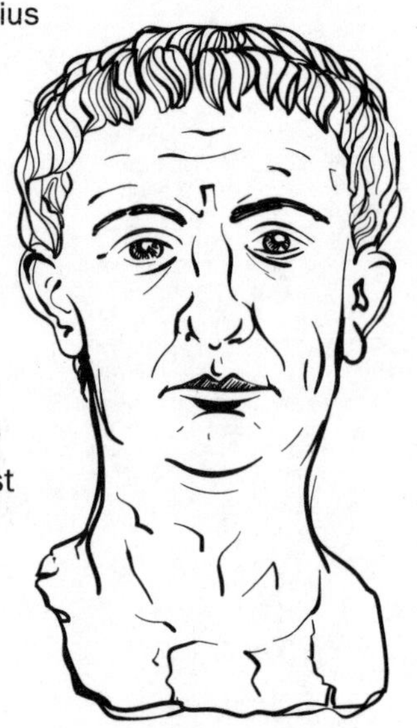

BRONZE IMPERIAL PORTRAIT OF ROMAN EMPEROR CLAUDIUS. FROM AD 1 TO 50

PRISCILLA THE TROUBLEMAKER?

It's possible Priscilla and Aquila had something to do with those disturbances. They may have hosted a church in their home, just as they did later in Corinth, Ephesus, and Rome. But as Jews, they still attended synagogue services.

That put them face-to-face with tradition-minded Jews who considered them heretics who deserved to die. These Jews persecuted Paul throughout his ministry. They had Paul arrested, imprisoned, beaten, and stoned many times.

Scholars debate when Claudius expelled the Jews. One popular guess is in about AD 49. But dates suggested among history scholars span a decade, from the early AD 40s to the early 50s. Any of those dates would have put Priscilla and Aquila at Corinth in time to have met Paul, who arrived in roughly AD 50.

MEETING IN CORINTH

Paul met Priscilla and Aquila in the southern Greek port town of Corinth on his second mission trip, around AD 50. Priscilla and Aquila settled there after Emperor Claudius expelled the Jews from Rome.

By the time Paul arrived, Priscilla and Aquila were working at their trade: tentmaking. That's the same trade Paul learned as a young man. Paul stayed in Corinth for a year and a half, starting the church there. He lived with Priscilla and Aquila and paid his way by making tents with them. When Paul moved to Ephesus, Priscilla and Aquila followed and started a house church there. Ephesus is where they met Apollos.

When Apollos, an internationally famous Christian orator from North Africa, arrived on a speaking tour, Priscilla and her husband pulled him aside after his sermon and "explained the way of God even more accurately" (Acts 18:26 NLT). That took chutzpah. Apollos knew about "John's baptism" (Acts 18:25), but he apparently hadn't heard about baptism in the Spirit, which Jesus taught. Priscilla helped enlighten him. Some scholars describe her as the Church's first-known woman teacher, and some have even suggested that she could be the anonymous author of Hebrews.

When Claudius died, Priscilla and Aquila moved back to Rome and started another house church. Paul sent them greetings in his famous letter to the church at Rome (Romans 16:3). He said he hoped their church would help fund him for a mission trip to Spain (Romans 15:24). It's unclear if Paul ever made that trip. Early church writers say the Romans executed him sometime around the AD mid-60s.

Church tradition and early church writers indicate that Priscilla and Aquila were also martyred together in Rome, perhaps around the same time as Paul.

NAMED FIRST

Paul and Luke, writing in Acts, usually name Priscilla first. They may have named her first out of respect for her position, possibly higher in Rome's caste system than that of her Jewish tentmaker husband. She may have been born into the ruling upper class, known as patricians, who were rich landowners. Aquila may have been a commoner, known as a plebeian. Plebeians were people who made a living as artisans, as farmers, and by working other common jobs.

On the other hand, maybe Priscilla's name comes first because she was more active in church work. Aquila may have focused more on tentmaking. Though our Bible translations typically call her Priscilla, Paul called her Prisca.

HOW TO MAKE A TENT FROM LIVESTOCK

It usually took goats, dead or alive, to make the kind of water-resistant tents Romans preferred. Alive, goats provided hair, which was spun into thread. Their tanned hides were also used to make tents. In fact, the Greek word for tentmaker, *skenos*, gave us the English word for "skin."

The Roman army preferred leather tents over goat hair because leather tents were lighter and less bulky. One replica based on the Roman army's design for an eight-man tent weighs about 100 pounds (45 kg). It took the hides of seventy-seven goats to make a tent that size.

Tentmakers could buy tanned hides from tanners. Tanning was a dirty, stinky business often left to specialists living outside of town and downwind. Simon, the tanner mentioned in the Bible, lived outside of town "near the seashore" (Acts 10:6 NLT). The stink came mainly from dead animals, but there was also the rotten fruit, mulberry leaves, urine, and other chemicals tanners used to soak the hides. Tanners soaked hides for weeks to remove the hair and soften them. Tentmakers stitched leather hides together, which was a bit like making a quilt from different patches of cloth. The hides could come from a mix of livestock, such as goats, sheep, camels, and cattle. But goatskin was cheaper, lighter, and easier to work with.

Paul, however, may have preferred working with goat hair. He grew up where it seems goat hair tents were invented. He learned tentmaking in Cilicia. That's a Roman province where a Roman writer named Marcus Varro (100s BC) said tentmakers first practiced shearing goats to acquire the raw material used to produce goat hair cloth. Goat hair cloth adopted the local name and became known as *cilicium*.

Artisans spun the hair into thread. Then weavers worked the thread on looms to produce goat hair cloth, which they exported throughout the empire. Paul probably didn't carry his own loom as he traveled. But he may have bought cloth in towns along the way and stitched them together and shaped them for draping over tent poles.

Goat hair tents were better ventilated than leather tents because there was space between the fibers of the fabric. Yet the tents didn't usually leak because when it rained, the wet goat hair swelled to fill the gaps, producing a water-resistant barrier.

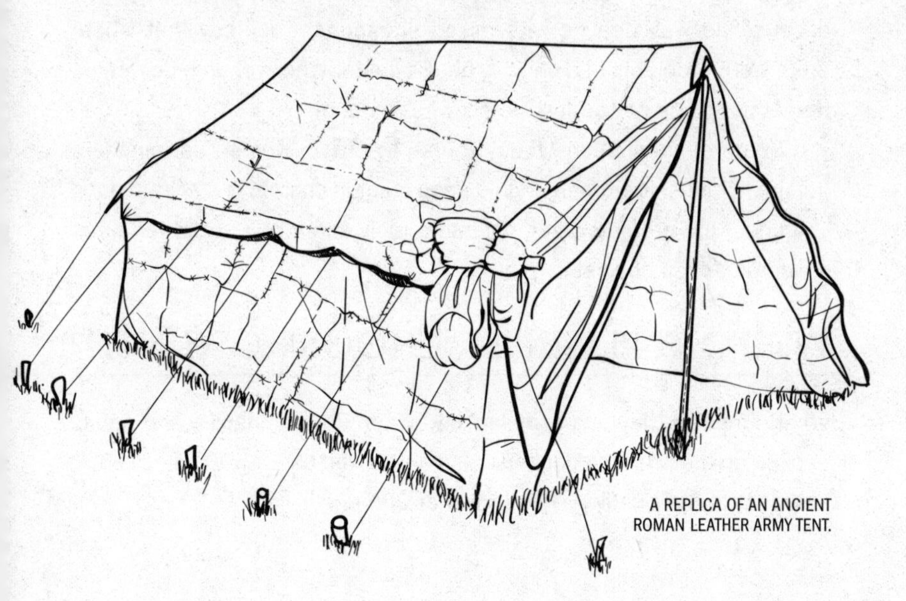

A REPLICA OF AN ANCIENT ROMAN LEATHER ARMY TENT.

PAUL'S MESSAGES ABOUT WOMEN

Paul's writings about women in ministry seem direct and unflinching.

- "Women should be silent during the church meetings. It is not proper for them to speak" (1 Corinthians 14:34 NLT).
- "I do not let women teach men" (1 Timothy 2:12 NLT).

Yet there's no indication Paul objected to Priscilla tutoring the famous orator Apollos. She remained Paul's dear friend and associate for the rest of his life. And she became a local church leader who hosted church meetings in her home.

Paul had good things to say about another woman too: Junia. He described her and another Christian as top church leaders: "very important apostles" (Romans 16:7 NCV). Some Bible translations tone that down by saying they weren't apostles but only "highly respected among the apostles" (NLT). Either way, some might argue, Paul likely wasn't commending them for their silence but for their active role in church ministry.

MIXED SIGNALS, MIXED SITUATIONS?

If Paul was sending mixed signals, some scholars suggest it was because he was dealing with mixed situations. They say that where there were problems in a church, he set limits. Where church became a respectful place of worship, he allowed freedom.

Some denominations today refuse to ordain women as ministers because Paul said women should keep quiet in church. But even among churches that ordain women ministers, only about one out of ten hires a woman as lead minister.

WHY DID PRISCILLA CHOOSE CORINTH?

When Emperor Claudius expelled Jews from Rome, Priscilla and Aquila packed up their tentmaking business and sailed about 800 miles (1300 km) east to the bustling Greek town of Corinth.

They may have picked Corinth for some of the same reasons Paul did—and why Paul stayed there for a year and a half, when in most of the other towns he visited he stayed only a few days or weeks.

Corinth was one of the Roman Empire's biggest cities. Corinth didn't have just one port in one sea. It had two ports in two seas. That made it perhaps the busiest crossroads town between Rome and the eastern half of the empire, which includes what is now Greece, Turkey, and the Middle Eastern nations of Israel, Syria, and Jordan.

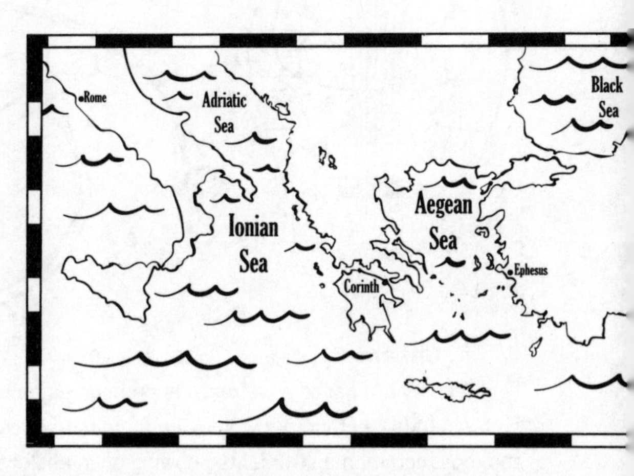

Some merchants sailed their ships into one port of Corinth and then had their products hauled across a four-mile long (6 km) strip of land to the port in the other sea. This gave them a shortcut to Rome, cutting 200 miles (320 km) from their trip. This allowed the merchandise to bypass the wild and unpredictable waves at the southern tip of Greece. With all this activity in Corinth, Priscilla and Aquila probably saw plenty of opportunity to sell tents there.

Corinth was a rich town. By the time Priscilla and Aquila and Paul got there, business was booming at markets, taverns, theaters, and bathhouses. There were a lot of temples too.

One other bonus: Corinth and the local region hosted Olympic-like games every two years. This attracted athletes and spectators from all over the Empire. Those visitors needed overflow facilities. Paul probably figured they needed Jesus too.

After his stay in Corinth, Paul started using athletic imagery in his writing: "I have fought the good fight, I have finished the race… And now the prize awaits" (2 Timothy 4:7–8 NLT).

ROMANS MADE MUSIC WITHOUT A FIDDLE

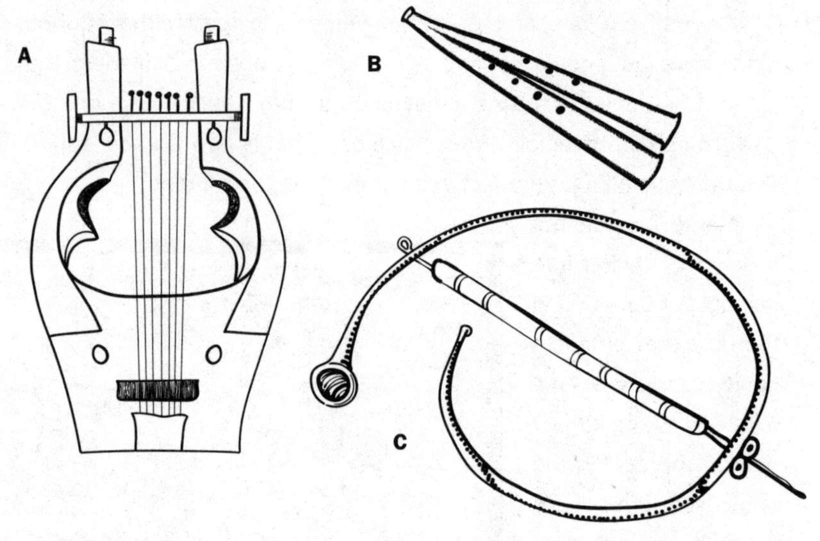

A. Cithara

A mini-harp called a *cithara* was perhaps as popular in Roman times as the guitar is today. In fact, our word *guitar* comes from *cithara*. The cithara is one of the most common instruments showing up in ancient Roman art. If Nero played any kind of a stringed instrument while Rome burned, it probably would have been a cithara. Designs varied, but the seven-string cithara looked a bit like a four-string lyre. The cithara produced soothing music much like a harp, though not quite as rich in tone.

B. Flute

Flutes traveled well, didn't cost much, and sounded sweet when played with grace. They were popular at plays and gatherings of all types, if their frequent depiction in ancient Roman art is any indication.

C. Cornu

Cornu is Latin for "horn." Our word *cornet* is a modern linguistic descendant, just as the instrument itself descended from the Roman cornu. Romans played a variety of horns when they needed loud, bracing music, such as while honoring the emperor, introducing gladiators in the arena, or signaling soldiers during a battle. One of the loudest was a brass horn nearly ten feet (three m) long, and curled into a giant "G." It sounded like a bugle.

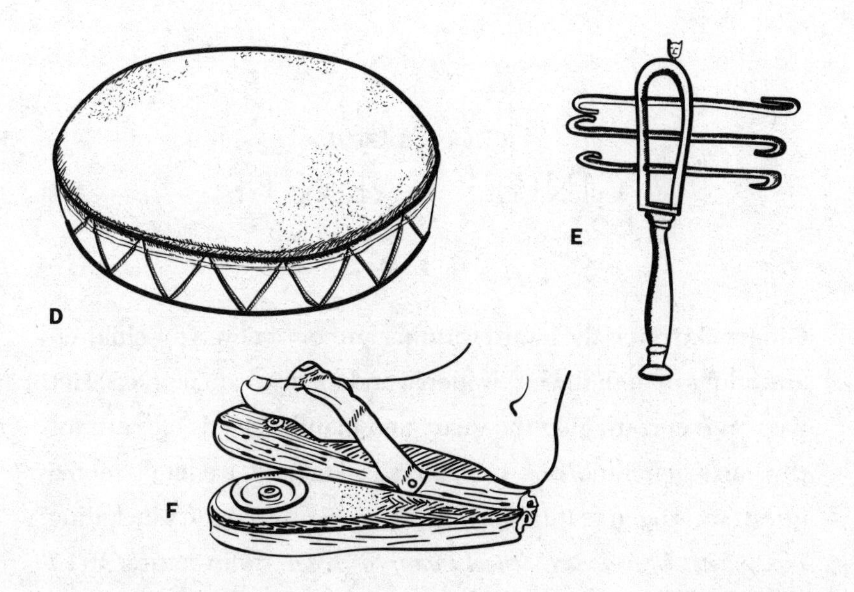

D. Tympanum

Romans added a toe-tapping beat to their music with percussion instruments such as the *tympanum*, a hand drum that looked like a tambourine. Musicians beat the drum with hands or sticks.

E. Sistrum

To add in some rattling rhythm to their percussion section, Roman musicians played a sistrum. Some sistrums (or *sistra*) looked like a small metal frame set on a handle. Loosely attached to the frame, metal rings strung across metal bars created a rattle when shaken.

F. Scabellum

Music conductors sometimes kept the beat by wearing a clapper sandal called a scabellum. It sounded a bit like a tap dancing shoe and looked like a tiny pair of cymbals secured into the toe of a hinged sandal.

Fiction Author
GINGER GARRETT

Ginger Garrett is the award-winning author of novels for children and adults in both the inspirational and mainstream markets. Her passion is encouraging the weary and planting seeds of truth for the next generation. A popular speaker and frequent media guest, she's been featured by media across the country including Fox News, *USA Today, School Library Journal,* radio station 104.7 The Fish, Atlanta, Billy Graham's *Hour of Decision,* and more. Ginger lives in Atlanta with her family and her twenty-seventh rescue dog, Watson. You can learn more at gingergarrett.com

Nonfiction Author
STEPHEN M. MILLER

Stephen M. Miller is an award-winning, bestselling Christian author of easy-reading books about the Bible and Christianity. His books have sold over 1.9 million copies and include *The Complete Guide to the Bible, Who's Who and Where's Where in the Bible,* and *How to Get Into the Bible.*

Miller lives in the suburbs of Kansas City with his wife, Linda, a registered nurse. They have two married children who live nearby.

Read on for a sneak peek of another exciting story in the Ordinary Women of the Bible series!

BEFITTING ROYALTY: LYDIA'S STORY

by Elizabeth Adams

Lydia pushed on as the crowds pressed close. The streets were filled with merrymakers already celebrating, as well as women leading donkeys pulling carts laden down with supplies. She waved at Leia and Asuman, indicating for them to stay near. She probably did not need to fuss at them, as they knew these streets as well as she did. But the parcel they transported today was irreplaceable, and she would not be at ease until they had delivered it safely.

"Some people must not realize the festival does not start until tomorrow." Leia ducked her head as a man, already stinking of much drink, leered at her as he passed by. She moved closer to the wagon, protecting the parcel inside. Asuman nodded and spoke softly to the donkey, urging it on.

Tomorrow already. They were late making this delivery. She had hoped to get the cloth—possibly the finest cloth her workshop had ever created—to Felix last week, but the special weave on the fine-spun wool had proven trickier than she'd expected. His seamstress would have to work quickly to turn it into a robe. But it would be worth it when he saw how it shimmered in the sun.

"We will be there soon." Lydia pushed through the crowd and soon emerged into the agora teeming with people. Vendors selling fish, fruit, or spices called out from their stalls, and the tables where men gambled were full. The fortune-teller called out from her regular booth, trying to lure customers to hear her predict the future. To the left, the municipal building stood. It was imposing, made of marble blocks and fluted columns. A statue of the emperor guarded the steps. To the right was the library, which the magistrates sent from Rome had filled with books and manuscripts of all kinds. Crowds spilled out of the temple to Saturn, making their offerings for the holiday. Saturn was said to be the god of crops and growing, and many in the area believed they depended on his mercy. Lydia knew better and tried her best to guide the cart through the crowd. A woman, laden down with baskets of meats and vegetables, pressed into Asuman, who stumbled against the wagon.

"Sorry," Asuman said, ducking her head. The woman stormed off as if she had not heard.

"It is just up ahead," Lydia said, pointing to the far side of the agora. She was grateful it had not been Leia. Leia was loyal and dedicated, and she was a master crafter at the loom, but she had a sharp tongue and was quick to pick a fight. Lydia just wanted to make this delivery without incident.

They finally made it past the square and entered a side street lined with large homes. This was the part of the city where the government officials preferred to live, with its hilly streets that gave them the best views over the city. The donkey's hooves clapped along the stones.

Lydia had supervised deliveries to this house before. Felix, a high-ranking magistrate, liked to be well dressed and was one of her most loyal customers. The house did not look like much from the outside—just blocks of cut stone pressed up against its neighbors—but Lydia knew better. While Asuman tied up the donkey, Leia knocked on the door, a heavy wooden slab carved with intricate scrollwork. Lydia hoisted out the heavy bundle of fabric.

"I can help with that," Asuman said, coming up next to Lydia, but Lydia shook her head.

"I do not need help," Lydia said, balancing the heavy parcel in her arms. Asuman knew better than to argue.

They were quickly ushered inside the house by a servant girl with glossy black hair and high cheekbones. The late-afternoon sun filled the central courtyard with light. They were ushered upstairs to Felix's private chambers at the top of the house. As soon as the three women were inside the room, the servant stepped out and closed the door.

"Lydia." Felix sat behind a wooden table, writing on a strip of parchment. He set his quill down and pushed back from the desk. Light streamed in through the arched windows that showed a dramatic sweep of the town. "It is good to see you again."

"It is good to see you too. You look well." Felix wore linen robes of a deep indigo, and his beard was neatly trimmed and oiled. She had learned that it was wise to flatter Felix, who liked to be admired. "That color looks very good on you."

"It is a beautiful color, isn't it?" Felix laughed as he stood. Behind him, an open door led into his sleeping quarters and revealed his bed, beautifully carved and layered in deep purple coverings. "I got the fabric from a beautiful woman. One who makes the finest cloth in Macedonia."

Lydia forced herself to keep the smile on her face from faltering. She had learned to ignore the way he studied her form whenever she saw him. He was a powerful man in the city, she reminded herself, and one of her best customers.

"I would like to meet this woman who is my competitor," Lydia said, keeping her voice light. Of course she recognized the fabric as one of her own, but she knew better than to fall for his flattery.

Felix laughed again. "See? That is why I like you, Lydia. Clever and funny as well as beautiful." He gave her one more appraising look and nodded, and then he stepped forward. "Let me see this cloth you have kept me waiting so long for."

He crossed the stone floor, inlaid with strips of marble, and indicated that Lydia should set the parcel down on the table in the corner of the room. Lydia moved toward the table, positioned next to an arched window that looked out over the theater and the aqueduct. She set the package down and then unwrapped the heavy cloth covering that protected the fine fabric within. She gently pulled out the finely woven wool. It was the color of ripe eggplants, and it was shot through with threads the color of gold. Her team had rarely worked so hard on a piece, and she was pleased with the result. She lifted the bolt of fabric and unwrapped a section, letting it hang free. The golden threads gleamed in the sunlight that streamed in through the windows.

"I don't know how you do it, Lydia, but every time, you make me something more beautiful." Felix stepped forward and ran his fingers over the wool, nodding at its smooth touch. "It was very clever the way you wove that gold thread in."

"My weavers are the best in Philippi." She was not. It was true, and everyone knew it. While it was quicker and easier to purchase and dye whole strips of cloth, Lydia's team had dyed this wool in its raw form and had it spun and then had woven it after the color was fast. This meant they were able to weave the shimmering golden thread in with it. "Leia worked on this piece." She nodded at Leia, who kept her eyes focused on the ground.

"You are very talented," Felix said. He trailed his fingers along the fabric one more time and then moved his hand and placed it on Lydia's arm. She forced herself to not flinch. She was mindful of Leia and Asuman standing just behind her. "You have handled the business admirably since Andreas passed."

"My husband built up a strong business, and I am doing my best to honor him." Lydia had largely run the business herself while Andreas had been alive, but she could not say so.

"It has been, what, two years now?"

"It will be two in Martius."

The way Felix looked at her, she felt as if she were a goat being appraised at auction. "You are a beautiful woman. You would make a fine wife for the right man."

"I am focused solely on my business at the moment." His hand felt heavy on her arm.

"You would not have to run a business if you married me. You could spend your days as you wished, sitting in the shade and talking with the other women. Your every need would be met, and you would attend all the best gatherings and be much admired in the province." It was hardly a declaration of love. She took in a deep breath and let it out slowly.

Felix trailed his hand down her arm. "You are still young. We would have many fine sons. Surely you want sons."

Lydia would not let her face betray her emotion. "I am focused on my business at the moment," she repeated.

"I am a Roman citizen," Felix said. "You would be protected."

Protected from the laws that Felix and the men he worked with enacted, he meant. After Caesar's armies had conquered the whole Hellenic region and installed their own system of government, the officials had begun to bestow special privileges on residents who bore Roman citizenship. These citizens had freedom from many taxes and had special status within the colonies. If Andreas had been a Roman citizen, they would not have had to pay many of the local taxes that had saddled their business, and the dye works would have been even more profitable. Felix, a Roman patrician, would need to obtain special permission to marry her, a citizen of Macedonia, but she had no doubt a man in his position could obtain whatever he needed. And yet Lydia could not imagine marriage to Felix being worth the gains.

"I am afraid I must focus all of my energies on my business for now," Lydia repeated and stepped back, pulling her arm away.

Felix's brow creased, and he continued to watch her.

"Come here tomorrow for the feast," he said. "Celebrate with us. We will have much food and wine and dancing, and all the best people in Philippi will be here. You will see."

"That's very kind." Lydia tried to keep her voice even and steady. "But I do not celebrate."

His gaze did not falter. "That is right. I had forgotten. You worship with the Hebrews."

"I worship Adonai."

The quiet stretched out just a moment too long before he spoke again. "Even still, you would make a fine wife."

"I thank you, truly," she said. "But I must be going now." She gestured for Leia and Asuman to follow her, and she started for the door. "You may send payment for the material."

"It came quite late," Felix said as she walked away. "My seamstress will have to work very quickly to finish the robe before the festival begins. Because of that, I will not be able to pay the full amount, you understand."

Lydia understood that he was punishing her for her refusal. A part of her wanted to insist that he could and should pay the agreed-upon price for the fabric he had already told her was her finest. But she was more concerned with getting out of here with her dignity intact.

"I am sure you will pay what is fair," she said, and then she pulled open the door and walked out into the hallway. The same servant girl who had led them upstairs stood outside the door and now ushered them downstairs.

As soon as they were out onto the streets again, Leia seemed unable to help herself. "That man is insufferable."

"Please do not let him bother you, Leia," Lydia said. "We cannot let him worry us. He is one of our best customers, and we must speak of him with respect."

"Not such a great customer if he doesn't pay," Leia said, but a look from Lydia silenced her.

Asuman untied the donkey and they started back toward the agora. The crowds were thicker now, and the women were pressed together as they walked.

"I don't know," Asuman said. "He is not bad looking. He is rich. And if you married him, you would be one of the finest couples in town. Would you not consider it?"

"No, I would not." Lydia's voice was firm. For so many reasons, she would not. "Now let us forget about that man. We must get back to the workshop. There is still much to do."

After they passed through the city gates, the crowds thinned, and they had more space to walk. The stones were hard beneath their feet, but there was a breeze, and it carried the scent of eucalyptus and jasmine. The workshop was housed in a stone building not far off the Egnatian Way, the road that linked the western sea to Byzantium, far to the east. Andreas had taken great pride in the construction of the new workshop building when he had taken the business over from his father many years before. Andreas had never had much interest in the actual work of dyeing, spinning, and weaving cloth, but he had enjoyed the prestige that came with the lucrative trade and had spent far more than he should have on making sure the building was the largest and finest of the dye works in the area. Lydia supposed she should be grateful. While he had lacked business sense, he had left her with a strong, well-built workshop, the envy of the other owners of the local dye works.

"Leia, would you please check the loom room?" Lydia asked as they neared the workshop. "Please make sure they are close to finishing that linen I promised Miklos. Asuman, will you make sure all is in order with the thread?"

Both women nodded, and after she opened the heavy wooden door, they scurried off. They were good workers and loyal. Giorgio stepped in from the storage room and greeted Lydia as she crossed the small front space where she handled her business dealings. The room was cool and well lit from narrow openings Andreas had had built into the top of the walls. They were meant for ventilation, to let the stench of the dyes out, but they also brought in sunlight.

"Was Felix pleased with the fabric?" Giorgio asked. His gray hair was matted to his head, wet from the heat of the vat room.

"He was," Lydia said, settling onto the stool. After the long walk, it felt good to rest. "Though he threatened to withhold part of the payment because it was late in coming."

"That man would take a denarius from a starving child if he could get away with it," Giorgio said. Lydia shook her head, stifling a smile. It was dangerous to say such things about the magistrate—there was no telling who might overhear and report the words—but Lydia had long ago stopped trying to tell Giorgio what he could and could not say. Lydia did not know how old he was, but he had deep wrinkles and his hair and beard were gray. He had worked here at the dye works, supervising the boiling of the dyes, since Andreas had been a child. He did as he pleased, and as long as he continued to make the most stunning dyes in the region, Lydia would not complain.

"You had a visitor," Giorgio said. "Damon came by to collect payment for the latest shipment of wool. I told him you would return shortly. He will come back after he visits the other workshops." Giorgio winked. "Wants to get paid before the holiday, no doubt. Saturnalia is not much fun without some coins in your pocket."

"Thank you, Giorgio." Giorgio had been one of Andreas's most loyal workers, and while he had always treated her with respect during Andreas's lifetime, he had not been pleased when Lydia took over after Andreas's passing. It had taken many months before he would look her in the eye, and many more before he started to accept her orders as valid. But over the months, he had come to tolerate working for a woman and had even begun to chastise other workers who defied her. He even tried to joke with her from time to time. "If you could start to clean out the vats, I would appreciate it," Lydia continued. "It is almost time to close."

Giorgio often stayed here overnight when there was a dye on boil, but because of the holiday, the vat room was empty. Giorgio nodded and then turned and walked back through the doorway toward the storage room.

Lydia sat at the table and pulled out the strip of vellum she used to track her costs and income. Andreas had not been much for numbers, so early in their marriage Lydia had taken on the task herself, taught at a young age by an indulgent father who let her look in on his own business dealings while she was a girl. She marked that she had made the delivery to Felix and that payment was still due. She added up the amounts due to her various suppliers. The largest payment, as always, was due to the man from Neapolis who supplied the seashells used to make the costly purple dye. Then she counted out the coins she owed to Damon, who sold the finest wool. She became so absorbed in her calculations that she didn't hear the door open again or notice that Damon had entered the workshop until he stood in front of her. She saw his frame before her, started, and then laughed.

"Damon. Goodness. I didn't see you." He was a tall man, solidly built. How had she missed him coming in?

"You were concentrating hard on something." Damon smiled. He had supplied wool to Andreas for many years, and she had gotten to know him since she had taken over the business. He was a kind man and charged fair prices.

"I was looking over the accounts," Lydia said. "I guess I was more wrapped up in the numbers than I realized."

Damon shook his head. "I have never met a woman who found business accounts so intriguing." He was teasing her.

"You must not have met too many women responsible for making sure they can pay their workers, then." She set her quill down and sighed. It had grown darker in here as the sun had slipped lower in the sky.

"No, I suppose that is true." Damon tilted his head just a little. "There are not many women who are brave enough to take charge of a business."

"I am not sure whether it was brave or stupid." Many had urged her to let Andreas's brother Tobias take over. Tobias would have gladly stepped into running the profitable workshop, but Lydia had fought to keep hold of the business she herself had helped build. She had grown up learning this trade, and she did not need anyone to help her manage the dye works. She had held firm to the business, even though many would have liked to strip her of it.

"Perhaps a little of both." Damon laughed. "But you have proven that you are better than most men at this."

"You flatter me. You must want your money quite badly."

"I do want the money. I have my own workers to pay." Damon stepped closer. "But that is not why I flatter you. I do that because I like to see you smile."

Coming from another man, it might have sounded disingenuous. But there was something about Damon that made her trust him. She reached for the coins and held them out.

The face of Caesar Augustus glinted in the soft light. "Flirting with me will not make me pay you more."

"See? I told you that you are better at business than most." Damon took the coins and counted them before slipping them in the leather bag at his waist. He smiled at her again and then turned back toward the door. "Have a nice holiday, Lydia."

"You as well." There was no need tell him that she had no intention of joining in the raucous debauchery that Saturnalia inevitably became. Damon cast one last look back at Lydia and then pushed open the door and walked out into the early evening light.

Good. That was one account settled, Lydia thought, marking the payment on her vellum. But somehow, she still felt a twinge of disappointment that he was gone.

A NOTE FROM THE EDITORS

We hope you enjoy the Ordinary Women of the Bible series, created by the Books and Inspirational Media Division of Guideposts, a nonprofit organization that touches millions of lives every day through products and services that inspire, encourage, help you grow in your faith, and celebrate God's love in every aspect of your daily life.

Thank you for making a difference with your purchase of this book, which helps fund our many outreach programs to military personnel, prisons, hospitals, nursing homes, and educational institutions. To learn more, visit Guideposts Foundation.org.

We also maintain many useful and uplifting online resources. Visit Guideposts.org to read true stories of hope and inspiration, access OurPrayer network, sign up for free newsletters, download free e-books, join our Facebook community, and follow our stimulating blogs.

To learn about other Guideposts publications, including the bestselling devotional *Daily Guideposts,* go to ShopGuideposts.org, call (800) 932-2145, or write to Guideposts, PO Box 5815, Harlan, Iowa 51593.